The Last Great
Susquehannock Chief

I wrote this story for the Indigenous Susquehannock Americans who don't exist today. This story is for people I'll never meet but who cannot speak. It is for the Susquehannock peoples who made contributions that were never appreciated in their time. Out of a sense of guilt and gratitude, rivers, schools and roads are imprinted with the name Susquehanna. This story is about the people of that name. This story is also for the many tribal nations that no longer exist. They too are lost to history. Their voices are also heard in these pages. They live on through others, if we choose to remember them.

In *The Last Great Susquehannock Chief*, readers paddle beside a man who grew from white settler to warrior to chief, teeming through the waters of a history that brims with courage, cruelty, and adventure. A lively and tender journey that traces a historic thread of many colors, Rose's novel paints vivid scenes of battle, parlay and negotiation, plus the glories of a new love found in a new land. This book delivers a scent of history that should be savored and remembered. Motivated to make the New World a better place for others, Judah's story in this sweeping novel shows readers the adventures that made a native people great.

— Ron Seybold, author of the historical novel *Sins of Liberty*

Radiates an impressive verisimilitude...Blue Eagle's psychological conflict is artfully rendered. Historically edifying. — *Kirkus*

The Last Great
Susquehannock Chief

How Judah Joseph Became 'Blue Eagle'

C.A. Rose

For reprint information, address crpatriot@gmail.com

First paperback edition, 2025

Cover Designs by René van Druten
Interior Layout by Maureen Cutajar, gopublished.com

Names: Rose, C. A., author.
Title: The Last Great Susquehannock Chief / C. A. Rose.
Description: Austin: Trampoline Press, 2025.
Subjects: LCSH: Susquehanna Indians—17th century—Fiction.
Jewish men—17th century—Fiction.
Indians of North America—Northeastern States—Fiction.
BISAC: FICTION/Historical. Fiction/General.
LCGFT: Historical fiction.

ISBN: 979-8-9995504-0-8 hardback
ISBN: 979-8-9924198-6-3 paperback

This novel is dedicated to my wonderful and tireless wife, Jan, who spent countless hours reading, editing, and guiding me through this effort. This project would never have happened without her.

Contents

Prologue

The real story of the first Susquehannocks dates to about 1550. The Algonquian-speaking Powhatans had been fighting with the Iroquois and later the British in northern Virginia since 1608. The Susquehanna River played a significant role in their movement and settlement. Initially, the nation spread along the river from Philadelphia to New York State.

History has recorded a few cases of colonists rising through indigenous American ranks to become clan leaders called sachems as well as tribal leaders. Their backgrounds have yet to be registered. Some may have been born to mixed marriages, unions where their fathers may have been traders, and their mothers may have been cast out from their villages. They are, for the most part, the stuff of stories and legends.

Judah Joseph is our protagonist. His family roots date back to the Spanish Inquisition, where his ancestors were forced to convert to Christianity, leave the country, or perish. His family moved to Amsterdam and later to Recife, Brazil, because the Dutch had established control there through the Dutch West India Company.

Judah's early life is told through flashbacks. You will see his personality and the incidents that shape him and mold him in these incidents. The flashbacks in this story are separated by breaks in the text. This young man was an adventurous and curious boy who saw his father's occupation as a company trader as exploitive and harmful. Judah's mother raised him in a traditional Jewish home, but the Hebrew stories of the bible left him callous and disbelieving. Yet, in his heart, he was genuinely motivated to make the world a better place for others. To his mother's chagrin, he fell for a beautiful non-Jewish au pair. Together, they schemed to teach street boys how to read. But fate and history intervened, and the family was forced to leave Recife when he was twenty-four.

After a storm changed their course, the ship with twenty-four Jews aboard was rescued by a French privateer. Their ship was rejected by several Caribbean countries including Curacao and Cuba. They were rescued by a French privateer named Lamotte and finally landed in Peter Stuyvesant's New Netherland which the English later called New York in 1665. This landing was factual and duly recorded by several historical sources.

Judah lived with his mother and father there as tenant farmers. Bored with farming, Judah found work tanning hides. Although he liked working with his hands, his sense of adventure drew him to his surroundings, and he loved to explore his world. Judah was well educated, and spoke Portuguese and Dutch fluently and some Hebrew.

Judah and his family fractured on his upbringing. He wanted no part of his father's trading career and only a small part of his mother's Jewish heritage. His feet were firmly planted in how the soil, tress, animals and sky were all connected to human beings that inhabited the earth. His moral and ethical compass was now firmly established.

While Stuyvesant was away displacing the Swedish, a large group of indigenous tribes, including the Susquehannocks, invaded New Netherland, destroying homes, killing settlers, torching crops, and taking prisoners. Judah was taken prisoner, and rather than be involved in a prisoner swap, he chose to become a Susquehannock warrior. There, the book's story begins. Judah identifies with the Susquehannock warriors and their people. The nation and the village gave him honor, courage, and strength. In turn, he brought them knowledge, skill, honesty, and adventure. A quick learner, he picked up the Algonquin language easily and a story unfolds.

The story of Judah Joseph is purely fictional, yet he could have existed. Colonial history weaves through the story like a thread of many colors. Some of the events are true and as accurate as possible. Others are made up out of my imagination but certainly could have happened. I hope you enjoy following Judah as he faces challenges and rewards to become the warrior Blue Eyes, and then Blue Eagle—The Last Great Susquehannock Chief.

—C.A. Rose

PART I

Becoming

CHAPTER 1

Capture

Women, children, and old men fled in every direction at the New Netherland settlement. Gray clouds covered the sky in September 1655. Tomahawks slashed and smashed everything in their path. An old man turned and ran, but he was too slow and too late. A woman pushed her door ajar. A warrior's pained grin with slash marks across his cheeks greeted her and threatened a rape that did not happen. These warriors were more intent on destruction, fire and mayhem. Her scream attracted the attention of another well-built warrior. They lashed her by the neck, tied her hands behind her back, and led her to a chain of women prisoners. Old men were scalped or killed, while fields and homes were burned at random. Peter Stuyvesant's home—the governor's mansion and furnishings—went up in flames.

Judah could hear the warriors before he could see them. He opened his door of his house slowly, knife in hand, then circled the house looking for an attacker. With a low stance, bowed back, and arms extended, he turned his head side to side. This position gave him a quick jumping point, as the knife was positioned to the rear. Judah could not know that two tattooed warriors watched his movements before they leaped on him and pushed his face to the ground. He struggled against their grips, but they threw him against a tree, kicked his feet out from under him, and pushed him to the ground.

Without saying a word, they had him lashed and lifted by the shoulders for marching in line with others. Judah thought that the best decision he made before opening the door was to put on boots. Overcome by victory, a warrior shouted, "Ayee…Ayee" and threw Judah's knife against a tree. Another warrior held his tomahawk against Judah's face and traced its edge along his cheekbone. He thought that his young life would be over very soon. The noise of shouts and screams rang in his ears as he walked, corralled like a wobbly mule in line with others.

Judah was dazed but started to breathe deeply and control his body and his mind. If they were going to kill him, he would be dead by now. That meant they intended to keep him alive, perhaps in trade for something else. He tried to get a better sense of his surroundings as they moved further away from New Netherland. Judah was thinking of his parents and whether he would ever see them alive again, but he could not let those thoughts cloud his judgement.

His job at New Netherland of tanning hides and working with his hands was not rewarding, but it taught Judah a lot about the life of tradesmen and tools. That place of tanning, along with many others, was probably burned in the melee. Dismissing them from his mind wasn't easy; he was on his own now. The other men killed or captured would have to survive on their own. He could see his guardians once he was in tow with older men and women. Judah's forced march was plain ugly. He counted eight in his group but did not know how many prisoners the warriors took. One had two feathers on top of his head and a decorated headband. He stood before a leader whose face, chest, and arms were streaked in black. He spoke very little, but when he did, others obeyed his every word. Judah tried to pick up the meaning of his words and actions, but it was not easy. *Focus your mind, learn the language through gestures,* he told himself, *always stay focused.* They were heading downhill, maybe to a body of water. The chattering of birds became noisier and the chirps more numerous, but they knew the land and walked without complaint.

A certain sympathy was building in Judah's mind for his captors that he had not thought about before. Judah admired their loyalty to their leaders, their straightforward strength and courage. The way they moved impressed him as well—there was grace and dignity—no wasted motions. One characteristic impressed him the most above all the rest. They were not savages like he had been told. They were a free people. This nation of people obeyed the land and tied themselves to their heritage. Freedom was what made them who they were. For the first time, Judah understood who they were, and he wanted to be like them.

The warriors packed their captives into canoes for a trip downstream. He had to steady himself using only legs and his stomach muscles. Even bound, his mind was in motion. He ignored his hunger and thirst. A strong easterly breeze blew off Long Island Sound and into the Delaware Basin. The black lining of the clouds hinted that rain could soon be on the way. The sun was still high, and the clouds drifted southeast.

After what seemed like hours of rowing, the canoe came to a rest stop at an island in mid-stream and broke the monotony. There was no place to hide, and escape was impossible, yet guards kept a vigil. Judah listened to the night sounds of the owls, the scurrying of small animals and even the creeping beetles. Two warriors built a fire while others fetched wood or broke out food. They were well organized and said little. They settled after a brief break, then ate and talked before resting. The prisoners were segregated and bound to trees after they drank from bladders and ate. The tree binding was akin to torture, lashing the settlers to a trunk with their hands behind their backs.

"Where did they think we would go?" Judah said in Dutch to

no one in particular. "Do they think we would steal a canoe and paddle to somewhere out here?"

Judah tried not to rub his hands, saving such gestures for when the warriors were not staring at him. In his mind, he was grateful that he did not have to row, but if he were to act like a warrior, he should refrain from showing weakness. Judah set his mind to earning their trust and confidence by being compliant without being subservient. The trick was to follow directions while using hand signals for communication, staying out of trouble to keep a low profile. Without warning, a soft rain began to fall and soon everything became wet. As hands and clothes were drenched and soaked, their bindings to the trees tightened.

After three days and nights of paddling, they arrived at a sizable village. Judah could tell by the twenty-eight canoes parked on the bank. He was escorted from the canoe and hustled to a holding area which included other male hostages. There was one consolation— at least they were dry. A guard kept watch inside a barren longhouse. He untied Judah's bonds and gave him water in a cup, a soup mixture in a bowl, and some hard-tack deer meat. While he sat on a blanket next to the soup on the dirt floor there was no speaking, although an older man tried to begin a conversation in Dutch. The guard gestured for him to be quiet by putting his finger to his mouth, but nothing further was said.

Women of various ages came in to pick up the bowls and cups and to pour more water. They disappeared after a time. A younger warrior with no feathers in his headband replaced the older guard. He gestured toward a bed on a shelf that overlooked the fire that the women had started. The men wrapped themselves in blankets and tried to sleep. Everyone seemed to have a job to do.

No one knew what to expect or how long the group would remain in place, since they were away from everyday life. Judah figured it made sense to collect and treat them like negotiating bait; trade them for what they might bring. One old man managed to mumble something about a prisoner release. Judah remained clueless, but his plan was developing as he waited—he was in no hurry. An idea formed that would stay with him the rest of his life. He, Judah Joseph, would become like them, Susquehannock warriors. Even better, he would become a leader of these men, a sachem and tribal chief. Why go through with the agony of body and spirit? The answer was easy: without pain there would be no reward. To suffer and survive with success would equal respect and gratitude for himself and others.

Judah and the captives were held in longhouses along three Wappinger and Susquehannock villages along the Delaware and Schuylkill Rivers. Stuyvesant appointed Captain Adriaen Post to negotiate their freedom. Post spoke Algonquian and knew the ways of the tribes. He arrived in Susquehannock village to negotiate for the release of the prisoners in trade for ammunition, wampum, and blankets. After talking with the captives, Post was shocked when he learned that Joseph wanted to remain with the Susquehannocks.

Post, who was in his early thirties, spoke to Judah in Dutch. At six foot two, Post was two inches taller. With his right hand clenched in a fist and his left index finger extended in anger, Post asked, "Why do want to do this? It is a child-like fantasy, that will end badly and in great pain. You are too old to learn native ways of survival, hunting, and living. In the end you will suffer great pain and may even die from this foolish misadventure. You will have accomplished nothing but embarrassment for your people."

Judah's deep-blue eyes widened, his brows came together in defiance, and he stared hard at Post. "You are wrong. I'm young and strong and can stand their pain and earn their trust. I will succeed because I can help these people live free—free from the colonizers like you and Stuyvesant who want to buy freedom for price of a few blankets and ammunition. Free from those who want to take their land and their way of life from them. I can show them how to protect and defend themselves against enemies and live with dignity and honor."

"Nice words," Post said. "I will take them to Flowing Waters, the chief, and see what he says. If he lets you stay, you will be on your own. If not, you will go back with the others, understood?"

"I understand," Judah said.

The chief and his circle of elders, with the village mother, sat cross-legged at one end of the longhouse where they had just finished negotiating the terms of the release of the hostages. That negotiation had taken three days. His headband had multiple feathers. The group looked tired and worn when Post approached them and asked to talk.

Flowing Waters sat motionless, smoking a long pipe with a small bulb of tobacco, which he gestured to Post take a puff from. The smell of smoking was pungent and astringent to his lungs, and he forced himself not to choke. Post told them of Judah's intent to stay. "Let us talk," Flowing Waters said, and Post left.

Post waited for about an hour. Finally, Flowing Waters met Post man-to-man. The old chief's deeply-lined face was etched in wrinkles and scars and looked like a worn treasure map. From the corner of his mouth, a wry grin curled enough to show one missing front tooth. The chief faced Post and told him without hesitation that this story was not amusing. "A hostage white man wants to stay in the tribe to learn the ways of the Susquehannock. For what purpose?" The reasons Post gave him did not seem to sink in at first. "The ways of the Susquehannock and their language should be left to the Susquehannock, not to a white man who wants my job." Flowing Waters re-loaded the tobacco, tamping it down and thought on the idea several minutes more. Post, by this time, was getting agitated.

At last, Flowing Waters spoke. "This man can stay as long as he can provide food and pelts for the tribe, does not complain, and listens to the clan mother and his elders. He must obey. He will die if he fails to do any of these things. He will learn what it means to be a Susquehannock warrior."

Post shrugged, turned on the balls of his feet, and turned to the chief sachem. "Flowing Waters speaks excellent wisdom," he said. His cold, gray eyes gave no hint of disapproval. "I will pass along this message to the man at once."

Post and Judah squared off like two prize fighters at a boxing match weigh-in, standing in a corner of the longhouse as they sized each other up. "The chief said that you can stay, so long as you listen to the village mother, provide pelts and food to the village, and obey the council. I think that you're as dumb as a rock in this foolish fantasy, but I respect your will and determination."

Judah spoke without blinking and without the anger he once held. "I appreciate the fact that you were straightforward in your approach to Flowing Waters. I will do my best to become the Susquehannock warrior I want to be." They looked at each other with respect they had not shown before. Post told Judah that he had more stops to make and about one hundred and fifty prisoners to return home at four different locations. They shook hands, each with a clear goal ahead.

Judah began a search for firewood. No matter, it was too dark to be helpful. He walked around his longhouse. The walls were bracketed with long sticks. It was a short hut, maybe six paces long, domed and oblong. With only one blanket, he was chilled, and his clothes gave almost no protection against the wind and fall chill. The hides on the outside of the longhouse helped but did not block the winds. He picked up the tiny embers in his hands, blew on them softly and raised a small fiery glow. By placing the kindling atop them, he managed to get a few sparks of fire. He fed the branches which quickly led to a small fire, but more wood would be needed.

Just as he rose to leave, three young women came through the leather opening in the front of the longhouse on silent moccasins. One carried a small bundle of firewood. They giggled as they approached their prey. Circling like hawks, each examined their quarry to see which one would jump first or maybe all at once. They did not speak to each other or to Judah. The taller of the three moved first, followed quickly by the other two. They attacked the buttons on his shirt first and then on his trousers. Judah fought their hands off at first, but there were too many, and they came fast, too fast to resist. Besides, it tickled, and he was laughing as it happened. In what seemed like less than a minute, he was stripped naked, and the three women backed off together to look at their handiwork.

Judah leaped toward their feet and stood before them. His sex was half-hard and pulsing. His hands covered his groin in a reflex action to their manipulations. He turned his tall, muscular body in a vain attempt to thwart their stares. The three giggled, cupped their hands to their mouths, and ran one-by-one out the front entrance; the last one pointed to a small pile of clothes near the entrance. It was quite a scene; words were not necessary. He got the message. These were the buckskins to wear for his first challenge. He put on the clothes and found that they fit, albeit a little tight in the shoulders. Judah would not wear colonial male garments again. They left him a knife together with the bundle of wood—all the conveniences of home. He turned his attention again to the fire for relaxation and slipped the knife into his belt. This time, he fell into a sleep without dreams.

Judah felt a strong hand push hard on his chest. His first instinct was to grab the arm and reach for the knife, then swing down from the bunk. The hold on his chest was strong, and another hand stopped his knife from moving. Judah looked up to see the face of a painted warrior glare at him with a menacing look. He raised his palms outward, facing the intruder, gesturing that all was good and the warrior's hands relaxed. Judah slept in his buckskins, and when he reached for the belt with the knife and sheath, his intruder ripped the belt from his grip and tore it from its sheath. In less than two seconds, he had the knife out, its tip pointing toward Judah. The two squared off, and the warrior grinned, showing teeth that glistened white in the fire. Judah's fists were closed, his legs crouched, his head bobbed, and his body weaved in defense.

The warrior began to laugh. He stood erect and pointed to the front of the longhouse while thrusting the blade in his belt. Judah led the way. The two feathered warriors were still laughing and grinning. Judah calculated that he was jovial because he had disarmed him and now led Judah for a trial of pain and courage.

The warrior pointed toward the village center. It was a vast expanse with several circles of fireplace rocks, built-up racks for hanging hides, pots, ceramics, wheels, and large stones for sharpening. At the end of the long row, Judah spotted two long rows of people in various forms of dress. There were many warriors: old men, women, children, and teenagers. They appeared to be armed—all of them. It was difficult to believe how many were there. They seemed to be chanting in unison as he got closer. A northeast wind blew cool against his buckskins and the longhouses flapped in response. He began to shiver as he approached the two lines of jumping, agitated villagers. To Judah's ears, the villagers all seemed to be saying the same thing. The group held sticks, hatchets, and war clubs. He knew he was going to take a beating, a very severe whacking. The lines were about two paces apart.

Judah let the women and children hit and poke him at will. Although some could hurt him, the warriors could kill him. He felt his feet slide in the soft, clay dirt as he weaved, dodged, and crawled in a muddy mess. By twisting his body to reach the legs of the warriors and attacking their knees with his forearms he was able to throw the warriors off balance without fighting them. Although his shoulders, back, and legs were bruised and battered, he managed to keep moving, crouching and even crawling. But he still had a long way to go. Forced onto his knees now, the

crazed crowd yelled at him and spit what could only be obsceni-
ties at him. He must show them, he thought, the warrior spirit
must come through. Two warriors came in to crush him to the
ground, but he fought back using only his bare arms and legs
without weapons. After more blows and harangues, he grabbed
a teenager's staff and raised it to deflect oncoming assaults, but
that move lasted only ten paces, until a war club broke the staff
in half. Exhausted and crawling near the end of his strength, Judah summoned what remained of his courage, rose, and took
more hits as he staggered forward.

There, at the end, stood Flowing Waters. Judah looked him in
the eye, face-to-face and spread-eagled, and spoke in broken Algonquin, "I am a true Susquehannock warrior." He turned to the
crowd. "I am a true Susquehannock warrior."

CHAPTER 2

Bear Smile...A Warrior

B ruised, beaten, but not broken, Judah could barely walk, yet this place drove him. Judah grabbed a bladder at the village center and held it high to slake his thirst. A small group of children then watched as he clutched at the gruel and soup on the fire. Judah almost singed his hands, gulping it down in amounts that surprised even him. He nearly vomited up all that he consumed, but after he righted himself against a wooden rack to keep from falling, the children ran away back to their longhouses. Now recovered, he straightened up and walked to his yet unpainted longhouse. More tests would follow, he knew. It only strengthened his resolve to see his ambition through. For now, it felt right, but he had to rest.

Judah's longhouse was stocked with a few surprises: additional blankets; a bladder of water; a knife, belt, and scabbard; and bowls of what appeared to be ointments ground into fine powder. Judah suspected that they were for his bruises and contusions and slowly spread them on. They felt soothing to his skin, and he spread them like butter. The effect was magical. Sleep came to

Judah almost instantly, and he curled into the blankets as if he were in the womb.

When he awoke he did not know how long he had slept, but it was as dark as tar outside. The northeast wind had blown cloud after cloud over the camp and a thick layer of river fog enveloped the grounds like a giant paw. Night sounds such as chittering squirrels filled the trees nearby. Judah thought deeply about the day's events and the generosity that followed running the gauntlet. To him it could mean only one thing—this village had a heart. There was at least some acceptance of who he was—he owed them more than they owed him. Of that, he was sure he knew what he had to do to earn their respect.

Other trials were coming. Judah knew that the damage caused by the blows of the gauntlet demanded rest, despite his obsessive desire to prove himself. Stone Face, the village mother, sent young boys and women to see if Judah's supplies needed to be refilled. To the villagers' surprise, they reported that he was up and walking around, pacing the longhouse and looking for firewood. They said he had even asked for a bow with arrows, and he seemed anxious. They reported that his language had improved, that he had been talking with the women at the village center, and that he had been practicing his skills with weapons.

Bear Smile thrust into Judah's hands a bow and a quiver of arrows. The warrior was dark, very dark, and stood before him with legs apart wearing a single, feathered headdress, loin cloth, long bow, and a decorated quiver. The man was frightening to look at. His visage bore an angular, narrow, and scarred face, with dark, piercing eyes and almost black pupils that stared without moving like a crouched, treed panther before it pounced. Bear Smile gave orders to the two other warriors, and with quick gestures of his hands the three were moving out of camp into the early morning haze. From where he stood, Judah could not see the claw marks on the warrior's neck and back.

Bear Smile earned his moniker when he was attacked and clawed as a young man by a mother grizzly bear after he came between her and her cubs. He tried to stab his way out of the bear's hug, but sustained permanent claw streaks down his back and on his neck before fellow hunters ended the bear's life with several arrows. The deed saved Bear Smile, earning him and the hunting party legendary status. The tribe ate well for a week and used the fur in trade as a bargaining chip with the French. Unfortunately, the cubs also gave up their lives after the melee, since survival in woods would be doubtful without their mother.

A modest ceremony preceded the launch of a small beaver hunting party. Flowing Waters said, "A white man was captured more than three days away at a place called New Netherland. For reasons known only to him, he wants to be a Susquehannock warrior. Since then, he has proven to have courage and will. We see in him a bright future for our people. I will now call him Blue Eyes and wish him good fortune and may our ancestors bestow their blessings upon him." With that, he placed a headband with a single eagle feather upon Judah's head.

Judah bowed slightly to Flowing Waters. The small crowd nodded their appreciation, but Bear Smile just grunted in boredom. Judah stood as straight as his back would allow and exited toward the crowd. Those who were gathered patted him on the shoulders and back as he left proud and slightly misty-eyed.

Judah was in the middle of the group led by Bear Smile, the warrior moving silently through the brush, looking up and ahead and rarely stopping. He was confident and always knew where the next step was taking him. Judah was several paces behind him, sometimes more. The three-feathered Bear Smile moved on wordlessly through the brush to a tributary.

There was no doubt that they were a hunting party looking for game and beaver, but the Susquehannock also had Indian enemies. It would not be unusual to come upon other tribes doing the same thing in these woods—feeding their families. Judah did not know that the two warriors behind him were looking for signs of enemy warriors while Bear Smile was up front looking for signs of medium-sized game such as deer, muskrat, quail, turkey, and beaver. Bear and moose were also possible but much less likely.

It was in the middle of fall now. The leaves had changed to their brilliant autumn colors. Rutting season for male deer was well underway, and beavers were as busy as ever building their dams for winter. In short, it was an ideal time for hunting. They were hours away from the settlement now; the sun was not yet at midday when Bear Smile spotted a stream that ran westward from the tributary along a bank about seventy-five paces below. They headed down slowly and quietly. The ground underfoot became softer and almost soggy. It seemed to please the Indians very much. Beaver territory, Judah thought, but did not dare to speak. Judah's experience with bow and arrow was limited but he often ventured into the woods by himself and with friends. They walked in slow, deliberate steps, making the extra-long landing as soft as possible. Each step was muddier than the last.

In about ten strides, they came upon a beaver dam stretching almost six paces across the stream. Under the water, the hunter had no chance against the beaver, but the bow and the knife could be deadly above the water. Bear Smile crouched, using a tree trunk to stabilize his shot. The others crept around the back and crouched low and silent, waiting for the beaver to pop out of the water. Judah positioned himself at about five paces from Bear Smile, tried to copy his movements, and drew his bow, aiming for the cluster of limbs at the end of the jamb of the dam.

As the first beavers popped up on the surface, Bear Smile took his shot. His body was almost erect and as taut as his bowstring. His right arm was parallel to the ground, two fingers under the string, one above, and his eyes locked on the target in a line with the arrow tip. He was perfectly still when he let the notched arrow go and stayed erect to follow through for a split second after release and then fell into the crouch and quiver for another shot.

The sequence of moves was smooth and fast.

The arrow tip with small point hit the beaver square on its right side, went through the body, and stuck into the timber inside—a perfect shot. Bear Smile retrieved the beaver and the arrow and waited on the bank with a bow in hand, just in case. The two warriors on the back side, along with Judah on the far bank, also readied their bows and waited, but nothing happened after what seemed a long time. Hunting requires patience. Judah had not hunted beaver before, so his job was to alert the others and observe. Judah heard splashing in the water near the dam and signaled for the others to be ready.

Beaver heads bobbed up, then down, then up again, and then two bodies on the far side came up. Judah heard arrows whoosh and strike wood along with some misses. Then two more arrows flew, and one found a mark. A hit in the shoulder, but not a kill shot. The warrior tried to pull the wounded beaver to shore. The younger warrior jumped into the icy cold water to retrieve his wounded prey. He was waist-deep with a knife held high. He grabbed the animal by its thick tail, but it flailed. He lost his grip, and it swam away—a dangerous move. Tackling a beaver underwater is never a good idea. Judah did not have a shot and seriously doubted he could hit one, even if he did. The wounded beaver did not surface, and Bear Smile told Judah and one warrior to swim to the other side of the beaver dam to see if the quarry was there.

The warriors did as told, even though the temperature of the water was almost as cold as the air above. They swam the twenty paces across to the stream and to their surprise the wounded beaver had floated under the dam and surfaced on the other side with the arrow intact in the shoulder. With every stitch of his body shivering, Judah jumped in the water again, retrieved the wounded animal on the shore with the arrow plunged into its side. He held up the valuable carcass by the arrow for all to see from the other shore. They raised their bows in jubilation.

When Bear Smile returned to the village, he did so with only two does, a few turkey, and other small animals. The hunt was with five warriors and meant for beaver. The beavers that were returned with Judah and the other warrior were quickly gutted and dressed for trade. Beaver skins were valuable in trading, and although their carcasses were quite edible, they did not go as far as deer or the larger game such as elk.

Flowing Waters asked to see Bear Smile. Once seated, he uncurled a crude map. "A small raiding party of Esopus and Lenape Indians pillaged a Susquehannock settlement many hours south of their village but along the Delaware River. They killed two warriors, one old man, and two women and children. They destroyed some crops and left them by canoes."

The chief was very upset and said that retaliation was in order.

Bear Smile replied, "How many men do you want me to take?"

A sly grin crossed the chief's face. "Take only as many as you need. What kind of warrior will the white boy be?"

Bear Smile snickered. "He has the heart of a woman, the will of a warrior, and the body of a man."

Flowing Waters smiled. "Hmmph," he said. "What is your plan now?"

"It's one thing to kill an animal; it takes quite another to kill another man."

"Test him."

Outside of his longhouse, Bear Smile unfurled the map that Flowing Waters had given him and met with six warriors. Judah recognized two of them from the beaver hunt and sensed that it was going to be a serious affair. Bear Smile said that this was going to be a quick raiding party on a village south of their own. They were to prepare for a few nights out and would leave at dawn. Essentials included dried meat, weapons, extra arrows, blankets, and water. Warriors traveled and lived with a minimum of needs. Thinking of himself as Blue Eyes, he reasoned that this trip might give him that opportunity if he mustered the courage to be ruthless. The party's raid might give him a chance to talk with Bear Smile and the others in a campground setting, now that his language had improved.

Judah knew that he had a lot to learn and absorb. He had been at the village they called River Walk for about three months and still had a lot to learn. Although his language was better, it was still basic. He was able to recognize Susquehannock warriors and how they wore their clothing, their feathers, and greeted each other. He wanted to learn about the ways of the other tribes.

They made camp on a small island in the middle of the river for safety. At that campfire, Judah asked for help in recognizing the differences in the Lenape and the Esopus warrior headbands and dress. Only one young warrior had the patience with Judah's language to tell him about the differences in the feathered headbands of the Susquehannock worn atop the head, versus the Lenape warriors' worn behind and back. Judah thought he would call the young warrior Sad Eyes, because his eyelids were hooded. No one else seemed interested enough to answer Judah's question. Bear Smile curled inward to his blanket and went to sleep.

Five warriors and Blue Eyes slipped into three canoes when the frost hung low on the Delaware riverbank, and they headed south. The sun hid behind ominous clouds, preparing to spew an over-laden store of misery. A robust wind blew the canoes downriver, bringing the driving rain mixed with sleet and the nor'easter with it. The wind carried the canoes toward the shore, and the warriors had to fight the water and struggle with their loads to keep them pointed in the right direction. The lead canoe with Bear Smile changed its position with the next in line to avoid fatigue in the storm. They did this every few hours on the trip with Blue Eyes in the trailing canoe with a young warrior he did not know.

The wind and rain began to lessen, to Judah's relief, and so did the convoy's efforts. Even the sun peeked out from behind two puffy clouds shaped like a meadow. The riverbanks were muddy and broken. Beaching the canoes here would not have been a good idea. Judah knew this was all new territory, and his eyes were wide with anticipation. He marveled at the growth of the riverbank, the vast trees whose branches hung over the river like great guardians to keep intruders from disturbing the quiet solitude of the forest. The tiny convoy pulled to a break stop alongside the bank for dried meat, water, and urination.

The area was ripe for hunting, and it was easy to see why so many hunters were eager to take advantage. It was also easy to see why several tribes, such as the Lenape, settled in this area: game and fur. The lead canoe slowed, sending a signal to the others who were closing in on their objective. They rowed for about another hour, looking for a good spot to land and camouflage the canoes.

The canoes were beached and dragged into the brush. They were covered with branches and leaves and scattered into the wood. Judging from the sun, it was early afternoon when the party reached the outskirts of the enemy camp. Getting to a suitable striking point beyond the settlement by foot would also take time. They could not, however, risk water travel and the chance of being seen.

Bear Smile gathered his group and told them he planned to launch an ambush in the woods well before the hunting party entered the settlement gate, kill all from the camp, then head back to the canoes. It had to be quick and lethal, and it had to be well away from the settlement. Each warrior was to cover the victim's mouth first, then slash the throat, stab the heart, and take the scalp. There were a lot of unknowns, such as the size of the hunting party, but it was a calculated guess that there were no more than four warriors and maybe a sled. It was a good plan but depended on surprise, stealth, timing, and luck. A jutting rock formation around a blind corner provided a suitable launch and strike location.

Bear Smile guessed that the settlement was about a thousand paces away with trails splitting the woods from where he stood. No words were exchanged. A field mouse scurried across Judah's position near his leg, but he willed himself not to move or say anything. Judah saw a line of ants make their way across a small hill in front of one of the warriors, but the man didn't move or wave them aside. Branches and leaves concealed heads, eyes, and feathers, all blended with the surroundings. They waited in silence while the chirping, movement, and noises of the forest surrounded them.

The sun arced toward the horizon but was visible from the river. Bear Smile could hear the faintest noises as leaves and twigs rustled and snapped along the trail. He used hand signals to alert his party to be ready. Within two minutes, human figures approached the rocks. Hands gripped knife handles tight, and then Bear Smile leaped and whooped as the lead warrior passed him and turned at the corner of the rock. The ambush was a total surprise, and the melee followed.

There were four hunting and fighting warriors plus one litter bearer against six Susquehannock warriors including Blue Eyes. Bear Smile shouted, "Ayee...Ayee," and killed the lead warrior and took his scalp in less than two minutes. He held it up and whooped again in bloody triumph for all to see. Sad Eyes was locked in a struggle with his enemy. The Lenape warrior had deflected the knife blow of Sad Eyes aimed at his shoulder and squared to face him. Judah kicked at the back of the warrior's knees, rolled him on his back, and stabbed his blade into the warrior's heart. Sad Eyes took the blade from the warrior's heart and returned the weapon to Judah, hilt first. He then took out his tomahawk and scalped the warrior with two semicircle cuts to the hairline.

Judah was stunned, but only for a second. He looked for other enemies and found none. He found the litter bearer get up and start to hobble away. Another warrior saw the same act, drew his knife and threw it at the boy's back. The teenager went down before he could get twenty paces away. The warrior hurried to kill and scalp the boy and retrieve his blade. He wiped the blade on his leg as he walked back to the group.

Bear Smile signaled everyone to gather in a circle, collect their prizes and weapons, and return to the canoes. It took just minutes to complete revenge for the havoc in the woods and avenge the murder that their people suffered. It would be a slow and careful trip back to the canoes, an overnight trip in the woods, followed by a long and hard canoe trip upriver.

There was little talk among the warriors returning to the canoes and camp. They did not boast about scalp-taking and kept them in a sack only as proof of what they did. As they sat around the campfire before turning in to rest for the night, Bear Smile thanked everyone for coming back alive and fulfilling their role as warriors to the tribe.

Sad Eyes pulled Judah aside as they came upon River Walk and Judah's hut. "No need your help, I kill myself."

Judah had a hard time processing this until he realized that instead of preserving Susquehannock pride, he was denying Sad Eyes the chance to kill his enemy on his own. What he believed to be a rescue act was an indignity. He could never make up for such a humiliation.

Chief Flowing Waters called a council meeting the night after the revenge party returned to give his thoughts on what happened. The village mother spoke first.

"This raid tested our word and reputation," Stone Face said. "We are proud of our warriors for the honor they have given our village. Other clans and tribes will now think twice before they attempt to take advantage of our people."

Chief Flowing Waters spoke next. "Thanks to our brave warriors, our tribe has been avenged, and the Susquehannock name will remain throughout this land. People will know that an attack on our people anywhere will not go unanswered. We suffered no losses," he added, to cheers all around. "I will now pass out battle feathers to our brave warriors for their part in this raid." The chief handed each warrior a battle feather but gave Bear Smile an eagle feather. The crowd gave out shouts and whoops. No other feathers were passed out.

Blue Eyes walked back to his longhouse and lay on his blanket and couldn't sleep. Judah counted the ribs in his hut and still couldn't sleep. There was so much to think about. He had to calm down—but how? He ventured outside. The night was clear and cloudless. The stars splashed their patterns across the sky like a pattern of moving glass. Judah fell to his knees and cupped his head in his hands, bowed his back, and sobbed from sheer exhaustion and frustration. He knew he could become a sachem, even a chief, but he had a long way to go. He was only twenty-seven, yet he would have to find a wife if he was accepted and show responsibility.

He would also have to show how he believed the earth, sky, and animals were connected and related in a grand design and plan. He would have to reveal how his inner self would help the tribe succeed. These were not easy tasks. He would have to do all this while keeping his native-born fellow citizens at bay, living away from frequent contact with the tribe. All a tall, tall task. Especially for someone seeking acceptance. After a minute or two, he stood erect and walked into his hut, fully relaxed and ready to sleep.

The moon outside was waning with very little natural light. The sleeping Blue Eyes did not hear or see the lone girl open the flap and move silently into his longhouse. Her touch was light and soft as she reached for his arm, but he rolled over on his back and gripped her arm in his hand. Judah's other hand twitched closer to his knife as he rolled her to his right. A flicker from the fire cast a shadow across her face and outlined her shape. Judah felt her other hand cover his mouth signaling for him to be quiet. She straddled his body and slipped her hands underneath his buckskins while caressing his chest. Her moves were quick and silent; no words were spoken. Her other hand pulled at both of their waist thongs. His sex sprang to life as her long hair caressed her chest. The thought that he should push her away now, never to return, crossed his mind. That thought left his brain almost as fast as it entered.

The pair was fully naked now with Judah on top warmed only by the fire. There was no need for words or tenderness or kissing, just sex. With his erect member in her hand, she encased it in her warmth. They remained motionless for a few seconds and then began a slow, rhythmic motion, like leaves drifting from trees in the fall. When they closed onto their climax, the pace quickened to an excitable explosion. Judah could feel her release before his own and the two remained locked together in silence for a moment. She dressed and slipped away in the quiet, as silently as she arrived minutes before. Judah rolled over for some much-needed sleep. After putting more wood on the fire, he fell into a dream about a trip to Curacao and the banker's daughter, Skyler Culper. It was memorable only for the fact that he was nineteen and it was his first lovemaking experience.

CHAPTER 3

The Trap

Judah stepped out of his longhouse and looked around at River Walk. The village he now called home was huge. His best estimate, including the cultivated fields and many longhouses, was well over thirty hectares down to the river. More than forty canoes of different sizes—some of which could hold up to four persons—lined the shore, flipped over to prevent snow and ice and unwanted varmints from making a home. The fields of vegetables alone covered at least half of the cleared land and seemed organized into many clans.

About one month had passed since that visit in the night from what was certainly a young woman. Judah had used that time to sharpen his bow and knife skills. Winter was making itself known and villagers were preparing for the certainty of cold weather by stockpiling wood, sharpening weapons, drying and smoking meat, gutting and skinning animals, storing meats and vegetables, and planting winter crops. Since much of the work was done by women, Judah busied himself by fishing.

The practice of building a weir and trapping a fish was not

new to him. He had been doing this since Brazil and then at New Netherland. The only thing that had changed was the size and shape of the rivers and the weir baskets. The most effective kind was a box or a cone within itself with the bait inside. Fish were trapped in this way without a pole or line and could not escape. After building several traps, Judah made his way upriver and placed his traps at bends or near rock drops. Blue Eyes was successful to a point in trapping fish and built a smoker to dry his fish for the winter. While this was interesting, another conversation occupied his mind and his time.

The reputation of Stone Face preceded her, and Blue Eyes was fully prepared to let her do the talking. She wore a buckskin skirt and blouse with black, braided hair and beaded moccasins and her stride was purposeful and deliberate as she ambled his way.

She told him to come inside, pointing to a longhouse about one hundred paces away. It was late fall, and unless spoken to, Blue Eyes dared not speak. She was speaking using Susquehannock and Algonquin.

"Now that Flowing Waters has accepted you into our clan as a warrior, there are a few things you need to understand. First, your past life is over. You might never see your mother and father again. You will not be welcome if you decide to leave the village on your own. Do you understand?"

"I understand," Judah said, obedient and answering directly in a mixture of Susquehanna and Algonquin.

"What you do now is for the village's sake and not for yourself. If you hunt, fish, marry, or go to war and have children, all your actions and behavior will be for the betterment and benefit of all. Do you understand?"

"I understand," Judah said once again, this time with reverence.

"You must learn the ways of the Susquehannock and its

people—our history, our language, what makes us special, and the reasons we are here. You must earn the respect of your elders and be honest with all, even your enemies. I know that a young woman came into your house not long ago to try you out. You cannot dishonor her. I will send her to you again, and you will marry her. Is that clear?"

This last part took Judah aback. He was now in a trap. If he said no, he would have to leave and return home; he did not want to do that. With only a slight hesitation in his voice, he said, "Yes, Village Mother." He realized then and there that he was caught like the fish in the weir and Stone Face had set the trap with the girl. He would have to marry the young woman or leave the village. That was her plan all along, and like the fish in the trap he could not get out.

"Good," Stone Face said. "Now, I will tell you the legend of the Three Sisters and teach you why we plant."

"When the Great Father first created the earth, the Sky Woman fell through a hole in the sky toward an endless sea. The animals of the endless sea saw her coming down, so they brought up soil from the bottom of the sea. They put the earth onto the back of a giant turtle to create a safe place for her to land. Sky Woman was pregnant before she fell. After landing on the turtle's back, she gave birth to a daughter. Then, the daughter grew into a young woman and became pregnant. She died while giving birth to twin boys. Sky Woman buried her daughter in the new earth. From the daughter's grave grew three sacred plants: corn, beans, and squash, known from then on as the three sisters. Each of the plants provides for each other. Then, a young boy took the sisters back to the lodge individually, starting with the squash and then beans and corn. The three spirits have unique gifts of support, giving, and protection."

She told him how to plant the three vegetables. Corn's tall stalks emerge first from the mound, growing tall and straight, offering support for the beans, acting as a pole-like structure that the beans can wrap around to climb up to reach the sun's rays. The bean plant tethers to the corn stalk, keeping the corn standing straight even in the strong winds. The squash's large leaves shade the soil, preventing the moisture from evaporating, holding the moisture in the ground, and depriving weeds from growing for lack of sunlight.

"The lesson is to keep the plants growing and growing," she said. "The danger is too much contact with the white man. We have seen how his pox can kill our people without warning. We must grow tall and strong and not give in to his diseases."

Judah, in turn, told Stone Face of his transformation to a connected earth from his previous beliefs. He now believed that the world around him was all connected. Trees, the earth itself, animals, grass, and even bugs had a purpose in the grand scheme of life. Judah told her what he did not tell Abraham and Ruth—about the vibration and buzzing sensation he felt on the ground and the tree. He also believed, like many natives, that we return to earth after death in another form.

Stone Face listened patiently and nodded without uttering a word. She looked at Judah for a long time. Her cold black eyes did not reveal emotion. At last, she said, "I believe you, young man, but the marriage will take place in ten days." She walked away.

The wizened old woman had shared a lot of knowledge. Judah knew he had to learn and prepare himself for an inevitable marriage. He was told by his mother in New Netherland that many of the native populations in the area held onto matriarchal beliefs, and village mothers were traditional positions that were very influential in council decisions.

The air was chillier on the way back to his longhouse; Judah thought the villagers seemed to be busier than before. Winter was approaching and harvest time had almost everyone gathering, preparing or storing food in grain houses for the cold months ahead. Judah wanted to pitch in, but he was obsessed with the looming marriage. Sleeping with peace seemed out of the question; possibilities swirled in his head like an eddy. There seemed to be no way out for this one-feathered warrior. Judah tossed and turned on the bench in his longhouse until a boy runner told him that Stone Face wanted to see him.

Stone Face told Judah that that the girl's name was Singing Bird, and her clan was the Raven. He needed to prepare to wed in just five days.

"How old is this Singing Bird?"

"It does not matter," Stone Face said without changing expression, "but I think she is fifteen."

"That is quite young," Judah countered. "I'm twenty-seven, almost twice her age."

"There will be no more questions. After the ceremony, you will move into Singing Bird's family longhouse. There will be no more discussion." Stone Face dismissed him.

The shock had passed. Judah knew what he had to do now, and he started to get ready. It was too late for remedies. As Blue Eyes, he was being forced into a marriage he did not want. Given Stone Face's push, he guessed that she believed that Singing Bird was pregnant by now, even if she did not show. He had a good sense about know how these arrangements would work, and he would not have any control or say in the matter—that was the worst part. Singing Bird's father, mother, and Stone Face would make all the decisions and choose among the details. The bride and groom were mere specks of grain in this harvest. She woke up his body that night, he accepted her, then she left. Now, she was to be his bride. He did not know who she was or even what she looked like, what her family was like. All he knew was that she was fifteen, a mere child. But not a mere child in the eyes of the Susquehannock. In the tribe's way, she was a fully grown woman ready for a family.

Desperate to latch onto some information, Judah decided to volunteer to store and hang meat in a longhouse. He approached another warrior with one feather and spoke in a friendly Susquehannock tone. "I will be glad to help you with that if you let me," Blue Eyes said.

"Hmmph," said the younger warrior. "I guess it's all right."

"What do they call you?"

"Beaver Teeth," the young warrior said.

"How did you get such a name?" Judah asked without mocking as they worked.

"I guess it's because my top front teeth lap over my bottom teeth."

"Ah, that's nothing," Judah said. "Sometimes I get called porcupine because of my curly hair."

They both chuckled at that and continued to drape the meat over racks for smoking in the winter. After some time, Judah asked Beaver Teeth if he knew where he could find the Raven longhouse. Beaver Teeth pointed to the far end of a row close to the river. That helped because all the longhouses were marked with an animal's symbol on the side except his. He did not want to go poking around the village looking for the right place. Two stacks of meat were finished, and Judah thanked Beaver Teeth for letting him help. They nodded in appreciation and went their separate ways.

Back in his longhouse Blue Eyes went through all the options in his head: marry Singing Bird, take her away to another Susquehannock village, take her away to New Netherland or somewhere else, flee elsewhere by himself, or commit suicide. There were other possibilities if Singing Bird stayed with her family. Only in the first option would he be able to remain at the village.

Judah thought through marrying Singing Bird with serious intent and asked himself whether it was the best choice. Would he be able to fulfill his ambition of being a sachem and becoming a leader of these people? The answer was problematic with an unlikely outcome. A forced marriage to a white man with a mixed baby would carry a stigma that would force them out of the village. He dismissed going to New Netherland because it did not satisfy his goals and ambitions. That left the option of taking Singing Bird with him, or fleeing on his own, as the only viable ways out. Fleeing without the girl struck Blue Eyes as being less than honorable because it put the burden of the child back on the parents. In any case, he would need to pack a canoe with supplies for two for an extended trip and then hide the canoe out of sight for rapid departure once the need arose.

Sleep was difficult and seemed to come in fits and spurts. Judah would often wake and reach for the warm, wooden handle of the tomahawk which rested under his blanket. Somehow, the nearby feel of its smooth, cool blade edge calmed his mind and nerves. He knew he could run, but what kind of man flees from that trouble? There were just days left before the wedding of Blue Eyes, and he had to face this head-on as best he could.

Once word got out about his pending marriage, Blue Eyes was treated like an outsider, a shunned stranger with no friends and he sensed the next step. Stone Face sent a young boy with new buckskins for him to wear, for it was time to face the father.

The setting sun cast a sideways shadow on the Crow longhouse. Two angry brothers confronted Judah within seconds, after he entered. Both were armed with knives and tomahawks, as was Judah; the brothers wanted to challenge him outside in the haze of twilight. They stood about ten paces from the longhouse in the open and squared off in front of Judah. They were ready for a fight, their feet shoulder-width apart with one foot slightly in front of the other, arms on hips with their hands on their weapons. Their faces were snarled and teeth gritted, jaws tight set. The one shorter and younger shifted hands for no reason. The two circled Judah like wrestlers looking for an opening. Judah crouched and moved his body between them. Words were not exchanged, but Blue Eyes sensed either he was going to take or give an ass whipping in this confrontation.

It was at this point that the flap on the longhouse opened, and a dark, booming voice was heard over the darkening shadows. "I am Black Feather, the father of these boys," the voice said.

"What is going on here?"

Judah spoke up, wanting to relieve the tension and avoid a fight. "These two young men want to defend their sister's honor and believe the best way to do that is to fight. I admire their spirit but think there is a better way." Judah wanted this whole affair out in the open and not hidden.

Black Feather, who had a three-feather headband, replied, "You disgraced Singing Bird, our family, and the village. Our people have long memories, and this stain will not go away like ice in the spring. Having grandchildren here that are half white and half Susquehannock will bring shame every day to the village. She is just fifteen. If you take her away, I will miss her every day, for I have no other daughters."

"Hear me out before you say anything else," Judah said. "Yes, Singing Bird is only fifteen, but she came into my longhouse and Stone Face sent her. My regret is that I did not push her away. I cannot undo that night. We were both being used and tested. I failed the test and should have known better. I will marry her and take her away and return only if you want me to, but not with the baby. That is my offer to you. I have no quarrel with you or your sons. Fighting will not resolve anything. Do you accept my offer?"

"Blue Eyes, you are not so young," said Black Feather. "And you are guilty about the night with my daughter. After you marry, take her away and never bring her back. She and the baby are your burden now, she is not my daughter any longer. I have my sons who will give me Susquehannock grandchildren. They will not fight you now." He pointed to the sons and to the longhouse and everyone went home.

At a rock-strewn outcrop, in the chilled morning air on the day before the wedding, Singing Bird stands atop a prominent rock overhanging the running water. There is room on the rock for only one person. The water below is clear and shallow. Just to the right, there is a steep drop. To the left are multiple rocks where the water is not deep. The three maidens on the shore point urge Singing Bird to dip in the water on the left side for her wedding bath. Singing Bird will not turn sixteen for another six months, but knows she is pregnant because she has missed her time. She slips out of moccasins and lets her beaded skirt fall to the rock. Her bronze legs quiver as she unties the leather string that holds her top together. Her long black hair flows down just past her hips, and her arms shake as she jumps to the deep side. She waves to the maidens on the shore, watching in horror as her hand disappears into the moving water.

Among the maidens, no one they know has ever witnessed what they have seen. After a stunned silence, one of the girls suggests they collect the clothes and return to the longhouse. Another suggests they simply run to tell Black Feather.

Meanwhile, Judah finishes dressing in his best clean clothes, picks up his quiver of arrows and bows, belts his knife and tomahawk, and heads toward the Crow longhouse to meet his bride face-to-face for the first time in the light. Just as he arrives, he sees the backs of what appear to be Black Feather and several others running toward the river. When he asks a warrior what the commotion is about, he is told Singing Bird has drowned herself.

CHAPTER 4

The Flight and Journey
Part I

rmed only with his knife and hatchet, Judah took off running toward the river. Once he reached the line of trees at the river, he turned north, nestled amid a grove of thickets and well shielded from the river. He threw off the camouflage, tossed his weapons inside, and slid the canoe down to the river, following his plan of escape.

Anticipation was key. Blue Eyes followed his knowledge and his logic. Certain that Black Feather and his sons would consider him their responsibility, they would try to track him. They would believe that he was the cause of Singing Bird's demise. Unless several canoes on different paths were after him, though, he had a good chance of avoiding just one canoe. In that case, a sure death would await him on the river. Instead, he paddled north and headed to a new journey. When he looked at the sky ahead, it darkened to the east and to the north in early morning December light.

Judah could see the flat top thunderclouds looming ahead like great anvils to Thor's hammer. There were many tributaries that led north from the river, but they were not marked. Even as Blue Eyes, he had no way to know how far north they were passable. He would simply have to choose one and wait for the storm to pass. Judah beached and covered the canoe under a desolate grove of oak and pine trees and waited. The hunt was on.

The clap and roar of thunder overhead overshadowed all the noise of the grove. Judah cupped his hands over his ears and pulled a blanket over his head to help deaden the sound that seemed all around him. After several minutes, the noise abated but rain continued, first as hail pellets then as stinging drops and finally as a steady downpour. The once calm tributary trans-formed into a raging stream that overflowed the riverbank. Entry into the tributary to hide was a mistake that would not be re-peated. The way back to the river was blocked by water that was now faster moving than before the storm. The canoe was too heavy to portage. His only solution was hide in the woods, cam-ouflage the canoe, and hope his pursuers would check the tributary and pass him by.

Judah hid the canoe and covered his entry working very hard to leave no trace. He would rely mostly on his hearing and wait, even if he had to wait a very long time. Bright sun after the storm turned into twilight when Judah heard paddling on the water. He spied the outline of two warriors in a canoe rowing past the spot where he beached his canoe. It had to be them, he thought—just had to be them. He poked his head through the branches to see they kept paddling down the tributary until they were out of sight. A wry smile crossed his face. Now all he had to do was wait until they reached the end of the branch, turn around and head back to the river and explore more tributaries further upstream. When they and Black Feather got tired in a few days, he could head back upriver with peace of mind. All he had to do now would be to dry out and wait a few nights without a fire—and hope it wouldn't get too damn cold.

Wrapped in two blankets and comforted by the tomahawk underneath, Blue Eyes' fingers drifted to his feathered headband. He began to stroke the eagle feather that made him so proud to be a warrior. Stroking that feather set his mind into a dreamlike state and returned him to his childhood. He was just six years old and was with his friend Noah, sailing aboard *The Finger* on Judah's first voyage to the New World from Amsterdam.

On that ship, Judah and Noah poked their heads out from under the duct cover of the longboat to watch the action on the masts and spars. Sailors were alternating their arms and legs through rope loops like nimble mountain climbers ascending to the heavens. The boys spotted Niles, the captain's cabin boy, halfway up the mast. He was sporting a new cap with a small feather in it as he made his way up the main mast to the top—maybe he'd make it into the crow's nest. They shouted out their vitality, but wind and rain made that impossible to hear beyond a foot's distance. They watched him as he reached the lower sail, spun around the mast and crow's nest, and climbed to the top of the upper sail in no time. At the topmost spar, he and three other sailors gathered in the sail, lashing the ropes around the bundle while the ship swayed thirty degrees east and west in solid wind. It was dangerous work for anyone.

The boys looked up and down the ship. There was no hesitation in the steps of the sailors as they moved along the spars to the mast and down the ropes through the pouring wind and rain. Their bodies seemed to move in unison to the ship even in these conditions. Every so often, you might see a foot slip from a wet rope loop only to be caught by the next one down, but not very frequently. Halfway down the main mast, Niles spotted the boys in the longboat. There was no one above him. He held onto the rope with one hand and one foot and let the wind sway him to and fro while his other hand reached back, took off his feathered hat, and waved it to the boys in a gesture meant to delight them.

At that exact moment, a gust of wind loosened his grip on the hat, and it flew from his hand into the air, floating high above the longboat, and settled onto swells over at least three hundred feet of water. Noah was out of the longboat and almost over the boat rail before Judah could stop him. Judah yelled, "Noah no! Don't jump! Don't do it!" He lunged for Noah's legs but managed to grab only one shoe as Noah went overboard. The rain poured down now in heavy sheets like swirling and twisted whirlwinds. A sailor yelled, "Man overboard! Man overboard!" He grabbed Judah under the shoulders and lifted him back into the longboat for safety. More sailors came to see if they could rescue Noah. Judah stood up in the longboat shouting, "Please do something, he'll drown!"

Hammershield, the first mate, scampered down into the longboat and searched for anything that would float. He found a net with some pieces of cork tied to it for fishing. He tied a rope to the net and, with the help of the nearby sailors, tossed the contraption overboard, hoping to save the boy. Meanwhile, Noah struggled to keep his head above the waves behind the ship, some hundred feet below the deck. The net and rope dangled over the side. The feathered hat went under in the pelting rain at the aft of the boat, gripped solidly in Noah's hand as he went under for the last time. Hammershield retrieved the rope and net and put them back in the longboat. Judah wrapped his arms around the mate's chest and sobbed. Hammershield covered him with a blanket. He then lifted Judah out of the boat, carried him down the steps, and put him into dry clothes on the cannon deck, where he explained to Ruth and Abraham, Judah's mother and father what had happened.

The boys were likable; even Hammershield thought they would grow into fine men. They were sailing into a growing gale rapidly turning into a full-blown storm, and they could not spare any energy for sympathy now. Knowing the drill, the whole crew was needed at their stations to keep the loss of life and property minimal. There was no way to know just how long the storm would last. It could blow like this for two more hours or days. The wind and the water were merciless.

The helmsman had almost no control of the ship. There were times it seemed the devil himself possessed the rudder. Captain Bucker had been through worse storms, but this one lasted longer than most. They took a pounding for nearly two days before it finally let up. By then, their best estimate put them off course by a little more than five degrees latitude. This severe correction probably added two or three days to their voyage.

Judah was inconsolable. He did not want to eat or hardly drink for days at a time. He kept blaming himself for Noah's demise, saying that he should have stopped him sooner. Nothing that Judah's mother or father said helped. Nothing Noah's mother and father said helped. Noah was just gone, and nothing was going to bring him back. To Judah, he was more than a friend; he was part of his soul.

"I'm sorry about Noah's drowning," Niles said. "He was a good friend, a great fellow. I know you miss him. I want you to keep this as a memory of him." Niles reached into his pocket and gave Judah another feather. It was much like the one that Noah had chased into the sea.

Judah's eyes welled up in tears. "Thanks. We won't forget him, never." With that, he hugged Niles, and they parted, never to see each other again.

That feather was much like the feather that Judah so proudly held in his hand now, a symbol of his allegiance as a Susquehannock warrior. The past cannot change, Judah thought, but the future can; the immediate future was before him now and he had to set a plan in motion. Even for two days he was going to need food and a temporary shelter while staying hidden. Winter was settling in—nights were longer and even a small fire further inland might be detected by a passing canoe. Using his sense of woodcraft, Blue Eyes set up the canoe further under the trees to shield it from the wind while he huddled against the cold. A blanket with branches served as a temporary shelter. Finding small amounts of food like berries and squirrels in this grove wasn't difficult, but waiting two days and nights to pass was extremely hard.

Sleep, without the comfort of a fire, proved the most difficult part of all. The intervals of sleep were interrupted by disturbing dreams. A few of those nightmares were haunting, guilt-ridden memories of Noah's hands protruding from the water that caused Judah to awake in a shivering cold state. His only remedy to get back to sleep was to look at the world around him and hope that his protections against the cold were enough to keep him from freezing.

After his second undetected day, Judah awoke cold, dry, and hungry, but happy to be alive. It was time to leave. Singing Bird's drowning would live with him forever, and Judah believed that Black Feather and his sons would never forget the incident no matter what happened on the river this winter. It would remain unsettled until it was avenged. There was no time to reflect on the past or what happened at River Walk. When he was at the village Judah heard stories from the other captives about villages being spread out all over the river that was later called the Susquehanna. Now was the time to find out where those captives were.

The distance back to the river was shorter than anticipated, only about a half-day's paddle. Even though his supply of dried meat was stowed away, Judah had to conserve his food and energy. By necessity, he was constantly on the lookout for likely signs of good hunting along shore like tree rubbings, footprints in the mud, clearings, water collections, and pine tree clusters. He kept his bow close by. If he were looking for these clues there were good chances that other tribes were also looking for the same thing, even in winter.

The whoosh sound of an arrow sounded like a snap and missed sticking in the canoe's bow by inches. With the instinct of a cat, Judah ducked and paddled hard against the current, and less than one second later another arrow whizzed by his head, followed by a third that stuck in the side of the canoe. Bent low to make himself a smaller target, Judah paddled upriver as hard as he could, but the arrows kept coming fast. Although he zigged and zagged like a snake, one shot was bound to hit its mark.

When it did, fortune was on his side. One arrow found his shoulder while the other pierced his food supply. The arrow stayed in his shoulder until he left the danger zone, about fifty paces upriver. Panting from exertion, Judah had to attend to the wound. He was lucky, the arrow did not penetrate fully to the barb of the arrowhead, and he was able to remove it. He pulled over, applied pressure and used gum from tree bark to stanch the bleeding. The canoe resembled a porcupine with all arrows stuck inside and out, and he could not recognize their design. He collected the arrows for future use and moved on, thankful the incident was not crippling or life-threatening.

Paddling against the current was difficult and the wound to his shoulder only worsened this task. He would have to pull over and rest in more frequent stops. He told himself to slow down to let his body rest but pushed on despite the need for a slower pace. Judah found a dry spot in a grove of trees where he could pull over and put up temporarily shelter. Here he could light a fire, hide his canoe, and perhaps shoot a deer or trap small animals for a few days.

Mid-winter was soon upon him like an icy blanket. His mind was focused on improving his chances of survival during the frost that was certain to come and ice that would be possible. After months of life learning the skills that had transformed him into Blue Eyes, he built snares for animal traps from flat rocks and twigs. Since berries and mushrooms were hard to come by, he tried but failed to catch fish using arrows as spears, tied to strings from clothing. Instead, he built a conical weir he made from branches to trap the fish. The weir yielded five fish in three days, and ten fish in eight more days which sustained him through bitter cold nights. Just as important, those nights gave time for his wound to heal and built up his confidence to sustain himself when alone. The fire could not keep Judah warm by day or night. He knew he had to move on, but at the same time he had to find some form of permanent shelter. He simply had to survive.

Snow had started to fall as he got further north, and at this time of year the winds and clouds were especially unpredictable. Blue Eyes continued to paddle and there were only a few scattered signs of human settlement along the river, and nothing significant. He moved northward, always northward. The river stayed passable, but the banks accumulated some ice at night. Judah relied on his dried meat stores for protein and the energy to press on. He knew that his supply would need replenishment soon.

The river widened up ahead, and Judah spotted two canoes with what appeared to be three warriors inside. They were far too distant to distinguish markings, and he was sure they hadn't seen him because they had not looked his way. Judah pulled over to the bank behind the fire where he could not be seen. At this point he was out of sight of his targets. He circled around and silently grabbed the arrows from his quiver and held them alongside his bow. Blue Eyes walked through the woods and around to their position for a closer look. It was a small hunting party. They did not post any guards, meaning they were probably less than a day from their village. He would have to be very quiet. As he crept closer, he could spot what appeared to be beaver and possibly some deer in the one canoe.

One of the men had two feathers in his headband; the others had one each. He knew which one he would shoot first. In either case, he could not let the other two get away. The one with two feathers gutted the deer, and the other two worked on the beavers. All three were using knives and had tomahawks at their belts. The men were bent over their prey. All three talked and joked in Algonquian, an Iroquois-based language he mostly understood. He lay the arrows beside his bow, notched the first one, and took aim. He had a clear shot through to the warrior canoe except for some small branches.

Twang…thud…Twang…thud…Twang…thud… Blue Eyes fired three arrows rapidly with full draw power at his target. He then pulled back and fired a fourth arrow. When the second target turned on instinct to see where the arrows were coming from, he took an arrow straight to the sternum and dropped backward. Judah notched and aimed a fifth arrow at his first target, who wheeled around with an arrow between his solar plexus and asked the third warrior to pull it out. The first warrior staggered to his feet and then stumbled to his knees. Blue Eyes moved from his kneeling position, notched another arrow, and aimed to stand behind a tree for support. He fired at the staggering warrior, who had risen to see where the arrows were coming from and took the fifth arrow square in the upper left ribs that were protecting the heart. He bled where he stood. He stared down at his wound in stark disbelief. He died in less than one minute.

Judah went after the third victim with his tomahawk. Although wounded in the back, the warrior was not dead. He ran him down in about five paces. Blue Eyes jumped on his vulnerable back and struck his spinal cord with two blows to the back of his neck. He did not feel victorious or satisfied after surprising and killing these warriors. He didn't even feel relief. What he did feel was regret. Regret that he had to take the lives of three probable family men who could no longer provide for or love their families. All of this was necessary for his survival. They would have known that he was Susquehannock despite his arrows simply by how he dressed and cut his hair, as well as the design of his canoe. They were enemies. They would have cut his throat before giving him help.

CHAPTER 5

The Flight and Journey Part II

Judah's next task was to take on the image of and persona of a warrior from a tribe identity he did not recognize. He took the clothes of the warriors and stored them in their canoes. He wore the clothes of the two feathered warriors along with his headband. They had five beaver pelts plus one doe, nearly wholly gutted, and he finished the job. He then loaded the remainder of their canoe into his, stripped them, took the arrows back, wiped them off, and drug the stripped bodies into the woods. He cleared an area in the woods and then set fire to the bodies and their canoe to lessen the chances scavengers would not feast on them. All of this took time, several hours, but he had to move on since warriors would begin their search soon.

When Judah entered the river again, he was in a mixture of clothes and arrows from tribes he did not recognize but he had nourishment in the form of meat and beaver for trade. He also had the burden of three more lives that dwelled on his conscience.

To add to this, he had to fight the elements, which were not friendly. The sky grew darker by the minute and sleet pellets began to pound the overloaded canoe.

Since he was only four or five hundred paces from the killing zone, he paddled furiously to find a safe landing place. An island was only about fifty paces northward and he paddled with all his might to reach the rocky shoreline. When he came close he tugged the heavy load, walking backward on the rocks. His feet slipped in the pouring sleet, and he almost lost the lead rope but, in the pull ashore, his ankle twisted, and a ligament sprained. The pain shot to his brain like a bolt, and he went down on his rump. He struggled, pulling the laden canoe back with his good foot and tying it to a tree on the muddy shore. His chest was heaving in spasms when he finished and the ache in his ankle overpowered everything else. He repaired his ankle using clothing and branches, even fashioning a crude crutch.

Injury in the woods during winter usually spelled disaster, but in this case, he would make the most of a bad situation. He had food and clothing and could make fire for warmth, and he could hide inland for days if needed. A smoker to dry the meat before it went bad was next, but he'd need to hide it in the trees. He was lame but not immobile. In total, he'd spend about five weeks on that island before his ankle healed well enough to use without a crutch or bandage. That doe was just about gone by then, but the fishing technique still worked.

Judah's goal was to reach the largest and most northern Susquehannock village he could find. He had no idea where along this river he would find it. Stone Face, Flowing Waters, and traders had told stories about such a village, but no one had ever seen it. Eventually he was bound to find someone who knew of such a place, so he paddled on. A cold northeasterly wind pushed the canoe into yet another mid-river island. It seemed to him that his past was long behind him, but in truth, it was not so long ago— just over two months. After a river's bend he happened upon a trader's shack near a fork where a tributary met the river.

Judah then pulled his canoe up the inlet next to the trading post. Inside the shack a man spoke first in Dutch and introduced himself as Dirk Dietrick, a trader. It was bitter cold, but he was a person at the right place and time. They spoke in Dutch, which surprised and excited Dietrick. The small cabin was crammed with tools, blankets, buckets, and furs.

"Do you have beaver pelts?" Dietrick asked.

"I have five, all dressed out," Judah answered.

"What do you need?"

"I need a good fur coat, needles, lots of strong thread, stout, thin wire and plenty of fishhooks."

"I have the thread, needles, wire and fishhooks, but only blankets—no coats," said Dietrick.

"Then it's no deal."

"I can't give you what I don't have."

"What about that coat on your back?" Judah asked.

"I'll throw in a musket instead of the blankets," Dietrick said.

"No deal," Judah said, starting to walk away.

Dietrick really wanted the pelts. They were worth at least the price of two or three coats. He relented and whipped off his coat in disgust.

Judah went to the canoe for the beaver pelts. They were soft and furry to the touch and worth a handsome price in Europe. Dietrick knew it, and Judah knew it. A deal was a deal.

Judah could feel the warmth of Dietrick's coat the instant he put it on. The fur collar around his neck shielded him against the brisk wind and the seams were tough and tight.

What Judah wanted even more than the coat was information. "Let's talk," he said in Dutch.

"Do you know of a large Susquehannock village in the north along the river?"

Dietrick's eyes were deep set, and his face was lined with scars. He was now wearing a lighter coat, more suitable for spring.

"My trader friends tell me that there is a larger village further north into Iroquois territory, but I've never been there myself."

They said their goodbyes and Judah headed north. When he moved back into the wilds, he could think of himself by the name the chief gave him, Blue Eyes. The wind had shifted and came out of West and gave him a little push to the eastern shore as he paddled in a steady rhythm.

He didn't see any signs of life as he paddled forward but saw animal tracks as he passed the woods on the right. The ankle on his right side was still bothersome but he had grown accustomed to its lingering ache. The woods on both sides were heavily forested with oaks, pines, cedars, and thick brush. The trees were so thick and close-grown that a squirrel's legs would not have to hit the ground until it reached high mountains. The damn packrat could just jump from tree to tree and collect nuts in this beautiful and pristine country. The sun would be setting early now in winter, and Blue Eyes looked for a clearing to set up camp.

His canoe was lighter now that he had many of the things he needed to survive alone. Even though his movement was still limited by his ankle, he knew what he needed most—food. The bank where he decided to make camp provided some protection from the wind, together with his clothes, his fire, and his coat. But despite the signs and tracks, food on four feet was hard to come by. The dual threats of hunger and cold made sleep for him even more precarious. When he finally did sleep it was punctuated with another disturbing guilt-ridden dream about drowning.

A huge hand pushed Noah first up and out of the water—he waved the hat with the feather and danced on top of the water as if nothing had happened. Next, the hand reached below the surface and pushed Singing Bird up over the water for Judah to see her, as if she were standing next to him with her long black hair, high cheekbones, and smooth bronze skin. But then she dropped back under the water, lost in the foam. At the last, the hand dipped in the water, lifting the three warriors back to their village where they were welcomed with open arms. Judah watched all of this from the sky over and above them.

Judah awoke to a clear sky filled with stars hovering above

him in an endless diagram of light. Some dreams required action, and he hoped that this one did not. In the darkness, deep in his heart, he knew the dream meant that he could now get on with the rest of his life, but he still carried the heavy burden of guilt about Singing Bird's death. Noah and the three warriors were easier to justify in his mind. Singing Bird, however, would live with him as a part of his being; it was a hard life lesson that would never leave. He made a promise to move on with the rest of his life, regardless of the obstacles.

In the morning, he made two weirs for fish and set out the traps. Berries in the winter were non-existent. He put out pinecones with the thought that deer might follow but other than bugs, ants, and a few squirrels, there were no signs of life anywhere. Frustrated after a few days with no fish, Judah set out with his empty weirs and an empty stomach looking for signs of game. While exploring his surroundings, he spotted smoke in the distance toward a nearby hill. He gathered his packs and canoed closer to what had to be a man-made fire. On foot and closer, he discovered the remnants of a small village and a smoldering fire.

No children, women or old men greeted Blue Eyes as he walked to the first partially burned longhouse that he came upon. Curiosity gripped his senses as he approached the fire in the center of the village, a place which reminded him of River Walk but burned to a much greater extent.

Finally, a middle-aged woman and small child approached from behind a burned-out longhouse. "What do you want here?" she said in Susquehanna dialect.

Judah replied in the same tongue. "What happened here? I am looking for a large Susquehannock village in the north, and I am very hungry."

"Our village was wiped out by the Haudenosaunee and their friends. Several of them took our families and fled to the woods—only a few survived. This is all that we have left."

Judah was surprised but not shocked by what he saw. "How many of you are left and do you have any remaining food?"

"I am not sure, mostly women and children, maybe one or two old men. Some of the meat and grain are not burned."

"Where is the food stored" Judah asked.

In two longhouses over there," she said, pointing to two partially burned longhouses near the planted fields.

"Bring the survivors here, if you can. I will see about the food. We are leaving here, if we are able," said Judah.

The survivors came, one-by-one out of the woods to the village center. All together there were four women, one baby, one old man and two young children.

When Judah returned from his canoe, he brought with him all of his clothing, blankets and some of the tools and weapons from the warriors he had killed. In the winter, when warmth mattered more than fit, the clothing was welcome. Three of the least damaged canoes were repaired and the food was collected and stored. After three days in the burned village Blue Eyes headed north with four canoes laden with food and survivors.

It was a new mission, for Judah, possible because he was a different man than before. He had found a new purpose and a way to make the world better. The trip north took on meaning as never before, because this time it wasn't just about him. It was about the eight people he had in tow. Eight people whose lives he hoped would change because he had taken the opportunity to change what would have been a miserable life that most probably would have ended in the woods, forgotten.

Unlike before, Judah now had responsibility for those behind him. Sometimes, they felt like an anchor weighing him down and he wanted to cut them loose—never to see them again. It was easier when he was alone, fending for himself and making decisions that affected only him. It was much harder with the eight behind him. This was his new mantra, his new purpose, and they depended on him to make the right decision—all the time.

Relief came in the form of overnight camping. The river narrowed slightly after a major tributary to the west forked in. This area looked especially tempting to Judah, who was anxious to catch some fresh meat, something that the eight had not eaten for days. With bow at the ready, Judah heard a rustling noise a few paces away which stopped him in his tracks. He notched an arrow, holding the shaft in his left hand against the bow low on his thigh. Judah reached a small clearing, dropped to one knee, and waited. He saw a thrush peck in the corner under a bush, but the prize he was hoping for soon came from one of the trees in the corner.

A good-sized turkey waddled, and Judah drew back on the tight gut bowstring and released the notched arrow. The arrowhead caught the body of the turkey square in its wide belly and took the turkey a whole pace from where it stood. He notched another arrow and shot at the thrush, but it was a glancing blow that only wounded the bird, who fluttered into the brush. Judah went after the bird—then put his hand on its back and twisted its neck with a quick turn of his wrist. He went after the turkey, grabbed it by its legs, and carried it to the clearing.

Judah gave both birds to the women for cleaning and gutting. Instead of prancing like a rooster, he collected firewood with the boy and prepared for camp to do his part for the outing. The eight villagers and Blue Eyes had come quite a distance in the last several days. This campfire had a family feel to it with everyone gathered around the fire eating fresh meat and talking about the future. They spoke to Blue Eyes in soft, hushed tones.

The old man asked, "Do you know where you are going?"

"North is all along the main river, we will not take the small stream."

"What will happen to us when we get to this village?" asked one of the women.

"I will see that you are treated and fed well and taken into their clans, so you will live useful lives there." Blue Eyes said with a half-smile, "A little voice deep in my soul tells me that we are going to meet with our people soon in this village, and all of us will be taken care of and work out our days there." They huddled close to each other around the fire and slept.

Ice chunks on the river increased the farther north they went up it. Winter's last gasp wasn't finished and no matter how hard they tried, it was not possible to escape the cold when outside. The northerly wind whipped them like a vengeful master determined to steer them off course. Blue Eyes was resolved to keep his tight little group intact and on target, pushing ahead against the odds, always hoping for a break in conditions. Finally, after hours, the wind abated and shifted toward the west. A feeling—and that was all it was, a feeling—emerged that the worst of this long journey was over, like a branch bending in the wind that finally lies still.

PART II
Bear Village

CHAPTER 6

New Start

After disembarking from their canoes, the cluster of eight around Judah looked like an unholy assemblage of the needy. They bore a bedraggled mixture of blood-stained clothing, blankets and rags, many ripped with knife and arrowhead slits. Women and children from the village could tell from their language and greeting that they were Susquehannock kin. Judah asked them for their help, and they gave it quickly, hustling them off to nearby clan longhouses for assistance and re-clothing.

Winter was losing its icy grip on the village, but in March the winds still rose from the river, reminding the people in the longhouses that there were still weeks of bitter cold flapping at their doorways. Blue Eyes asked a young woman in her language to speak with the village mother whenever she was able. While waiting for her at the village center, he looked around at the very large expanse of the village. There were dozens of clan longhouses of varying lengths and widths each with its own animal facsimile on the side. On the far end were hectares of agricultural fields which bordered the river. When they pulled into the riverbank of canoes, they could hardly find an open space for their three canoes amid the rows of already stacked ones on the riverbank.

As he approached the villagers, Judah did see a beginning construction of gates surrounding what appeared to be meeting places for the council and clan leaders.

"Village Mother, please forgive my shoddy appearance," Blue Eyes said as he greeted the woman called Peace Maiden. "I have come a long way." His buckskins were ripped and torn in several places; he looked unshaven, and the smell from his unwashed body was unapproachable. Yet despite his appearance, he wanted to present his case to the village mother in the hope of understanding. He mustered all the respect in his condition, wearing a grave and serious expression.

She cut him off. "I can see you are tired and weary. I have been told that you brought eight villagers with you from a village to the south that was burned and pillaged. That was commendable. We have arranged a longhouse for you nearby." She pointed to a small house close to the center of the village. "We will talk later." Peace Maiden left him, without further discussion.

The greeting cards at his longhouse were fresh buckskins, a bladder of water, clean blankets, and ample wood for a fire which had already been started. After a rinse he slept for a few hours, awoke to twilight, then went back to sleep for what seemed like a long time. It was a peaceful sleep, cocooned in his blankets, wrapped in warmth like a silky moth. Judah relaxed, with his knife near his head. At a bathing spot in the early morning twilight, he rubbed soapwort and lavender to bathe in the still, cold water. He was glad to be alone. Going back to rest by the fire felt like a luxury and gave him time to think about what lay ahead for him at this place.

It was dark when he awoke, but no one had disturbed his rest. Blue Eyes was wary of what was in store for him now—he could only guess. If they wanted him dead, they would have killed him already. Perhaps there would be his banishment from the village with minimal survival supplies, or another grueling trip through the gauntlet. He began to prepare himself for the possibility of return to New Netherland. He fell back asleep, but did not want to think about the latter. He was resigned to his fate.

When he awoke, his decision was to remain as positive as possible, because he was at a place where his dreams could be fulfilled. He might earn their trust and confidence as leader and inspire their hopes to rise up against their enemies. By making their lives better and improving their future, he would become their sachem, feathered warrior and leader. They had already shown him kindness. It would be up to him to repay them with his worth.

Peace Maiden contacted Long Trail, the chief sachem. "A council should be convened soonest, to discuss the next steps to deal with the new white warrior who calls himself Blue Eyes. He brought eight people from a burned and destroyed village in the south. We have proof that the clothing he gave them came from the Mohawks he killed before. The weapons he gave us also came from the Mohawks."

At the council meeting where Peace Maiden repeated her testimony, Wolf Eyes from the Porcupine clan summed up what many of the elder sachems thought. "Blue Eyes is clearly running away from something. Killing three Mohawk warriors for their food and clothing is understandable. He should be commended, however, for leading eight people from the burned-out village. I say he should be tested for his loyalty to the Susquehannock by running the gauntlet. He should come forward and tell us the whole truth afterward." Around the council, the sachems nodded their agreement in unison; the decision seemed fair.

Peace Maiden sent word to Blue Eyes to prepare himself. In the morning, two painted warriors entered his longhouse, and as before, he was mentally and physically prepared for what lay ahead. It was a cool March morning, with puffy clouds blocking a rising sun in the east. There was no sign of rain. The two lines of warriors that lay ahead seemed endless. The drums on both sides beat a deep, rhythmic echo that reverberated through the trees and woods. The booms were accompanied by the chants from a staff of seedpods shaken by the medicine man Storyteller.

The difference in running this gauntlet than the last one lay in the intensity of the blows. In the first one, the blows by the warriors at the end were brutal in their intent. Just as he reached the end, Judah stood as tall and straight as he could manage despite his wounds. He walked up to Peace Maiden and to the multi-feathered warrior who appeared to be the chief sachem. He was breathing heavily. His chest was heaving, and his feet were even with his shoulders. Judah's back was as straight as he could make it. "I am proud to be a Susquehannock warrior."

Long Trail and Peace Maiden simply grunted. The sun poked through wind-blown, puffy clouds.

During this trial by gauntlet, Judah sensed that the warriors were more restrained in their force, their blows a little less savage. Their jaws weren't tightened and twisted with contempt like in the other gauntlet. It looked more playful, almost like they were toying with a game. They weren't smiling. He took a beating, but it wasn't delivered with malice.

Back at his house and applying salve, Judah thought about the reasons the warriors did not go full strength on him as the gauntlet had the first time. Judah was reasonably sure that bringing the group to the village had a favorable impact on his image. He vowed to be totally honest with Peace Maiden when he spoke with her again. Judah did not have to wait long; he was summoned to her longhouse the same day.

"How are you feeling, Blue Eyes?"

"Beaten and tired, but I'm glad that ordeal is over. I'm not seriously hurt. I'll be fine in a day or so."

"Be honest and tell me what forced you to leave your last village."

"I was captured in a raid on a settlement called New Netherland," he said. "Instead of leaving, I became a Susquehannock warrior with one feather about eleven moons ago. Unknown to me, a maiden, sent by the village mother, came into my longhouse. She became pregnant, and over a month after that encounter, the village mother told me I was to be married to that girl. I told her father I would leave with her, and he agreed never to see her again. On the morning of the wedding day, she drowned herself and her unborn baby. I had to leave there in great haste. I was followed by three canoes. I traveled through the winter, killed three warriors for their food and beavers, traded the pelts for a fur coat, and found eight survivors in a burned-out village and made it here. That is my honest story, village maiden."

Peace Maiden looked at Judah for a long time and said nothing. Then she spoke, saying, "We have examined the clothing and tools you gave to the villagers you found and brought here. We know that they are Mohawk. The Mohawk are friends of the Iroquois and have been our sworn enemies for a long time. If they find out that you are responsible for their dead, they will seek revenge. Now that you are here, how do you intend to be a part of our village?"

"I traveled long and overcame many obstacles to be a part of something bigger than myself," said Blue Eyes. "I wish to help make this place better—I speak three languages and have experience as a warrior and a hunter. I have demonstrated my skills as a fighter, and I know the ways of the white man. My heart is with the Susquehannock people."

"Be prepared for a ceremony tomorrow morning by chief Long Trail," Peace Maiden said. "It would be better if you started a family here and created your own clan. It does not speak well for your future to remain unmarried."

Judah returned to his longhouse to think and prepare for the ceremony. A runner from Peace Maiden brought clean buckskins for him to wear, presumably at the ceremony since the previous ones were dirty and ripped from weathering the gauntlet. Judah also had to shave; this was no easy task. His knife had to be honed and sharpened using the village sharpening stone, since an obsidian blade was not available. The work took hours but with water on the wheel, the blade was finally sharp enough for shaving. He used soap leaves and deer intestines to soften the slide of the blade across his face, which made the smell awful but the result acceptable. At last, he felt presentable. On a bench of smooth rocks, Judah made a bed of blankets and reeds and laid down for a covered rest near a fire for the first time in months.

The ceremony was short, with only a handful of warriors and sachems present. In the crowd was a dark-haired young woman with a young girl about seven or eight years old beside her. The woman was about twenty-five or so, older and apparently unaccompanied. While standing tall and trying not to stare, Judah glanced over at her with interest. She was pretty with long black hair and high cheekbones, but there was something else as well. Her facial features seemed hard and set; her neck muscles were taut. He guessed that since her hands pressed against her hips she used them in her work.

Long Trail called Blues Eyes forward. "We are here today to present Blue Eyes, the newest warrior in our family, with another feather for bringing with him eight of our people from a destroyed village to the south. He saved their lives and showed courage and determination to give them a future. It is an example of true leadership." Judah stepped forward and Long Trail placed another feather in Judah's head bonnet. "From this day forward, Blue Eyes will be known as Blue Eagle, a true two-feathered warrior." Other warriors in the crowd raised their bows, tomahawks, and fists in the air to shout their agreement. Women and children in the crowd cheered on. Blue Eagle stood proud, turning to the crowd to raise his arms and cheer. But the woman with the black hair who Blue Eagle had spotted did not cheer.

After the ceremony, Blue Eagle presented Long Trail and Peace Maiden with an idea he thought would increase the safety of the village. He proposed that a longhouse be dedicated for the exclusive use of traders who came to the village and that he, as Blue Eagle, be put in charge of those trades.

"I am a natural fit for the job," he said. "I speak fluent Susquehanna, Algonquin and Dutch. I know how to trade, what the trader usually needs and what we need. The trader is dirty mess and carries white man's diseases wherever he travels. To keep from freezing, I traded beaver skins for the coat worn on the back of the Dutch trader. I know the ways of the white man and have his blood in mine. I can still catch the pox, but I am better at dealing with his diseases than you and less likely to catch and pass on the pox to others. You and your people will spread these diseases. I will keep them closed, like in a bottle."

Long Trail and Peace Maiden listened closely, and Long Trail replied to Blue Eagle. "We have heard what you say and will pass that on to the council and let you know the decision."

Although the riverbank still had ice and snow under the overhanging pine branches, signs of spring were budding everywhere. A cool northeasterly wind blew white caps along the broad running water that rifted slippery rocks jutting up from the fast-moving river. The water was named 'muddy,' but the current under and around the rocks was strong and flowing. Fish traps and weirs lined the waterways in this artery that flowed relentlessly south. In that country and among those people, spring is a coming out time of year—the bear comes out of hibernation, the beaver comes out of his dam, the deer and other animals give birth to their offspring, birds to their eggs and so forth. Spring thaw, plowing and seed planting were just beginning.

A hunter learns quickly that you must be patient in the woods; that was an early lesson for Judah. The waiting game for the council to meet seemed to take a long time. He did not know how many of the sachems would be on the council or how many would be friendly, enemies, or neutral. Success, he told himself, would come in deeds not words. He would make the village a safer, stronger and better place to live. A trading longhouse could accomplish all of that.

While waiting for the decision of the council, he spent his time making fish traps and weirs, catching, cleaning and eating river fish including trout, walleye and bass. Blue Eagle often used smaller fish like shad as bait for larger ones; another technique was to use traded string in gillnets attached to long poles to trap fish mid-stream. Like most fishermen, he found that fish are best trapped at certain locations, times and depths.

When not checking on his fishing nets and lines, he helped where he could in the village. He prepared skins, a paid occupation he held at New Netherland. He also sharpened tools and weapons. Since planting vegetables was a chore left mostly to women, Blue Eagle did not attempt this task. After weeks of waiting, he received a message from Peace Maiden that the council approved a small longhouse for use in trading for the village needs.

"Like yours," she said when he met with her, "this longhouse will have no markings, but will have a bench and central fireplace. Traders will not be permitted to roam the village. You will be their only contact, and they cannot stay more than two nights. We trust you to guard the pelts, baskets, and other goods to trade as if they were your own. You must know what each of the fourteen clans needs for their trade. Are there any questions?"

"No mother. I am humbled by this responsibility and will make the village proud."

At his longhouse, Judah lay on his blanket and looked at the chimney hole in the roof and thought to himself—*yes!* He pumped his fist in the air and thought, *I have stepped on my first ladder rung of success.*

CHAPTER 7

Traders and Kateri

B lue Eagle's longhouse was sparse and as barren as an un-occupied shell. The shell was about twenty paces long and eight paces wide with a flap on both ends with cross ties made of spruce and pine. The outside was covered with branches and freshly cut ribs and bark of oaks and birch. The inside was lined with smaller sized cuttings from the same trees. The whole place stank of dried and putrefied meat, aromas which gave evidence of its previous use. He sat cross-legged in a corner of his house, elated by the possibility of his new job offer, yet saddened by the prospect of failure. He believed the answer to his dilemma lay in getting to know his people's needs.

Time was needed to ready his house for visitors, but he would need even more time to visit with each of the clans. He would have to tell the clan mothers and sachems who he was and learn what they had to trade and what was needed in trade. This was Blue Eagle's responsibility: to know what was needed.

It took weeks to visit each clan and learn the particulars. They were a little different in their own way. The Squirrel clan wanted more blankets and had very fine pottery for trade. The Bear clan needed steel pots because they would last longer; the clan would trade woven baskets in exchange. The Deer clan needed beads and shells for wampum and were willing to trade buckskins. The lists went on, clan after clan, some items the same and some different. The Deer and Bear clans had two or three longhouses, while Squirrel and Porcupine each used only one. Together, there were fifteen clans in twenty-one longhouses.

Blue Eagle had met only a few traders from his first village in the south. As a group, they were rough, poorly dressed, smelled like rotten eggs and had the reputation of carrying white man's diseases wherever they went. The only trader he knew personally was Dirk Dietrick, with whom he swapped his beaver skins to earn his fur coat. He thought that to be a life-saving and fair trade.

The trading longhouse was designed to keep this rubbish from going into the village and spreading their diseases. It was further designed to keep the traders from taking advantage of the villagers in trades, since most used only sign language to communicate.

One of the first trades that Blue Eagle needed was for a notebook and quill pen. He figured he could produce the black ink using charcoal, water and tree gum. With the pen and a notebook, he could write down what the clans needed. The alternative was to have them meet to tell him what they needed and him to collect what they could trade. The power to read and write elevated his status when it came to dealing with the white man. It was one of the reasons he was the perfect choice in this job or the perfect choice to be a chief sachem.

Getting to know the clans and the villagers was an important way for Judah to introduce himself to the village and the village to know him. Meeting all the warriors and their families was not possible, but getting to know many of them was feasible. Since he was not born there, he was a stranger in their midst and building their trust was an important brick in their relationship. One of the friends he made from the Bear clan was named Brave Cloud. Brave

Cloud, like himself, was a two-feathered warrior who had seen battle and hunted.

"Tell me, Brave Cloud, how did you earn those feathers?"

"It was not me, both times," said Brave Cloud. "Many clans were hunting for deer and beaver down river on our territory, then many Iroquois and their friends came across the rivers from all directions. We had no choice. It was kill or be killed, a bloody mess. They lost many, we lost some. I do not know how many but less than them. We were given a feather when we returned. My fellow warriors and I gave chase. I was lucky to survive."

"I'm sure that you are being too modest in re-telling your tale."

In order to cement his friendship, Blue Eagle started to think of ways he could help Brave Cloud or his family. Knowledge and village experience and not possessions gave Brave Cloud an upper hand—a life lesson. This was disturbing to Judah, but true.

"I will be honest with you. Brave Cloud. I am very interested in a girl I saw in the crowd at the ceremony with Long Trail when he gave me my second feather. Were you there?"

"What did she look like?"

"She was thin, long black hair, very pretty, high cheek bones, not young, and stood next to an older woman who had a hand with only four fingers," said Blue Eagle.

"Her name is Kateri. She has a daughter and is very feisty and as you could see, is beautiful. She works in the tanning house with her mentor Four Fingers, who can be mean as hell."

"I must, absolutely must, meet them both," said Blue Eagle.

Brave Cloud chuckled as if amused at the thought. "Okay, I'll take you to them. It is your funeral."

Before seeing the tanning group, Brave Cloud told Judah everything he knew about Kateri, which wasn't a lot. She was born a Mohawk and captured by the Susquehannock in battle, had a baby girl when she was fifteen, then married a warrior. The warrior husband died in battle, killed in combat with the Lenape when Kateri was twenty. She was now twenty-three and said to be devoted to her daughter. The community of women, most of whom were married, seemed to have adopted and protected her.

Judah wanted to meet Four Fingers, her mentor, and get to know her story before meeting Kateri. Brave Cloud smiled at that and wished him luck. He then pointed to the circle of women at the tanning group and turned away, chuckling to himself.

"Who is the one known as Four Fingers?" Blue Eagle asked them as he sauntered into their midst.

A hush like a pale cloud fell across the girls and women, as if a demon had interrupted a meeting with their mother. A steady and firm voice from the background said, "Who dares to interrupt my children's talk?"

"It is I, Blue Eagle, a Susquehannock warrior who wishes to speak with the one known as Four Fingers." He replied in a deep, firm voice as he stood arms akimbo, facing the group.

"You will wait your turn and speak when I give you permission to do so, is that clear?" said Four Fingers in a voice that was disturbed and curt with displeasure.

Without apology, Judah said flatly, "I will wait."

Four Fingers continued to lecture to a circle of girls who sat below her from a raised platform. He could not hear the lecture but guessed that the girls' ages ranged from twelve to fifteen. They were all young and pubescent. He waited patiently in a corner for about ten minutes. He stood erect, legs at shoulder width, back straight.

As he waited, he saw Kateri in her worn buckskins. Her sleeves and trousers were ragged at the ends and on the bottom. As a rule, a warrior might need six sets of deerskins a year, women and children less. Stitching was done with animal sinew using rib bones with holes. It wasn't unusual for a two-thousand-person village to need five thousand buckskin sets a year. There were no beads on Kateri's front or leggings, as there were on the skins of some of the other women. She did not wear necklaces or adorn herself with amulets or decorations. In short, she dressed more plainly than those around her.

Four Fingers jumped down from her perch as if she were twenty, not sixty years old. She patted the girls on their heads—

she had to reach up to do this for some—and clapped her hands only once. They melted away to the outside. It was easy to see who ruled this roost. She signaled for Blue Eagle to come closer.

"I am known as Blue Eagle," he said as he strode toward the old woman.

"I know who you are," the old woman said sharply. "I am known as Four Fingers," and held up her right hand, minus her little finger, as proof of her moniker. "I was taken prisoner by the Iroquois at age six along with my father. I spat in the chief's eye, and he cut off my little finger as revenge, then killed my father." Her voice was steady now, and not sharp as before. "I learned about you when you passed the gauntlet test. Why are you here?"

"I see why the girls look up to you as a mother. You are both brave and wise," said Judah, his tone now even and not pretentious. "I was a tanner once at a place called New Netherland along a different river, distant from here. At that place they used a special knife called a fleshing knife to scrape the fat, bone and gristle from inside the animal's hide without damage to the hide. If we could trade for such knives, our work here would go much faster and cleaner than the stones and knives we use now."

"I would have to see those knives in use first," Four Fingers said.

"Of course, but their price in trade would be high."

"Is that all you came to tell me?"

"No, I wish to know about the woman that is called Kateri. I wish to talk with her and ask her to marry me."

"I will not speak for Kateri, she is a grown woman with a daughter. She lives with others, including another widow at the longhouse. They sometimes bring the daughter to work sessions. Kateri is a talented worker and devoted to her daughter that we accept as our own. You are a white man. If she wants to talk with you, you may do so in my house."

After getting directions to the tanning longhouse, Judah was certain that Four Fingers was going to be involved somehow in

71

the future between him and Kateri. He was not certain how, but his sense told him that it was an inevitability. There was a tone in her voice and the way she said the words 'white man' that seemed to say, "Don't think you're special because you're a white man and can speak our language." Judah had gained respect for these people. They were independent, proud of their heritage and cunning, and could live without the white man's intrusion into their lives.

At the tanner's longhouse he asked to meet with Kateri privately, outside at first without her daughter. "From the moment I saw you at the feather ceremony I knew that you were special," he said. "The way that you stood and held yourself was different. I could also tell that you worked with your hands. I think that I too am different. I want to help you and your daughter to become all that you can be. I want to make you and your daughter and this village proud of what I can do for them. I want to make their lives better, more protected and safer. I know I can do these things. I have skills and talents here, and also in the woods. I speak three languages and know the ways of the white man. I know how to lead and fight. With you by my side, we could do even more together. I have talked enough. Tell me about you."

"They call you Blue Eagle, right?" Judah nodded and she continued. "I have been told a little about you, and it frightens me. Warriors hunt in the woods, forget they are married and go off with other women when they feel like it. My daughter is reckless sometimes, and I lose control. Your blue eyes make me nervous. Up close you look like a demon." Kateri's eyes narrowed in fear. "Why should I trust you?"

"In my mother's and father's religion there is a tradition of loyalty to a family that lasts a lifetime. If a man breaks that tradition, he will always repay the family for the broken promise. I could never be disloyal to you or your daughter. To marry you would be a sacred honor."

Blue Eagle said these words as he extended his grasp to hold her hands. At first, she drew back from him. She then looked into his eyes and slowly grasped his hands in hers and held them tight.

Inside, Four Fingers told him what he wanted to hear. "I have spoken to Kateri, and she has consented to the marriage ceremony in four days when the sun rises. If you want her as a bride, I will arrange it."

Four Fingers then told him he must prepare before the ceremony, moving his clothing and weapons into the longhouse. "Bring in nothing else of yours," she said. "You must bring her fine bird feathers and flowers to show her your enduring love and admiration. You will join hands and promise to love and protect Kateri and her daughter, and we will light smoke to close the ceremony. The girls will prepare a ceremonial ring of flowers and stones. A place in the longhouse is ready for the three of you."

Four Fingers recited the words without emotion, as if she had been through this many times before— which, of course, she had. "Do you have any questions?"

If Judah had any questions, he was not about to ask. The most challenging part of the preparation was obtaining fine bird feathers for the ceremony. Killing an eagle or hawk for this occasion was considered bad luck and those birds could not be used. Blue Eagle would hunt for a pheasant, turkey, or something similar, but time was not on his side. That night he set up a small camp away from others, baiting his traps, and waited. He did not want to attract a vulture or a similar scavenger. It wasn't long before he had a small group of three frogs. He set these down in a clearing and waited. He saw hawks circling high overhead quickly, but he had no desire to kill them.

Leaves and twigs surrounded his open bait for camouflage. Judah could see the airborne hunters circling in closer. He spotted a thrush sitting in a tree only ten paces away. He notched his arrow, bent the bow thirty degrees, and let the arrow go. He saw the thrush fall more than halfway down the tree, the arrow still stuck in its side. He scampered up the tree to retrieve his quarry. In the meantime, a hawk overhead, wings splayed, swooped down to its prey with talons extended, and snatched up two frogs from the clearing. The second hawk swept up the third frog in less than a second. Judah saw all of this from his perch halfway up the tree. What just happened in the space of less than thirty seconds was breathtaking. He threw the bird and arrow to the ground. He then climbed down the tree and squatted on the ground. His chest was heaving with exhaustion and relief.

He might never see birds of prey pick up their quarry at that close range again. What they left behind, however, was just as precious. While snatching up their quarry, they deposited four wing feathers. Judah returned these with the thrush to the long-house, where he would prepare his final meal before the next day's wedding.

The morning of the wedding was bright and chilly. Everything and everybody seemed to be ready. Judah showed up with feathers and flowers in hand. He brought his few clothes and weapons as instructed and wore his best buckskins. Kateri was beautiful in her deerskin skirt and beaded blouse, as was her young daughter, who had flowers in her long black hair. The ceremony went as Four Fingers predicted. After Judah presented the feathers and flowers, Kateri handed them to the attending maidens. There was quiet whispering and stroking of the feathers passed around the circle. He then lit some moss and embers for the smoke and promised eternal loyalty and protection to the family, the clan, and the village.

Judah and Kateri held hands, and Storyteller, the medicine man, said a prayer, rattled his seed pod over their heads, and the ceremony ended. Judah gave her a hairclip made from a piece of deer antler. She gave him a beaded leather necklace made from hollow shells. Prayers for happiness and longevity followed. The pair danced in a small circle, and the short ceremony concluded. Then the general dancing and music began. The festivities lasted only a few hours since it was not a village-wide ceremony. The purpose was to induct Judah into the tanning group, forty families of all ages who lived in two longhouses under the Squirrel flap whose primary job was tanning hides. It was an excellent place to start, since his experience pointed him in this direction. The more warriors he could get to know, the more followers he could lead and direct.

There was no immediate acceptance because he had become married, but it was a first step in responsibility. His job now was to know his new bride and family. Since he was married, he and Kateri needed some time together to get to know each other. Each longhouse was well over one hundred paces long and over fifty paces wide, with several fireplaces. Blankets separated their things, and a fire was not too far away. Some privacy was available to almost everyone inside, but you had to be respectful and watch where you walked. An eating and sleeping area were also ready for them.

Judah spoke first. "Kateri is a fine name; it means beautiful in Mohawk, right?"

"Yes," she said in a shy tone.

"When I was canoeing down the river and thinking of marriage to you, I spotted a group of dragonflies dancing among the cattails. My thoughts went immediately to the two of us. If it does not offend, I would like to call you Little Dragonfly from now on." Judah pumped up his chest as he proposed this name.

Kateri replied, "As you will soon see, I am not a little girl anymore. I have been called Kateri my whole life, and I prefer that name now that I am married again. I will call you Blue Eagle or, if you prefer, my husband." She said this without a smile in her voice.

The comments took Judah aback. He was not expecting a reply of confidence and self-worth, but he respected the remarks for what they represented. Now he understood that he had not married a girl, but a grown woman who understood the world around her, someone who was not easily manipulated by others and would stand up for her beliefs.

Judah looked Kateri in the eyes. His own sparkling blue eyes met her deep-brown ones, and the pair gazed at each other at first and then began to speak almost simultaneously. They talked about their backgrounds, how they came to the camp, and why they were there. They talked for a very long time. They also spoke about what they wanted from life and each other. They laughed about why they would get married first and then talked about this later. There was still much to learn from each other. They had just met. They both seemed exhausted and fell asleep holding each other.

A peek behind the door flap revealed a spray of stars against a black sky with only night sounds. Owls were hooting, and couples were stirring under blankets. Fireplaces crackled inside the longhouse. Judah re-kindled the nearby fire. Kateri stirred half-awake, and the two stripped off their clothing under the blanket. He felt her body's heat next to his, and she felt his next to her. Their breathing became more labored as his hands began to search her body and her smooth, bronzed skin, and then the stroking began. There was no kissing. Her fingers inched across his muscular back and down his spine. Kateri urged him to be gentle as sweat formed over his rising chest and back. Her body enveloped him like a sheath to a blade. She whispered something in his ear but still there was no kissing.

The pair stayed together motionless on their sides, savoring the moment. Kateri then spoke softly. "This is private between husband and wife. You must not ever speak of this to anyone. Do you understand?"

"There is no shame here," he said in reply. They rested and slept, spending time together in each other's arms, wrapped in a blanket of contentment, warmed by the fireplace rocks.

CHAPTER *8*

Black Feather Returns
and Storyteller

In the morning, Judah said, "Kateri, you need to know my complete story, my background and the whole truth of what brought me here to this village. You are a mature woman and wise in the ways of men. You deserve to know the whole truth, but you are alone. I trust you not to repeat what I am about to tell you. One day, I want to be the only white man ever to lead a Susquehannock sachem. If my story were to become widely known, I might never reach that position. Do you understand?"

Kateri nodded in agreement.

Judah then began what was a lengthy account of his life. First, it was in Holland, and then in Brazil. That was followed by the voyage to the Caribbean and his time in New Netherland. The last part was as a warrior in the first village, the pregnancy and suicide with Singing Bird, the long voyage and murder of three Lenape warriors, and finally his arrival in her village.

Kateri said that it was now her turn. "I have not experienced the white man's exposure to education as you have. I was tiny when the black robes came to our village and tried to teach us about their religion and Jesus."

Judah interrupted her. "Black robes?"

She scowled but answered, "They called themselves French Jesuit missionaries. Now let me finish. I was never baptized or believed in the white man's ways. I was just six years old when the Susquehannock took me prisoner in a raid that killed my birth mother and father. I have known their ways and Four Fingers ever since. The education I received with my people prepared me to be not just a woman but an independent woman."

Judah's eyes widened at this. She added that she was married at fifteen to a kind and gentle warrior from the village's Fox clan in this village. "At sixteen, I gave birth to a beautiful daughter named Orenda.

"That is the word for Magic Power," Judah said.

"Yes, and my dream is for her to become a clan mother one day. She will grow into a tall and powerful woman. She will be honest and straightforward and carry forward our way of life for this clan and others. She is a young child now, the same age I was when I was taken captive, and she is learning fast. Four Fingers has taught me how to treat and soften the hides of almost any animal. Our way is a long and challenging process that takes time and care."

Blue Eagle looked closely at Kateri, noticing the intensity in her eyes and the intense emotion in her voice and body movements. "I know what you are saying is true. There is sincerity and meaning in your voice. I will help your wishes become reality."

"You are a strong and capable warrior, Blue Eagle," Kateri said. "Together, we will make unforgettable children."

She then told him of a dream. Not a vision. but a dream. Dreams are personal, but Kateri shared hers as best she could remember it. She was alone in a cave. When she tried to escape, wolves blocked the entrance. When they came closer, she saw they all had the same face: Judah's face!

Judah told her that dreams are profound, and he could not tell her what the dream could symbolize or mean. It could mean that she was thinking about him and had a natural fear of wolves, and they combined in some strange way in a dream. He asked her not to repeat the dream to Storyteller because he might have his interpretation, and the dream might not mean anything. "Dreams can be held deep and should never be mocked or laughed at," Judah said. "Although they can be disturbing, they are usually best left alone. To make them disappear, some people believe dreams should be acted out," adding that the idea was superstitious and dangerous. He told her not to dwell on the dream but think of more pleasant thoughts like a mother and her child.

"It's best to leave bad dreams to die on their own" he said, feeling himself more as Blue Eagle. "Dreams are often mixed good and bad and come and go really fast. I think there are a lot of fears tied to the bad ones and hopes tied to good ones. It's probably best to just let them go and release them completely, if you can."

"You are probably right, Blue Eagle," Kateri said.

The pair parted, each going back to work. Tanning, for Kateri, and talking with the clan members in Blue Eagle's work. Unknown to either of them was Black Feather's trip up the river to confront Blue Eagle. Singing Bird's suicide was a wasteful act in Black Feather's mind. He firmly believed that she sacrificed her life to avoid shame on the family, and he was therefore duty bound to take Blue Eagle's life in exchange.

On this revenge trip, Black Feather took just his oldest son, Hidden Tree. The pair started with their supplies when ice was still on the riverbank in March and took weeks paddling against the current. They had chased Blue Eagle when he fled the village after the suicide. They searched for days but could not find him. Now that winter had passed, they set out on a new mission to find Blue Eagle. Four villages and months later, Black Feather finally stopped at Bear Village and asked if they were sheltering the blue-eyed white demon who took his only daughter.

Spring was moving into summer; days were lengthening, and branches were sprouting. The change also meant rains, flowers and vegetation budding, animal impregnation, and swollen bellies. Black Feather and Hidden Tree were slack jawed at the size of the Bear Village. There was nothing to compare to their home, or anywhere else they had seen along the river. They were told by a passing warrior that they might be able to find Blue Eagle at the Porcupine longhouse.

The pair were armed with tomahawks, knives and bows. Their pace picked up as they neared the longhouse. Just then, Judah stepped out of the flap, spotted the pair and signaled for them to meet him at the woods nearby. He had to think fast. He knew that he wasn't armed as they were, and they could fight together and seriously hurt him. The question was how he was going to talk them out of trying to kill him. His options were few.

The pair came closer to him and Blue Eagle closed the gap—only five paces separated them. Judah put up both hands, palms facing out, and said without shouting, "Stop! Let us talk. There is no reason that anyone here must get hurt."

"Easy for you to say, demon, you have only a knife," said Hidden Tree. "I can kill you now!"

"Oh, we can fight," said Blue Eagle. "I can take away your blades and your father can carry your body home in your canoe in a blanket, but it won't change anything."

"Let's hear what the demon has to say first," said Black Feather, "we can always kill him afterward."

Blue Eagle lowered his voice, which was now strong and steady. "I was willing to take Singing Bird away and never to return. It is you, Black Feather, who said you never wanted to see her or the baby again because of the shame of having a half-white grandchild. It was Stone Face that set this whole thing up because she did not want me in the village. She is the demon here. She is the one who sent Singing Bird to my house. I am guilty of being a man, a man who would not send her away. That is my guilt. I have married in this village; I married a widow with a child, and I am very happy. Yes, I will fight you both, armed only with a knife if you think that will satisfy your thirst for revenge. If not, we can all eat and rest like true Susquehannock warriors."

After that speech, Black Feather turned to Hidden Tree and said, "We need to talk. What the demon or blue-whatever says is true. A fight now avenges nothing. Nothing changes. The real evil one here is Stone Face, but she is untouchable. We should eat, rest and go back home."

Black Feather, Hidden Tree and Judah ate stew mixture from the central cooking area near the tanning center. At the dinner, they told Blue Eagle that two of the villages where they had stopped had been infected with the pox and that many people there were sick and dying.

After an overnight rest, the trio walked down to the river. Hidden Tree was sullen and very quiet during their breakfast meal and did not speak at all. Judah was suspicious but carried only a knife on his belt. The father and son were about two paces ahead of Blue Eagle as they walked toward the river. Without warning Hidden Tree pivoted on his heels and turned, holding his tomahawk high in the air with his right hand. He let go a war cry and aimed his blow toward Blue Eagle's head.

Blue Eagle had his right palm on the hilt of his knife just in case something like this might happen. He leaned to his left to dodge the blow from Hidden Tree, then crouched and drew his knife in defense, grabbing the hilt and pointing the blade forward. Hearing the war scream, Black Feather dropped the gear he was carrying and tried to leap onto Hidden Tree to prevent the assault. He momentarily lost his footing on the muddy shore but managed to grab one of Hidden Tree's legs, while Blue Eagle tackled Hidden Tree from a crouch as he still held the tomahawk. In the scuffle that followed Hidden Tree managed to wound Blue Eagle in the back. Black Feather grabbed his son from behind and wrestled the tomahawk from his grip.

The three warriors were heaving and exhausted when they collected themselves by the river. Black Feather examined Blue Eagle's wound and apologized for Hidden Tree's behavior. Hidden Tree, still upset, jammed the tomahawk back in his belt with a sharp, defiant motion at the failed murder attempt. Black Feather left downriver with Hidden Tree and did not look back.

Judah was aware of his wound but could not reach it. It was then that a warrior who was dressed in an unusual way came over to him and asked if he needed help. He told Blue Eagle that his name was Storyteller. Then his hand went to Judah's back wound to stop the bleeding.

He told him that he could help him. "I may appear strange to you, but I'm really a serious warrior who knows a lot about wounds and customs and people. I'm the village medicine man and I'm going to stop this bleeding, clean the wound, and protect it from infection. It is not deep, and you should be fine with a few days of rest. You recently married Kateri, a widow with child, is that right?"

"Yes," Blue Eagle said in surprise. "How did you know that?"

"I make it my business to know many things," Storyteller said. "Follow me to my house and I will patch you up."

Storyteller's longhouse was a corner of Peace Maiden's and Long Trail's small longhouse, a building set apart from the council members' meeting place. Within minutes, Storyteller mixed onto broad leaves a concoction of plants, flowers with water, oils, and a foul-smelling potion that he said came from deer guts. "Just leave this wonderful brew on for a few hours and I guarantee success. I do not recommend matrimonial joining for a few days. The smell can be powerful."

Blue Eagle looked around Storyteller's space and was dazzled. In his little corner he counted four pairs of boots with amulets dangling like tassels—all different shapes and sizes, a headdress bespoke of giant antler horns and various strings hanging off the ears, two or three cured walking staffs bedecked with various feathers and strings, and innumerable seed pods for shaking and making noise.

Blue Eagle was amazed at all the stuff at hand. "So, tell me Storyteller," he said mustering a serious tone, "when you wear and use these things in your ceremonies, what mood are you trying to put us in?"

Storyteller's eyes were serious now. He furrowed his brow. "I am trying to connect my people with their ancestors. By dancing, chanting, singing, and moving, I am reminding them that they are part of the world around them surrounded by their ancestors, their family, the animals, the forest and everyone else. They are not alone—they will never be alone. They are all a part of a larger wheel of life that never ends."

CHAPTER 9

Family

know this is not a good time to say this, but I must. I'm only saying this because I care for you so much." Kateri used a serious tone in a way that gave Blue Eagle pause.

"Say it," Judah replied. "Say it if you must." Judah looked into her soft brown eyes. "You are a powerful woman, and I respect you for speaking the truth to me. Truth cannot be ignored. It makes our lives complete. My heart tells me that my destiny is to provide you, my future family, and this camp with the means to survive the future, whatever that might bring. I cannot ignore that. I must do my best to that end. I will keep your truth in my heart always."

Kateri was sitting upright this time, holding his hand tightly and looking straight at him. The fire made the rocks glow burnt orange, then a dull brown. He looked at her skin. The way her right shoulder and breast moved was entrancing. Her body seemed to beckon him, but he forced himself to listen. "I think I am with child, but I am not sure. I mean that I am late. I am usually never late," she said soothingly.

"I do not doubt that this is true," Judah said. He placed his hand gently on her belly and put an ear on it to listen for signs of life. "That is wonderful news. I hope for a healthy baby, boy or girl. It does not matter."

She cradled his head on her stomach, and they lay in this position for a long time until the fire lost its glow. Then, they slept, curled once more in their blankets.

Dirk Dietrick, the same trader that Blue Eagle had met when he was half-frozen on the way to Bear Village, was among the first traders to show up at camp. Judah was genuinely surprised and laughed heartily at the coincidence. Dietrick told him he had yet to acquire a coat like the one Judah had traded him for. "While I got a good price for the pelts, I often miss that coat."

Dietrick had to wash his hands and face in a pool of water near the longhouse before he could enter to sit down.

Judah told him of the precautions they had taken to prevent the spread of diseases. He then asked Dietrick a few questions. "I know that traders have their own network of information," he said. "They often find out what will take place before it happens and where rumors often come true just by listening to talk among tribes. Are the Iroquois and the Confederacy planning to disrupt our hunting or living here along the river? Finally, can you obtain two fleshing knives from the New Netherland forge? We can barter with beaver skins in exchange. The knives will make tanning hides much easier and faster than the stones and knives we now use. That Iroquois information and those knives will change our lives here."

Dietrick rubbed his chin with his newly washed hands. "I haven't felt this clean all year. It's no wonder that you keep us traders away from your people and away from danger. We lead a rugged and tough life, alone by ourselves in the woods, just us and the night and the animals to keep us company. Most of the time we just have wolves, coyotes and bears to keep us company. Is not an easy life, dragging all this stuff around village to village, never knowing where you're going to sleep—or even if you're going to wake up the next day. But I'll do my best to find out for ya those things that you asked. Now, you gotta do something for me."

"What is it?" Judah asked

"First, if you still have it, I'd like to have that fur coat back. I don't care what shape it is in. Second, I need someone to help me patch my canoe. And third, if I can find your fleshing knives, I'll trade you a good tomahawk and bow and arrow set for them."

"That, my friend, is a fair trade." The pair shook hands on it. Additional items that Judah had for trade included three woven baskets, two beaded skirts, a war club, a bear cape, and two handmade knives. In exchange he received a canoe, two iron pots with lids, shovels and axes, cooking spoons, utensils, and sharpening stones.

Judah told Dirk that he needed a writing pen and notebook in addition to the fleshing knives. Beaver, he assured the trader, were hard to find but he would try again soon. He called for Four Fingers to examine the cooking utensils and other items, just to be sure they were suitable. Four Fingers picked through some utensils and accepted the lot. Since beaver pelts were not available, Dirk was not satisfied with the trade.

The worn and soiled fur coat lay in a corner of the Squirrel longhouse amid a pile of unkept and torn buckskins. The coat's usefulness had long since passed. Judah snatched the coat from the pile. In a casual gesture that he was sure Dietrick would understand, Judah handed him the coat. "It's yours now, Dirk, wear it well. I will have someone help you with your canoe."

Later, Judah knelt by Kateri as she wove and tied lengths of deer sinew together from shoulder pieces for buckskin uppers.

She looked into his deep-blue eyes. "I need to tend to your wound, clean it to make sure it does not become infected."

He disrobed his upper body in full view of the other girls. They gasped a little but were not alarmed at his scarred hard body. It was the body of a tested and proven warrior whose white skin had been bronzed through many adventures in the wilderness. Kateri patted the wound with some water, then used rosemary and lavender oils along with bark to dress the wound. Since the wound was not bleeding, she thought another few days' rest would be enough for healing. Kateri moved away from the sewing and tanning circle and wanted to talk to Judah about Orenda.

"She seems bored and out of place with the womanly chores she is very adept at doing, like sewing and tanning. Her distaste for planting and sowing is also evident. Although she is obedient, she turns inward and moody at what displeases her."

"What pleases her?" Judah asked.

Kateri spoke in a low voice that could be barely heard. "She is only eight years old. At heart she yearns for the woods with ambitions to be a female warrior. She wishes she was born a man and regrets that she is a woman. It is a difficult situation for me and for us."

Blue Eagle gave this considerable thought before responding. "Orenda is very young and being alone there is out of the question. She needs mature guidance and understanding, a patient teacher who can focus her talents and energy in the right direction, a young person she can look to for protection. The problem is where to find such a person who would be willing to take on such a task. Until that person can be found, I suggest that she go on a short field trip with young boys about her age to learn basic skills in the woods like building fires, catching fish, frogs and trapping mice and rabbits. To know what plants are good and edible and which ones are not and the like. I will attempt to find her a mentor to her quest. It will not be easy."

"Thank you, Blue Eagle" said Kateri. "You know that Orenda means magic power in Iroquois. We will need magic power to make and set her on the right path."

"I am going now to ask Storyteller if he knows of someone who can help us," said Blue Eagle.

Storyteller recalled an ancient legend about a warrior princess who came down from heaven to save a people from destruction. She was a sister of Sky Mother named Sacho, a princess who fought off unfriendly tribes to free the Haudenosaunee. Blue Eagle reminded Storyteller that the need for Orenda was here and now, not an ancient story. Storyteller said ancient legends have truth in reality, and Orenda could become a female warrior one day with proper guidance.

Blue Eagle said, "This is where you come in—help us find someone who will protect and show Orenda the way of the world and the woods. Someone we and Orenda can trust."

"That, my friend, is very difficult, but I will try."

Judah went back to Kateri and told her of Storyteller's promise to find someone to mentor Orenda. Kateri liked the plan but was not hopeful that a warrior could be found to match the need.

Blue Eagle confided in Kateri that he also had a predicament. He was struggling to overcome a strong urge to provide the village with more game meat, beaver, and secure their living conditions. All three were high on his list of accomplishments. "To become a respected sachem leader, I must prove that I am a warrior capable of hunting and killing game animals," he said, "bringing in beavers as trading material and securing the village against attacks from unfriendly forces."

Summer was nearing an end and preparation for the fall hunting season was beginning. This meant that everyone in the village had extra duties in order to be prepared. Judah learned that he was to lead a party of fifty warriors from different clans going downstream and west in search of game and beaver. This was just what he needed and wanted. Word circulated among the clan that Long Tree was also going on the hunt, leaving

Three Hawks of the Bear clan sachem behind as chief in absentia. Peacemaker remained as the village mother. The clans pooled their resources and divided their hunting areas into five groups with three clans in each group. Blue Eagle led one of those groups.

The effort over the next few weeks was preparation for hunting. Nothing else mattered. Supply stockage, sharpening of tools and weapons, plus readying canoes and clothing were important, but so was spiritual and physical readiness. The mind and the body had to be prepared for what lay ahead—a grueling exposure that required a patient and focused mind and body, an ability to adapt and overcome unseen obstacles.

Each hunter, and especially leaders like Blue Eagle, would have to display a connection with their environment, using a keen sense of direction, sight, and smell to guide their men on the right path. To this end, he would meditate one to two hours a day. He would clear his mind then focus with his legs crossed near a small fire and rock until he was totally focused on his mission. He found this system most useful when he employed it early in the morning or late at night.

A huge bonfire was lit at the village center the night before the big hunt. Two concentric rings were formed around the fire with one circle dancing clockwise, the other counterclockwise. Storyteller was on the outside chanting songs in full regalia with his seed pod staff and fringed boots. He praised their ancestors in the hope for a fruitful hunt and danced for well over an hour. Children whooped and shouted their pleasure at the chance to throw any object into the fire that might touch off an extra burst of flame.

It was a memorable scene. At the side of the fire, Blue Eagle gathered his warriors for a prayer session to Sosondowah, the mythical hunter. "We pray for a bountiful harvest from Mother Earth," he said, "so our village may benefit from your blessing. We will deliver what the earth will bring forth. Deliver your wrath upon the enemy who tries to stop us. Praise be unto the

Great Father."

The sun peeked from behind clouds in the east, and a bright orange ball emerged shimmering over the horizon. The canoes were shoved off with a push and slid down the muddy bank, leaving a trail in the mud. Long Trail was at the head with the Blue Eagle group in the middle and the litter bearers last. A feeling of pride swelled in Judah's heart as he passed Kateri on the shore. He had a strong hand in putting this together. As a new father with a new bride, it gave him a sense of pride and purpose.

The crews paddled with ease going downstream with the current against them until they picked up a rhythm. The front boats started to hum to the hunting party's syncopated song. The other canoes picked up that song until all the boats chanted it in unison as they slid down the river in a syncopated chant that seemed unending. A group of young boys, warriors to be, ran alongside the boats, repeating the chant, whooping "umph-papa" as they went. They jumped and cheered until the boats were out of sight.

The boats split into two columns with the lead changing every so often to break the monotony. They kept the rhythm of the sing-song chant for a long time, but the fellowship soon faded, and the rowers got down to moving on. A rest period for water and food came every few hours, including dusk. To the hawk overhead, they looked like a twin trail of snakes.

CHAPTER 10

The Bear Village Hunt

D arkness descended on the riverbank as Blue Eagle's canoe split from the convoy. It moved into the forked tributary named by the Susquehannock as Snake's Tongue, because the stream continued for a long time without interruption then stopped without warning. The hunt for game would begin in the morning after camp was set up close to the river. The night around the campfires was peaceful, almost serene, except for the sounds of mice scuttering and the hooting of owls. He felt at home in the woods. A night watch was not necessary, since there was no immediate threat of hostile activity.

A lively banter aimed at those in the woods for the first time went back and forth at the fire.

"Bears like young and tender meat," said the first warrior. "They eat that before they eat old and tough meat."

A neophyte warrior asked, "There are no bears here—they don't like fire, right?

"Big mean bears are not afraid of anything," said a second warrior.

"I have a bow and arrows and can shoot the meanest of bears," said the neophyte. "Plus, I have lots of friends to help me."

"You think your friends will help? I don't think so. They will climb a tree like the bear—even make room for the bear. They will be afraid to shoot the bear and make him angry. Have you ever seen an angry bear?

"No," the neophyte said, "and I bet you haven't either."

At this, the other warriors were laughing. Banter like this could go on and on. Sometimes the talk would get more serious and lead to women, family, ancestors, death, and the afterlife. These were all private subjects but, in some cases, men would open up a little and express some of their inner emotions.

Before they started out, Blue Eagle had chosen Brave Cloud, Hawk Shadow, and Strong Oak as his team leaders. All three had experience in hunts, and all three had teenage litter bearers to shuttle carcasses back to the river's edge. After a hard-tack breakfast and dried nuts, the three teams fanned out.

Each had their own sector defined by natural terrain points— hills, ridges, valleys, streams, groves of trees and tree lines, saddles, and in some cases animal paths. They each knew how to tell direction by the sun using a stick planted on the ground and held upright with rocks. If there was little or no sun, they could tell east from west by the growth of moss on trees. Blue Eagle had his own way to attract deer using pinecones in a clearing and waiting in the trees. To avoid spoilage, each team agreed to meet at a spot on the riverside after two days of hunting.

Catching beaver by the canoe-load was the real objective of this hunt. It was the reason for going up the tributary. Beaver was becoming scarcer, and the pelts' value was higher each time a trader came by. Demand was high: five pelts could trade for a musket. Signs of beaver were easy to spot—they left a trail on land; their dams were easy to spot, but catching one was much more difficult. Judah retold the stories of trying to kill a beaver under water that ended badly for the shooter. The best way was to catch one out of the water.

Blue Eagle walked with Brave Cloud and his team searching for beaver, deer and turkey along the tributary. They stopped at midday under a partly cloudy sky at a reedy and swampy outlet stream of the tributary. Two other new warriors were with them. One of them spotted beaver sign, a trail of mud leading off the stream into the reeds on the other side of the stream. A third warrior walked around the stream to investigate while the others looked for a dam above water.

On one side, at the end, the stream had been blocked off by a beaver dam. Blue Eagle and Brave Cloud notched their arrows and scanned the area looking for tracks while crouching and walking slowly toward the dam. A warrior waded in the stream attempting to flush out any beavers under water. Blue Eagle had warned him about diving in and shooting one under water.

"The water will deflect your arrow, and you'll never get close enough for a clear shot with all that mud," Judah explained.

"I just want to chase them on land," the warrior replied.

At that point, Blue Eagle spotted a beaver climbing up and out of den only ten paces away. He pulled back on the bow's twisted sinew, aimed and fired an arrow that nailed the webbed rodent just above the hind quarter. The beaver spun around twice with the blow and fell over only one pace from the warrior, trying to get back in the water. This warrior retrieved the animal and used the club of his tomahawk to bludgeon the beaver on its head. The hunting group could not be certain how many beavers were engaged in building the dam, but before they were finished for the day, they managed to bring back five animals.

They trekked over the rest of the first two days, the four-member team meeting with the others, and walked back to the river searching for beaver. Beavers are heavy creatures. The first two days were taken with basic butchering of deer and beaver, shuttling carcasses back to the village. Judah made a promise to himself that when he became sachem and chief he would bring along women to help at the riverside with the butchering of animals. It was work they did at the village; they were more adept at it than the men—and they would feel closer to men and village by providing support and comfort to the warriors.

After he rested, Blue Eagle visited with his other teams to see if he could add value to their efforts. Hawk Shadow was little younger than Blue Eagle but also had two feathers, awarded for his encounters with hunting parties of Seneca and Mohawk warriors as a young man. He was familiar with the woods and had proved his worth to the Porcupine clan. Blue Eagle caught up with him and his team further west on the third day.

Blue Eagle and Hawk Shadow avoided the deep woods and skirted the heavy tree growth when possible. Movement, they agreed, was very difficult for men on foot. They kept to animal paths and open valleys, trying to find watering holes where game would congregate. The team spread out looking for game signs like scat, broken branches, and tree rubs. Game, especially deer, have herd instincts and feed on grass tops five or more times a day. At night, they sleep with their feet tucked under their bellies and are difficult to spot. The best time is during their feeding cycles when they come out in the open to forage.

As luck would have it, Blue Eagle and Hawk Shadow located a small herd of deer when the sun was low on the horizon. The herd of about ten does and two bucks were drinking water at a depression in the ground about thirty paces away. The team crouched low and moved upwind from the deer, working to avoid detection from the warriors' scent. When the ten warriors who were the closest came within range, they let loose a volley of arrows that felled the deer in seconds. Eight of the animals dropped instantly.

The hard work with the one litter carrier followed. By piling two animals on one litter and dragging the others, the teams were able to move the deer back to river by the end of day four. Exhausted from trudging through the woods, the warriors rested by the river.

Strong Oak was the older of the two and the only three-feather warrior on the trip. He was the sachem of the Coyote clan. Blue Eagle caught up with his team on day five, farther north toward a line of foothills. Strong Oak's team had already made two trips back to river and when Blue Eagle found them.

"We brought back four beaver, six deer, and eight turkeys," Strong Oak said of the work on river in four days with a team of fifteen warriors. "The area has been good but not great. I'm not sure how much more we can bring in if we stay out longer."

"We will hunt today and tomorrow and then go in," Blue Eagle told him. "Let's see how much better we can do." Grasses and draws dominated the land before the foothills, an area which folded into a valley and was dotted with tree lines on the east side. "Chances are good that you will find most of the game along those lines of trees to the east."

"I'm going to split my men," said Strong Oak, "with half going to west toward the foothills and the other half to east. I will see which half has better luck," he added with a stubborn determination.

After splitting up the teams, Blue Eagle followed the ones that went east. Their luck in finding deer and turkey proved to be much better than the warriors who went to the foothills. They brought in two dozen turkey and ten deer, while the ones in the west brought in one herd of ten wild goats.

After six long days and nights of hunting, Blue Eagle brought his teams together at the river to thank them for their hard work and effort. The teams lit three large fires, and Blue Eagle spoke to the assembled at dusk in a clear and commanding tone. "I do not know how the others are doing on their hunt, but I want to give thanks to all of you for your hard work and effort. You will be able to go home with great pride and tell your family and clan that we come home with full hands and hearts and nine beaver skins, twenty-four deer, twenty turkeys, and ten goats. These animals will help keep us through the winter months ahead. We give thanks to our ancestors to Sosondowah for the generous bounty of this harvest."

Much of the hard work of shuttling the partially butchered carcasses back to the village remained to be completed. About half of the dead animals had to be transported back to the village, going against the current on the two-day trip to the village. This was an unpleasant and difficult task that involved everyone's cooperation. There was no time for relaxation or celebration, since meat spoilage was a constant threat.

What troubled Blue Eagle even more was news from the other groups. On the seventh day, a warrior named Wolf Eyes from the Frog clan said that Long Trail had been killed by Seneca warriors. The Seneca tried to disrupt the hunting party by claiming that they were in Susquehannock territory. Two other Susquehannock warriors and three Seneca warriors were killed in melee. This news very disturbing.

Blue Eagle told all the warriors that remained by the river of the disturbing news. Not long after, a funeral cartage floated slowly by with three bodies draped in ceremonial clothing on raised platforms. Each warrior stood in solemn respect as the canoe passed. This procession gave Blue Eagle pause, his mind a whirl of thought. There were simply too many unexpected consequences for him to sort out right now.

CHAPTER 11

Eye for an Eye

A burial mound was built for Long Trail and the two warriors killed in the Seneca incident. Favorite items of the warriors were placed beside them inside the mound including their bows, the peace pipe, and the most-used blankets. A patch was dug out on the far side to give them a clear path to the next world. After a proper ceremony led by Storyteller and solemn dancing, their bodies were covered above ground in a corner of the irrigated fields. After the ceremony, Storyteller told Blue Eagle that he thought he had found a good fit for Orenda's mentor. The warrior named White Tail from the Antelope clan was married with one small child. He said he would be glad to help. Blue Eagle said that he and Kateri would make a point of talking to the man.

A council meeting of the clan sachems met, led by Peace Maiden. Blue Eagle was invited to attend because he too led a party on the hunt and so was becoming an important member of the village. Blue Eagle, however, did not vote on the council.

"We are meeting today first to select a new leader, a chief sachem after Long Trail met an unfortunate death at the hands of the conniving Seneca," Peace Maiden said. "May our ancestors watch over his and his companion's souls and return them to earth to avenge their loss." All present pounded the dirt with their fists or bows in uniform acknowledgment and grunted in agreement. "I propose that we choose Strong Oak from the Bear clan as the next chief—all those in agreement shout their favor."

A round of "ayees" was heard throughout the longhouse.

"Is there anyone who wishes to announce another?" Peace Maiden asked as she looked around, her face skewed as if twisted by an unseen hand. "Good, then it is so." She and the others pounded the floor again, stood and stomped their feet in approval.

When Strong Oak spoke, Blue Eagle could not believe what he was saying. Strong Oak said that he should have listened to Blue Eagle in the woods when he split his warriors with half going to the foothills. "All that I gained from that effort was ten goats," Strong Oak said.

Blue Eagle was praised for his leadership during the hunt for bringing in many beaver, deer and turkey. For this effort, Blue Eagle received a third feather and the rank of sachem in a new clan—by re-naming one of the Squirrel longhouses Groundhog. This was an unexpected boost for Blue Eagle, one that put him equal with the other sachems of the village and separated him from other warriors. His marriage to Kateri sealed the promotion.

Strong Oak then took a deadly tone and said that Long Trail was killed "because the Seneca thought we were weak and would not protect our hunting grounds. He said they believed we would not counterattack because they have the force of the Haudenosaunee Confederacy behind them. They were wrong. We will seek them out and we will avenge the murder of our leader, his death and death of his warriors. Their deaths will be ten—no, twenty-fold ours!"

Cheers of "Ayee! Ayee! Ayee!" arose from the council.

"Last, we will be strong at home. Our village will be a fortress.

Walls will protect our people from those who wish to invade. We will build walls all around our village. It will take time, but we can do this—we are proud Susquehannock of the river. No one can take our land or our hunting grounds."

At the end of the council meeting, Peace Maiden asked all who could hear her to gather in the village center. Strong Oak delivered the same speech as he did to the council, and just as well received and enthusiastic.

Without hesitating, Blue Eagle sought out Brave Cloud and told him he knew about the wall project. He told him that he had a plan and that he needed him to be the lead warrior to make it happen.

"What is your plan, Blue Eagle?"

"Brave Cloud will be in charge of the wall, but we must have the materials first. Pretty simple, really. We involve all the clans by taking at least eight warriors from each clan and dividing the wall into sections. I'll use the beaver and game we felled to trade for more shovels and axes. This is a long-term project that will take many months to complete. We know what must be done and we do not have to be told how to do it. We can get started with the planning and layout." Blue Eagle spoke in a deliberate way, but not at all excited.

Next in line of Blue Eagle's visits were to Kateri and Four Fingers. Without repeating what Strong Oak said, he told them that the wall project would require a lot of help from women and children. "In addition to all the tasks that you do now, and it's a lot, the men will need tremendous amounts of twisted animal sinew to tie the logs of the wall together. It is the only way that they hold them together after the supports go into the holes. The wall will collapse without them." Building up a stockpile now made sense. "Children can be involved simply by bringing the men water in the woods. In that way, more people are involved."

Blue Eagle asked Kateri if she could take the time now to talk with White Tail and his parents about mentoring Orenda. Kateri agreed. The conversation in the Antelope longhouse was

101

smooth and agreeable.

"Would you be willing to take Orenda out in the woods," she asked White Tail, "one-to-one to teach her how to live and survive by herself? She already knows some but needs to know more, a lot more. Which plants to choose and which to avoid, which trees to use, how to snare small animals, how to trap game, how to tell direction, how to build a canoe, which flowers you can eat, which you cannot, how to fish, and how to survive alone."

"All of this will take time, months or longer," Kateri said. "She is only eight years old, but she is a quick learner. You must never, ever touch her or try to molest her. This is why you have been chosen for this responsibility. She wants to be like a man and has been taught the ways of a woman, which for her is difficult."

"I can do all of this and more," said White Tail, "but I have but one question."

"What is that?" asked Blue Eagle.

"Has anybody ever asked Orenda what she wants?"

"The answer to that question is no," said Kateri.

The answer to what she wanted came when Blue Eagle, Kateri, White Tail, and Orenda all sat down in the Squirrel longhouse for a deciding discussion.

"We are here to talk about White Tail's help for you to understand life outside of this village, life in the woods," said Blue Eagle.

"I know almost as much as most warriors," said Orenda, her tiny chest heaving with confidence.

This statement angered Kateri. "You are only eight years old, what you know will not amount to my little finger," she said, holding up her outstretched hand. "What you think you know is another matter."

"I can teach you," said White Tail. "All about the plants, animals and everything that surrounds you in the wilderness, if you are willing to learn."

On the outside of the longhouse, Blue Eagle spoke with Kateri and reached the conclusion that if Orenda did not follow their direction with White Tail, she would have to remain with Kateri in the tanning group. Kateri told Orenda that her time in the woods would be limited, especially at first due to her age. While Orenda was not satisfied, she had no other options. Staying permanently with the tanning and sewing group, in her mind, was the same as a jail sentence.

Strong Oak called for a council meeting a few weeks after Long Trail's demise to discuss a counterattack. He wanted Blue Eagle there to help develop strategy. The important questions were when, where, and how many warriors was he willing to use? The Haudenosaunee and their Confederacy operated north and west from the village but were known to travel as far east as the Delaware River and as far south as Maryland. Blue Eagle warned the sachems that the Confederacy knew no boundaries and their chiefs were hungry for new hunting grounds, no matter where it took them.

"We must strike any of their tribes with enough force that they must respect the blood of our blades," said Three Hawks, a sachem from the Turkey clan.

"We can send warriors, fully ready to deal death," said Rain Forest, a sachem from the Moose clan.

The list went on until twelve warriors was picked as the number for the mission. Strong Oak broke off discussion and conferred with Peace Maiden before telling the assembled that Blue Eagle would be in charge of avenging the death of Long Trail. They knew how many would go but not where or when. A pipe with strong tobacco was passed around to seal the deal. Blue Eagle was anxious to go and distressed at the same time. Kateri was pregnant, and he needed to rely on Brave Cloud for the trades and for starting the fortifications.

"Tell him to get help," Kateri said. "You cannot do it alone. He cannot do it alone."

"Wise words from my beautiful wife," said Blue Eagle.

Help for Brave Cloud came in the form of two young warriors, brothers from the Fish clan: Four Rivers and Twin Branch. They were both young and dependable but not yet scarred by battle. It would be springtime before materials for the wall project would arrive, and Blue Eagle was more concerned about the revenge party to find the perpetrators of the Long Trail killing.

Clouds thickened the sky, and the air was laden with moisture. Tree branches, like bows, bent over the water, their leaves scraped the water's edge. Blue Eagle met the group then with each of the warriors to get to know them before they left. He had met a few of them before but not all. Now he took the time to talk to each one to learn of their experience and to encourage them on their journey. He picked two as team leaders that he knew. Moving Moon with two feathers from the Jackal clan, and Eagle Claw with three feathers from the Duck clan. They would each have six men under them.

Six canoes loaded with warriors and supplies slipped downriver in the misty December morning. They now knew when, but not the where.

There was no chant to pass the time and lift spirits as painted faces and lean bodies pushed steadily on the paddles. The canoes slid down the river in a steady rhythm. At a midday rest stop, Blue Eagle spotted signs of beaver slides along the muddy bank. If only he had the time to stop and check this out, it might yield success. They pushed onward instead. The second day was a repeat of the first. A stop at a Susquehannock village provided information about a hunting party that some of their own had spotted in a distant valley on their way home, southwest from where they stood. Now they had a kernel of news that fed their thirst for the where.

The party rowed for another half-day and came upon a tributary that led them southeast, a stream they followed for hours until the water dropped too low for the canoes. They disembarked and camped for the night.

Fires kept them warm and Blue Eagle felt the strain of rowing in his shoulders. He was not getting younger and needed rest. Curled in a blanket and wrapped in his thoughts, he had a flashback about the old man and the horse when about eight in Brazil.

It wasn't long before Noah joined Judah at the vacant lot, and the two began to chase each other around, trying desperately to catch the other. Judah, being slightly more prominent and long-legged, had a slight edge and was a little faster, but Noah cut corners and often caught up. Judah caught something strange from the corner of his eye in the middle of one of these skirmishes. Coming down the street at what seemed a lumbering pace was a single horse pulling a cartload of vegetables or something. An older man was running behind on foot, holding up his pants with both hands. The horse seemed to be gaining speed on the old man, shouting what sounded like "Help me!"

Judah turned to Noah and grabbed him by the shoulder, and both started to run toward the now-galloping horse. Judah saw the eyes of the brown mare bulge in horrid disbelief at what was happening. The horse had blinkers on and shook his head as he passed by. The two boys jumped into the street together and ran toward the horse. Seeing them both and fearing the worst, the older man flailed both and crossed both arms in the air, motioning them to stop. Judah almost instantly saw the horse, the cart, and the old man and had only one thought: the reins. Noah was a half-step behind him. As they headed down an incline, the reins trailed about two feet behind the horse's neck. Judah lunged for one flopping rein, and a half-second later, Noah leaped after the tail of the same rein. The horse slowed its gait but didn't stop. The older man was still huffing and puffing two blocks away. The boys hung on but seemed to be losing to the now sweating and bucking steed. Noah lost his grip on the rein, and his foot dragged down the cobblestone street like a rock splashing in a pond. He fell from the near-empty cart with a thud and rolled about ten feet.

Judah tried to pull on the reins, but his grip was almost gone. The horse's mane was flopping on her head, and her hind legs had now crossed. Judah feared she would fall over on him if he didn't let go. He freed the horse. The head snapped to the right, and the mane straightened out, but the horse stayed upright and reduced its pace to a slow walk. Judah fell to the pavement, exhausted to the bone. He picked himself up off the street and went to see about his friend. Noah hurried over to see if Judah was okay. They brushed each other off and laughed like this was one big joke. They were both a little bruised and dirty from their encounter with the cobbled street but were not seriously hurt. The horse stopped about one half-block down the street.

The cart had turned over about two blocks before and had been responsible for slowing down the spooked horse. By this time, the old man caught up with the boys, the horse, and the cart. Two men came over to see what the commotion was about and helped the old man put the cart back upright.

The old man contrived an angry scowl to scold the boys for acting foolishly in trying to stop the runaway animal that could have caused them serious harm. Deep down, he knew it was a "no harm, no foul" case.

"You know," he told them in Dutch, "that you two could have been seriously hurt."

Judah and Noah nodded, heads down and caps in hand.

"I'm happy that was not the case here. I have some squash here for you to give your mothers as a small token of my appreciation. Go home now and tell your mothers you will never attempt anything foolish again. Is that clear? Now wipe each other off and go home."

Judah's dream narrowed in on the old man. He smiled, and

his crooked, yellowed, and uneven teeth showed through. Judah and Noah looked at him with their mouths agape. A front tooth was never replaced, and silver outlined another. His breath could have killed a living plant.

He reached out to shake their hands. His was leathery and as hard as a horn. He swallowed both of their hands with his, took them in his, and they were awed by his presence. The old man tipped his straw hat and bowed with a slight bend. He told the boys, "Well, that was an exciting encounter."

"Yes, it was," Judah said in a quiet tone.

"You two need to go back home to your mothers," the old man said. "But if'n ya come back once in a while, I'll learn ya about ropes and knots. I used to be a sailor. But that's no life for boys like you. A sailor's life can be cruel and mean."

The dream felt real. Instead of feeling cold and alone, he only felt wet. Judah didn't know how long the dream lasted but knew it was real. He could feel the old man's hands as he touched the tree bark and looked up at the sparkling stars in the sky. Judah felt the dream was part of him. He remembered going back and looking for the old man, but they moved from Amsterdam to Recife a little while later. He missed hearing the stories that the old man could have told him.

While Blue Eagle's eyes popped open, his overtired body and racing mind could remember every detail like it was yesterday. He tried to let the memory fade to black, but it lingered in his brain until pieces of it seemed to fall from the starlit sky one-by-one.

The hoot of an owl jarred Blue Eagle fully awake. It sounded like a hoot, but not quite; more like a person trying to sound like an owl. Judah leapt from his blanket and poked at the blankets of his watchmen who were about fifty paces west of their position.

It was black outside, and Judah's eyes had not adjusted to the night; everything about him was in shadows. His eyes moved back, and the shadows congealed into shapes. He moved across the snapping twigs and brush and many of his team stirred at the sounds he made. When Judah came upon a watchman who was awake, he whispered, "Just now, were you trying to sound like a night owl?"

"I was," said the warrior watchman. "How was it?"

"It sounded like a human trying to imitate a bird," Judah said lightly. "Keep practicing, you'll get better. And tell your friend he also needs to practice." With that, Blue Eagle found his blanket and rested to the sound of men trying to imitate nature.

CHAPTER 12

Scalps and More

Tracking humans walking in the open is much more difficult than animals. Everything about humans is the opposite of animals, especially hoofed animals. Humans are unpredictable in their movements. In this case tracking was easier for Blue Eagle and his warriors by considering the humans' motivation, game and water. Find the game and water sources, then chances were good they would find the humans.

The group trekked westward looking for small streams, bogs, and tributaries. This tactic was necessary because that was the most likely place for beavers to build their dams. Blue Eagle knew, as did all the nations of the region, that the demand for beaver pelts was still very high. Their equivalent price in trade could easily be measured in terms of muskets, rifles and valued forged pieces such as knives and pots. The scouts that Blue Eagle sent ahead looked for signs of campfires and moccasin tracks in the dirt.

They found those signs in a swampy and reedy valley about a day's walk from their own campsite. All the signs, however, were cold and were used days before. The tracks gave sign that a split in direction occurred, and so their own chase party split up to follow in two teams. Each team knew that their pace would have to quicken to make up ground. Judah's team lost the track in a large grove of trees but picked it back up on the far side. Moving Moon, the team leader, was certain they were not far behind and their pace to catch up sped up even more. He and Blue Eagle agreed to an abbreviated rest overnight to surprise the enemy as early as possible.

From a small crest overlooking yet another stream they spied a circle of warriors engaged in the capture of four to five beaver building their dam and dragging wood from a nearby grove. Blue Eagle counted five warriors below. The two warriors agreed to watch until all the beavers had been taken, then attack at twilight when they would least expect it. The tension built as the sun disappeared on the horizon. At the pre-arranged signal, all seven warriors unleashed their arrows, and without hesitation, killed and then scalped their prey. Surprise was on their side and the attack was quick and efficient, lasting no more than two or three minutes.

Judah disarmed the three-feathered leader and shoved his face into the muddy reeds. While his knee was planted in the leader's back, he grabbed a lock of hair from the front and bent his neck backward. He demanded to know in Algonquin where the rest of hunting party was heading. Instead, his enemy spit into the air in useless defiance.

"The last words you will hear are these—don't fuck with the Susquehannock," Judah said into his ear. While still holding his hair and bending his neck back, he slit his throat with his knife from ear to ear. He ordered that the bodies be burned with their clothes on and left one arrow in a body so whoever found this group knew who was responsible. They took the scalps, the beavers, and the weapons back to a pre-arranged meeting place where they split into groups. The second team did not encounter the other second enemy team at all. They all feasted on beaver meat for their return to the river. Rain and wintry weather

slowed them and their canoes three days later. All thirteen returned to the village after four more days, unharmed but very
tired and hungry.

By this time, Judah had become Blue Eagle as a full-fledged
council member. When a meeting was called a few weeks after
their return, there was no question about what happened. Feathers were awarded to Moving Moon's team, and to Blue Eagle
recognition came in the form of a racoon tail. Their tomahawks
were awarded to Eagle Claw and his team. It was simply the
chief's discretion because they had not run into the enemy.
Bringing home the scalps and weapons of the Seneca warriors
gave closure to Long Trail's death, but everyone knew that the
Confederacy now had more than sufficient reason to come after
the Susquehannock, Blue Eagle, and the Bear Village in retaliation. The cycle of raid and revenge would continue.

Winter winds, ice and snow set upon Bear Village with a
vengeance. Unsettling weather came first in form of freezing
rain followed by light snow, and heavy snow was not far behind.
The months of January and February were the worst. Passage
on the river was impossible and made worse by the winds that
seemed to howl endlessly through the longhouses protected only
by hides and bark. The act of staying warm, even with a fire and
blanket, was a matter of survival when the temperatures plum-
meted well below freezing for extended times.

Almost nothing moved in Bear Village in those months but
work and chores still had to be done. Blue Eagle, the very pregnant Kateri, Orenda, and Four Fingers huddled in their
longhouse preparing and sewing buckskins, trudging for water,
tanning hides, hanging meat and trying to stay warm. Hardship
and death came for some of the very old and very young because
their bodies could not withstand the prolonged exposure to cold.
Some people in the village saw this as an inevitable consequence
in the cycle of life. Blue Eagle saw it as a lack of adequate protection for those that needed the most.

When Blue Eagle went to see Strong Oak, he and Peace

Maiden lay curled up in their blankets, unable to rise and greet anyone. When he talked with Strong Oak, he covered his face and mouth with a protective cover. Blue Eagle learned that a party of two warriors, including a sachem from the Susquehannock village that Judah and his teams had visited months before, had walked the long distance to Bear Village because the river was not passable by canoe. Just a week before, this party came to Bear Village seeking mercy and help from the cold for its people. They needed blankets and medicine from Storyteller to help stop the suffering. They had walked for days through snow, wind, and an ice storm to ask for aid.

After seeing the condition of the village mother and the chief, Blue Eagle hurried to get Storyteller, Rain Forest and Four Rivers to help. It was easy for Blue Eagle to see what had happened. Despite their intentions, the party from the village to the south had brought the influenza virus to Bear Village. The virus infected Strong Oak, Peace Maiden, and perhaps others that may have been around the leaders in the longhouse. What needed to happen now was to isolate those that the pair may have contacted and keep them quarantined for weeks, including the pair from the village.

Blue Eagle told Rain Forest and Four Rivers to locate teenage litter bearers and prepare litters with blankets and food and supplies to take to the village, on foot if necessary, to help them out. He added that he and Twin Branch would take the supplies to the village themselves.

Only the weather acted in the favor of Bear Village. By the time the quarantine could be put in place and shelter for the sick could be implemented, the snow and wind eased. By the end of February, the ice packs on the river melted and the rescue supplies for the village could be loaded on canoes and paddled downriver. This saved weeks of travel for Blue Eagle and Twin Branch. No one greeted them when the pair arrived in the village. It seemed devoid of life and vitality. Blue Eagle did find a few children and older men who showed him to the chief's and the village maiden's longhouse. He found them crouched and bent over wooden buckets of vomit they had expelled from sickness. Both visitors covered their mouths and faces, then Twin Branch laid blankets on top of both. The chief simply nodded his head; his face was drawn and worn like an old man about to die.

Blue Eagle found a longhouse with a symbol of a hawk on the side and found a fit-looking warrior who was named Lone Peak. "We cannot stay for fear of contaminating Bear Village back home," he told the warrior. "Can you have our supplies picked up and given to the sick?"

"Yes, we will take care of it. Use any of the canoes here to get back. We're grateful that you both came to help. We won't forget it."

Although the ride back took nearly three days against the current, Blue Eagle and Twin Branch were happy to return to Bear Village. What they came home to, however, was anything but pleasant. Despite their quarantine precautions against the virus, the disease managed to spread very fast to almost fifty people.

The quarantine did prevent the contagion from being widespread throughout the village population of over two thousand. By this time, the two warriors that carried the disease into the village had recovered and were sent with even more supplies back to their village to aid the stricken.

Judah was worried about Kateri and her unborn child. Fortunately, the Groundhog clan and the tanning group were not affected by the influenza. Strong Oak died on the day that Judah returned, and Peace Maiden died on the day after. An emergency meeting of the sachems was called, and Storyteller told Blue Eagle that the corpses of both of the leaders would have to be consumed by fire to satisfy the gods that their demise was caused by white man's disease. A fire was the only way to assure a true resurrection and return to the next life for such honorable leaders.

A raised funeral pyre was built in the center square. The

bodies of the six other women, children, old men and warriors accompanied Strong Oak and Peace Maiden on their flaming cremation to the next life. A long ceremony with Storyteller's accompaniment lasted two hours. He circled the bodies many times until the fire burned itself out. A burial mound in the corner of the fields was dug to lay the bodies at rest. The favorite weapons, toys, pipes, or cookware were placed next to the bodies there to give them comfort in the next world.

Afterward, there was much discussion at the council meeting among the sachems present. Since Peace Maiden had no children or immediate family members, a new replacement for her had to be chosen as well.

The Snake clan sachem, Sharp Point, suggested Four Fingers, from the new Groundhog clan. "She is well known, running the girls and women in the tanning and sewing groups like a mother hen with an iron fist. Yet, their loyalty and love for her knows no bounds. While we are choosing, I also suggest Blue Eagle as our chief. He is now a four-feather warrior who has brought the village recognition, pelts, meat, and knowledge of the white man's ways. He has shown loyalty to our nation, respect to our heritage and hatred to our enemies. What more could we ask?"

His suggestion of Blue Eagle brought out deep animosity toward white men. The Jackal, Moose and Fish sachems agreed that Blue Eagle had made contributions to the village but still objected to having a white man as their chief. They said that he would be an easy target of the Haudenosaunee Confederacy, and despite his language and fighting capabilities, he would endanger them all and not be able to protect the village. The objections stirred even more discussions. In the end, only the three objectors did not vote for Blue Eagle. All voted for Four Fingers as Peace Maiden.

A runner was sent by the council to spread the news about the selections. It was mid-morning, and the sun was high in the sky, with only puffy white clouds adding to the cold chill when Blue Eagle, Kateri, and Four Fingers received the decisions of the council. The trio sat in the longhouse in solemn silence and looked at each other, not really knowing what the other would do, at least for a moment. Blue Eagle rose up and invited Four Fingers to come with him to the council.

"We are going to thank the council for their decision," Blue Eagle said, "and promise to dedicate ourselves to welfare of everyone in the village. Kateri, please come along, if you feel up to it."

"I will be by your side," she said.

Three days later, under a cloudy and overcast March morning, a large crowd gathered in the center of the village to hear their new chief and village mother say a few words.

"I pledge on the faith of our ancestors to protect and defend the lives of everyone in this village," said Blue Eagle. "My goal is to destroy our enemies, improve your lives, and to make this place safer." He summoned himself as Judah by adding, "We can accomplish these things together, and together we can accomplish great things."

When Four Fingers spoke, she said, "When I was a child, I spat in the face of tyranny and paid for it by losing a finger." She held up her left hand as proof. "We will now go forward, confident in the future, always grateful for the path ahead. Our ancestors have been with us in the past and will be with us in the future to guide us to our destiny."

A small group of five Seneca and Onondaga warriors assembled unseen in a cluster of trees at the north edge of Bear Village, about one hundred paces from the village center. They lit a tiny fire and spread out from their vantage point. Each one notched a flaming arrow in their bow. Standing about two paces apart, each warrior pulled back the full length of their twisted bow string and let loose their flaming arrow toward the center of the village. They did not, could not, and would not know or care where their arrows would land. They did not linger to find out and sped from the trees to their canoes before the first arrow landed.

One or two warriors in the village crowd happened to be looking up when a cluster of flames landed in and around the village center. Blue Skies also saw them land and immediately turned to Four Fingers and Kateri and hustled them out of the way and into the nearest longhouse. Brave Cloud and other warriors reacted immediately to the arrows.

One of the arrows struck a woman in the leg but she was not seriously injured. Another landed atop a longhouse and was pulled down by a warrior; the other arrows landed harmlessly on the ground. Brave Cloud and three warriors armed themselves and leaped into canoes and chased downriver after the shooters. Blue Eagle was stopped at the riverbank by Four Fingers, who convinced him that if Brave Cloud and the others could not catch them, no one could. Blue Eagle and Four Fingers went to the injured woman to see if they could help.

CHAPTER 13

Preparations and Encounter

Brave Cloud chased downriver after the fleeing flamethrowers, but they were at least ten to fifteen minutes ahead and would not be easy to catch. Two canoes with four warriors paddled hard, breathed hard, raced hard and passed what could have been several small streams before they stopped up short at the mouth of small tributary that looked like it could have been an escape avenue.

The teams fanned out one canoe on each side of the small river searching for signs of use. Their pace slowed or else they might miss a sign. The warriors were looking for broken limbs, or footprints in the mud where a canoe could drug ashore. What's up ahead? Around that bend? The lead canoe bearing Brave Cloud pushed ahead hard, the trail canoe followed. Nothing ahead. Most likely the wind in the branches. They'd missed them. The party would have to turn around and go home. The four warriors were not accustomed to going home empty-handed.

Blue Eagle greeted them when they returned. "Be proud of

what you did and not disappointed. Even though you were not able to catch the cowardly bastards his time, we'll be sure to catch them next time. There will be a next time, and when we do catch them, there will be no mercy shown for their cowardice."

Spring seemed to crawl and not leap down the Susquehanna River in 1661. Traders like Dirk Dietrick used the bubbling river like a roadway to ply the goods through as short a time as possible to make every minute afloat count. When he stopped at Bear Village to see his friend Judah, he was surprised to find Blue Eagle, a now multi-lingual chief of the Susquehannock village. Business was conducted, as expected, in the trader's longhouse. After his clean-up in the near frozen river, they hugged and greeted each other.

"That river was cold," Dirk said. "I brung da knives ya were lookin' for, and da pen and notebook, and some shovels and axes and kitchen stuff ya asked for. Your mother is alive and well, but your father he did die defending his home against attack by crazed warriors. He's buried in New Nederland. Whatcha got fer me?"

"I have four beaver pelts," Judah told him in Dutch, "and two fringed buckskin sets, and three woven baskets. We need eight more shovels and axes, four iron buckets, and three iron pots. We need the shovels and axes right away. The rest can wait."

"So, what's the hurry?"

"We need to build a wall," Judah answered without hesitating.

"Okay. I'll pass it along to my buds—see what they can do."

With that, Dirk took off downstream in his canoe with another lashed behind him, covered and laden with goods. Blue Eagle gave his goods to Four Fingers and told Brave Cloud to get started on the fence project.

He spent the next few months looking after Kateri and her last months of pregnancy. Four Fingers wanted Willow Bend, a middle-aged woman from the tanning group and Groundhog clan, to look after Kateri in the last month of her childbearing and after the baby was born. She knew she would be busy with village matters and would not be able to look after Kateri.

Kateri gave birth without complications to a baby boy in early April. Sticking to tradition, Willow Bend would not allow Blue Eagle to witness the birth by the river. The baby was named Sosondowah, hunter hero, and was nursed by Kateri. The papoose was naturally spoiled by the tanning and sewing group women, and except for some time at night, Judah was hardly able to spend much time with the child.

The shovels and axes began to arrive at the village within months after Dirk's visit. Although preliminary work on the village palisades could begin right away, a council meeting was needed just to discuss plans for village security, since all the clans were involved. Brave Cloud and Blue Eagle told the sachems that the wall was to be a massive undertaking involving everyone in the village and lasting for many months, possibly years. Brave Cloud told the clans how each clan would be responsible for a given section and would appoint their own team leaders. Blue Eagle told them that all the clans would contribute to building secondary defenses, including ditches behind the wall which would be fallback positions for gunners and marksmen using rifles, muskets, and bows.

Brave Cloud took Blue Eagle out to a grove of trees to show him how warriors were felling trees, but it was slow, very slow. Judah suggested that they burn the base of the trees in a circle and build carts on the edge of the grove to speed up the process of moving the trees. Both ideas seemed useful to Brave Cloud. Digging the holes for the trees in a straight line was another area that could be improved. By using stakes on both ends and stretching twisted sinew between them, a crew could easily dig a line of straight holes in the ground by pacing off an equal distance.

Even given these improvements, the wall project would consume time Blue Eagle did not have when it came to defending the village against his most fierce enemies, the forces of the Confederacy and Angry Skies. Angry Skies was an Iroquois chief who had heard of the white warrior who had led the team that had killed five Seneca warriors. In his mind, Angry Skies had to even the score and go after the one who shamed his beloved Confederacy.

Blue Eagle told Four Fingers that he had a continuous concern that the village was insecure. He mentioned the incident with the flaming arrows and Brave Cloud's empty-handed return.

In a worried tone he said, "It's only a matter of time before the village might suffer a major blow. The wall has only just begun, and we are vulnerable to vengeance by the Confederacy. We must take immediate measures to be better prepared."

Four Fingers replied, "What do you suggest?"

A furrowed brow and worried face came over Blue Eagle as he said, "We should send two young and willing spies to get close to the Seneca and main camps of the Confederacy. They must be able to survive on their own for months and report back to us only when they have absolute knowledge of movement. If they are captured, they will be tortured and killed. We need to have a ready force in each clan to react to an invasion, regardless of other duties like wall building. If we can trade for muskets and rifles, we should do that and equip that force. A ditch will have to be cut before the wall is complete to give defense to the village for shooting and fighting. We cannot afford to be surprised."

"Those are difficult and dangerous tasks" said Four Fingers.

"Yes," said Blue Eagle, "but they must be done."

The eager brothers Four Rivers and Twin Branch from the Fish clan volunteered to be the long-range spies for Bear Village. Blue Eagle briefed them on their mission, and they left the village confines confident that they would bring glory that their information would save lives.

The older brother, Four Rivers, boasted to Twin Branch, "This spying job won't be easy, but it will be better than hauling logs for that stupid fence. When it's over we'll each get a feather."

"Don't count on it, shit-faced brother," laughed Twin Branch. "I would rather burn and cut cedar trees and curl up with a warm princess every night than sleep beside your ass."

The duo trudged northwest, sometimes in the open, sometimes in the woods, always in the general direction of danger. There was nothing to be seen but they moved onward, living off the land day after day.

The Seneca were a proud and forceful people with strong leadership. They respected the Iroquois but always chose their own camps and paths. When they found this valley surrounded by tree lines, they took it. Twin Branch spotted two men approaching each and judging by their appearance and walk, they looked important and in a hurry. He signed for Four Rivers to come closer. The two brothers edged as close as they dared to hear the leaders speak.

"We should wait for more warriors to give us a complete defeat," said the Seneca Chief, Broken Bow. "Won't their defenses improve after an attack of only twenty fighters?"

Angry Skies, an Iroquois chief, rose and spoke, raising his voice. "They probably will, but that is a risk we must absorb. This is just the beginning of a long struggle. I will loan you about five fighters. Do not use your best men. I will not use mine. We are going to test their defenses."

Angry Skies' voice rose as he laid out his plan of attack. "We will move in one day with about twelve canoes down this stream, what the English call a tributary, and then north on the big muddy river they call the Susquehanna to reach the blue-eyed village about four days' trip to the north. I will be with my men. I want to see the one they call Blue Eagle myself and taste his blood. We will attack from the river."

On the top of the ridge overlooking the tributary, the spying duo spotted the convoy of canoes lining up to leave with supplies and weapons. From the distance of well over five hundred paces they could tell if the tribe were friendly, but they were pretty sure they were not. Without an eyepiece, they could not be certain. An on-the-spot decision was made by the brothers to go back to the village with the news and let Blue Eagle and Four Fingers act or not act on the information. They gathered their stuff and made a beeline by foot back to the village, hoping to beat the line of canoes headed to the same destination. Extended sleep was not a commodity they could enjoy.

The brothers had to forego their light banter in favor of speed and accuracy to shave one full day of travel from their trip back to the village. Using the sun's position, their knowledge of the woods, and rationing of food, they were able to arrive back at the village in three days' time, shaving a full day from the trip going to the ridge where they first spotted the loading of canoes.

At the meeting with Blue Eagle and Four Fingers, they told them what they observed in detail. "We saw about twelve canoes being loaded with supplies and weapons getting ready to head down a tributary. From a distance we could not tell their tribe, but their faces appeared to be painted and ready for a war. They appeared to be young, and one or two had many feathered headbands. We counted about twenty-two bodies total."

Blue Eagle thanked them for their sacrifice and for overcoming danger and obstacles on their journey. He told the pair to get some food and to rest. He promised them a proper reward in due time. He turned to Four Fingers and said, "We must act quickly to defend ourselves and be prepared for an attack by water. Let's alert the clans."

Four Fingers agreed. There was no time for a council meeting, so Blue Eagle and Four Fingers went to each longhouse to alert the sachems of an impending attack from the river. The ditch had not been completed and was only a depression in the ground.

Throughout the day and night, shovels and tomahawks were used to widen and deepen the ditch about fifty paces behind the canoes. This would give the fighters some protection against the flight of arrows and a place from which they would launch a counterattack. When completed in the morning, it lacked log re-inforcement, but it did have a berm of dirt on top, plus debris from the bottom that could be used to deflect arrows. The fighters were also equipped with torches to see and fight at night if that became necessary.

About thirty warriors equipped with knives, tomahawks, bows and arrows, and war clubs stood inside the ditch in a curved line behind the canoes for fifty paces. They were the tip of the spear. Behind them, more than fifty armed men were ready to back up their brothers. Like all soldiers and defenders throughout the ages, they waited and waited. Then it began to rain, lightly at first, a spring rain in the early morning, just enough droplets to wet the ground and make it muddy. After a few minutes the rain intensified and began to soak the ground and the bodies that stood at the ready. Some of the painted arms and faces bled their colors a little at the wet onslaught, but no matter. The warriors waited patiently and listened.

As if on cue, the troublesome cloudburst that hung over the village swept out over the river and the morning sun shone through in the east and lit the longhouses in shadows across the mud. The sound of paddles touching water could be heard in the distance. Splat, swish, then a chant over the sound. "We're coming for you. We're coming for you. We're coming for you!"

When he heard the chant, Blue Eagle countered at the top of his lungs. "Come and get it, come and get it, come and get it!" The warriors picked it up and shouted in unison.

The canoes started in on the shore, smashing the existing canoes, with more shouts of "We're coming for you!" Upon the shore, they shouted, "Come and get it!"

Arrows then flew on both sides, from the canoes and from the ditch as fast as a man could aim, notch and fire. The onslaught was over almost as fast as it began. Blue Eagle ordered and led a charge to the canoes. Using his war club, he battered his way to the middle of the group when he spotted a multi-feathered warrior Angry Skies for the first time. Brave Cloud was to his left and the two brothers Four Rivers and Twin Branch were to his right. Angry Skies launched his tomahawk at Blue Eagle, who ducked, and the blow fell harmlessly aside. Blue Eagle also threw his tomahawk at Angry Skies, who by this time had his canoe and crew turned around and headed back downriver. Blue Eagle's tomahawk fell into the river.

Two other canoes followed Angry Skies downriver and Blue Eagle shouted for pursuit. After a short chase, Blue Eagle and Brave Cloud gave up their chase and returned to the continuing melee around the riverfront. The water was icy cold and deep in some places. The few warriors that were left alive were overwhelmed by the Susquehannock warriors. They quickly surrendered and were taken prisoner or were scalped and killed. In total, Angry Skies escaped with one Seneca chief and five warriors in three canoes but suffered two prisoners taken and fourteen warriors dead.

The village had lost four warriors and gained only two young prisoners who chose to stay with the villagers rather than go back to the Seneca. While the numbers were in their favor thanks to the spies and their warning, any loss of warriors was difficult to live with, because their replacement was never easy due to low birth rates and diseases.

Kateri was a big help that night. Blue Eagle unburdened his concerns about security, the guilt he felt about losing the lives of the young warriors. Kateri sensed his nervousness, held him in her arms, and soothed his jangled mind. She did not say much. She did not have to. Their lovemaking that night was slow, quiet, and long-lasting. The morning brought sunshine and renewed vigor. The warmth of the ground mixed with the sway of the branches in the gentle breeze that blew from pine to oak to cedar to birch. Some leaves had already turned from brown to bright green. A woody smell dominated the air and Blue Eagle breathed deeply. He picked up Sosondowah, held him in the crook of one arm, and wrapped his other arm around Kateri and Orenda.

For the first time in a very long time, Judah felt connected. He felt connected to his family, the earth, and the world around him. It was his time, his village, his destiny. He put Sosondowah back in his mother's arms. Orenda was on the other side. For the first time in memory Judah slipped into dreamless, peaceful sleep.

CHAPTER 14

To New Netherland

A council meeting was called with the sole purpose to present feathers and racoon tails to deserving warriors in the last incursion of Bear Village. In addition to those that fought in the ditch and behind the ditch, special recognition went to Four Rivers and Twin Branch because their information saved many lives. Brave Cloud also received special recognition for his leadership.

The four warriors who died in the battle were buried in a separate ceremony led by Storyteller in the traditional manner. Chanting and dancing accompanied the burial in a mound near the irrigated fields. Their families placed their bows, knives and tomahawks beside their corpses to symbolically accompany them to the next world.

As Blue Eagle, Judah announced that he was going to journey to New Netherland on personal business but would return as soon as possible. Kateri told Four Fingers that Blue Eagle was going to see his mother but could not take his wife or the Sosondowah with him because it was too dangerous. As a gift for his mother, Four Fingers hand-carved a small replica of Sosondowah for Judah to take with him for his mother. It was a carving of the baby wrapped in a blanket. Kateri gave Judah a bracelet made from river shells and strung with twisted sinew for good luck.

Judah set off in the morning with one large and one smaller canoe he had loaded with supplies. He left Brave Cloud in charge of the village in his absence since he had been made sachem of the Bear clan.

Judah did not know the precise way to New Netherland. But no one else did either. When he spoke to Dirk, he suggested a northern route as the quickest, and since it was spring he decided to go that way. It was a dangerous only because he had never been that way before and would have to rely on friendly tribes or trappers along the way. He took extra knives, tools, and sinew, because he might need trading material for the trip. He brought blankets and clothing and two beaver pelts to give to his mother as a gift she could trade for money but would not change from the Susquehannock dress. Judah remained a tattooed and feathered warrior.

The plan was to paddle up the river and continue after the fork on its eastern branch. At some point on the branch, Judah would have to ask directions from a trader or villager for the best way east to New Netherland, because Dirk told him that he could not follow the river directly north. He would have to walk a long way east; there was no other way to get there.

Clouds that blocked the sun all day gave him no clue about the weather except that it wasn't friendly. Exhausted, he knew it was best to make camp and rest for the night. Tomorrow would be another long day of paddling against the current. He pulled the canoe closer to a tree, set up a fire with stones in a circle, and huddled in a blanket for warmth. He felt a stirring before he could see it. The moon had not yet risen, but the woods seemed to stir and move around him. He was up in a flash, alert to the slightest sound, knife at the ready, moving slowly in a semicircle. He chose this place because it was a clearing. He could see only shadows, but his other senses were sharp. He picked up three to four branches and formed a crude torch, lit with the fire that he now stoked higher. The sound increased ever so stronger and closer.

Later, a strange noise awoke Judah from a sound sleep. He realized too late that his bow and quiver were in the canoe. It was a stupid mistake and too late to correct. Whatever it was, the sound faded, and he could hear only the expected noises of the woods. The sounds were so familiar to Judah's ears—the chirping of birds, the rustling of the wind through the trees. He could still see only spooky shadows. With a torch in hand, he decided to go the thirty feet to the canoe and retrieve the bow and arrows. If anything, they would comfort him and help him get some needed sleep. That completed, he rolled into his comfort position. His thoughts dismissed any animal predator. The fire and torch would have spooked the animal away if it were a four-legged variety. The two-legged kind would be another matter. If that kind wanted to wait and strike, it would do so on their time, not his. He could not control that. Overcome by exhaustion, Judah fell asleep.

After three days of steady rowing up the Susquehanna, he decided to pull into a small Indian village for a rest. He spoke to them in Algonquin and hoped they understood. After an awkward talk with hand signals, his conclusion was to leave the canoe there, make up a backpack, and head east on foot with the hope of eventually finding a trader.

After four days of walking east to the rising sun, Judah could smell water. At a crossroads with a small lake nearby he found a trader named Von Nuestrand. The Dutchman was only too happy to tell him that he was only about a two days' walk from New Netherland. The Dutchman was shocked that a white man could be speaking Dutch and be dressed and act like a Susquehannock chief. After exchanging introductions, he told Judah how to approach and get into the place without creating chaos.

Blue Eagle did not want to change his appearance. Speaking in Dutch, Von Nuestrand said, "Watch da tides and flow. Make a raft of sorts and if it's not windy, use the shore and go around the point then pole your raft across the river. After that, you're on your paces to New Netherland for about one hundred kilos. Good luck, kid." Van Nostrand said the words without hardly taking a breath.

Judah was speechless. It was a brilliant idea—make a raft with your supplies and pole your way across to the planted fields and walk in. They shook hands, exchanged incidentals, and Blue Eagle was on his way.

He could not afford a chance encounter. After camping, Judah looked up at the sky and saw a flock of geese heading south. From their direction, he sensed he was closing in on the mouth of the river where he would make his crossing. His sleep was disturbed by a cloudy dream. He dreamed that a rock talked to him. The rock told him about the story of creation and how the Sky Mother came to Earth and brought forth the animals, the water, the trees, and the mountains. The dream was not unpleasant but somehow mixed up and inaccurate. When he awoke, he was very thirsty, and it was very dark. He filled his pouch with water and drank from a small stream where he had camped. Gazing at the night sky instead of the bear's tail, he saw his mother's image. Her face was shining and smiling. He knew then that he would see her soon.

The new morning was different. Judah bathed in a little stream and cleaned carefully. Blue Eagle's woodman's habits took over. Everything was tidy and easy to access. He picked a distant point north as his aiming point and began a steady stride. He recalled the dream but did not try to re-sort it, only to see it for what it was. His mind was that of a person native to the land. Blue Eagle wanted to see how everything above and below him connected him to the land.

"No one owns the land. Not in the sense that the white man sees it. Their greed does not stop at the shoreline or the tree line. It knows no bounds." He was all alone, indeed, as he walked toward his destination. He felt ready to face whatever lay ahead.

When he drew close to the river, he began to build his raft. The wind was calm, and he needed only a few sturdy branches the length of his body, and he could tie them together with the twisted sinew that he still had in his bag. The floating raft was ready in about two hours. He fashioned a paddle to use as a rudder of sorts. From his vantage point, he could see the planted and unfenced fields downstream, that was his target. In the early morning, he floated toward his target, landed on the muddy shore, grabbed his backpack and began walking.

Blue Eagle hefted his pack, now much lighter than before. He carried only essentials—weapons, tools, food, souvenirs from Kateri and Four Fingers, fire starters, and little else. He knew from experience that the New Netherland towers were never operated unless an attack was underway. There were simply not enough people. He was looking for loose logs set into loose and wet footing. He knew the fortifications around the gates were the strongest, and he avoided those.

Finding his mother's house was not going to be easy, and he would have to make contact to do it. Judah was almost out of the cultivated fields when he spotted some woods to his left.

Judah let his mind drift again. He was back in Brazil with his mother and father. He remembered a severe conversation about no longer believing in the old ways. Judah's mind was floating, and he stopped to rest in the grove of trees.

In Recife, Judah sat with Ruth and Abraham when he was about seventeen. He was straying from Judaism's rules and restrictions.

"Please hear me out," he pled. "I no longer believe in the stories that the rabbis told us about how the Earth was formed by God in seven days or that Methuselah lived for over nine hundred years, or that Sarah became pregnant after she was over one hundred years old, and all of the rest. They are made-up stories for children. Our real purpose on earth is to connect all living things. The dirt, the trees, the animals, the birds. All living things are connected with purpose and have life."

"Judah, it is not unusual for boys your age to doubt your parents and Judaism," his mother Ruth said. "It's part of growing up. You will see the wisdom of what I say as you get older." She spoke in a way that was filled with love, yet with stern emotion.

Abraham, his father, piped in, "I will take you with me to the islands to show the ways of a man and the ways of the trader."

Judah countered, "I am not naïve or blind. I know what you both are saying. I know you don't want me to stray too far and want me to return soon to pray to Jehovah. I know the Jewish history, but I am not a part of that. I am indebted to you both for showing me a path—to make this world a better place. I will now take that path."

"Oh, my wayward son, I will pray for your return," said Ruth.

When he awoke, Judah prepared to face the past and the present. It was a mind game, and he knew what to expect. He had gone over the arguments his mother would propose for him to stay and prepared his answers. He told himself there would be no surprises. This encounter would be an emotional challenge. The only change to his appearance was to hide his cherished four-feathered headband. It held on to him and kept his thoughts level. He was now Blue Eagle, a proud Susquehannock chief sachem with a complete family. He knew his purpose in life and guarded those values close to his heart. He felt a deep ache for Kateri's embrace and Sosondowah's touch. His mouth was dry and pasty, as if he had swallowed a mouthful of sand.

He expected to see more people, but no one else was in sight. Judah kept a low profile as he turned west toward a grove of trees that took on a familiar shape and slope. No one knew of his mother Ruth Joseph. He knocked on three consecutive houses. At the fourth, a man looked Judah over carefully and invited him in for a drink after he looked into his blue eyes.

"I'll take water, sir," Judah said politely. His hand started to reach, but he pulled back, not wanting to appear too anxious.

"Then water it is. My name is Hector. What is your name, young man? And exactly who are you?"

"My name is Judah, sir, Judah Joseph. I was captured by the Susquehannock five years ago, and now I am a four-feathered sachem chief in a village far away."

"And why have you come to New Netherland?"

"I came looking for my mother," Judah said in Dutch. "Her name is Ruth, Ruth Joseph. I used to live here. I have news for her and came to see her."

"Well," Hector said, "your mother used to live near here, but I heard she's up and living with one of those Hebrew folks. She's renting a room not far from here. I don't know where exactly. Try over on that Hebrew street in town."

"Hector, thank you for the water," Judah said. "I will take another cup if you don't mind."

At a shop selling dry goods near the town square, Judah asked where he could find the street where Hebrews lived. A boy of about twelve pointed to a street four blocks away. On that street he asked an elderly woman where he might be able to find Ruth Joseph. She pointed to a solid-looking three-story brick house four doors away. He knocked on the first-floor door.

Good-bye and the Way Home

Judah embraced Ruth when she opened the door. His blue eyes were instantly recognized. The only thing that mattered to Ruth was that her son was home. She didn't care about dirty clothes or foul smells. Ruth would not release him for a long time, and

Judah knew deep down what that meant. It would make it that much harder for him to leave.

"What, what brings you back here?" Ruth managed through her tears, speaking first in Hebrew and then in Dutch.

"You, Mama, I came back to see you. I spent many nights of travel alone to see you." Judah's voice was cracking like dry straw. "To see your face once more." Judah spoke in Dutch; he was not comfortable in Hebrew.

She held his strong hands in hers. "Here, sit here," she said and pointed to the straw and moss bed. The questions that Judah knew were coming welled up in Ruth's Jewish bosom. "Can you stay a month? A week? How long? I want you here beside me forever, Judah. We belong together."

She said his father had been gone for over four years. "I'm lonely and desperate. I need you more than ever. I used to be strong and independent and could take care of myself. This place is shit. It will wear you down with work. Our small group of friends would return to Holland tomorrow, but we have no money. We live hand-to-mouth on this street. It's worse than Recife." Through her tears, she added, "I'm at the end of my rope."

Judah wrapped his arms around her in consolation. He reached beside his breast and woven into a pouch there was the Sosondowah carving. He showed it to Ruth. To lift her spirits, he told her his story. "I'm now a sachem chief in our village—a four-feathered, respected warrior. I'm married to a beautiful girl named Kateri. You have a new baby grandson named Sosondowah. We're happy. The carving is from a special person who is now the village mother, named Four Fingers who gave this to you to keep."

He said the tanning work team gave him a shell bracelet for good luck. "I would have brought the family here, but the trip was too dangerous. Please keep this always and think of them often. They are my life. The village is my home, the clan are my people. I belong there, not here." He said those words as if they were his creed.

Ruth looked at the carving and touched it to her lips. She said a prayer in Hebrew, covered her eyes, and her tears flowed again. "Sh'ma Yisrael, Adonai Eloheinu, Adonai Echad!" and then in a whisper, she said, "Baruch she'm avoid mulch-to l'olam vaed." The words meant, "Here O Israel, Adonai is Our God Adonai is One. Blessed is God's glorious majesty forever and ever." With his arms still enveloping her, they sobbed together, both knowing in their hearts they would soon be apart.

The practical Ruth of long ago came forth. "You must be bathed, reclothed, nourished, and refitted before returning to your village. That will take some time, some money, and some help. You must stay until we can put those things in place. You know I make sense and speak the truth," Ruth said, wiping the tears from her eyes.

Judah was surprised at how quickly his mother had recovered from the shock of seeing her son. He could not counter any of the practical obstacles. The most difficult of the preparations would be the buckskins. He would have to rely on someone other than himself, perhaps a trader, to get those.

Later, Judah bathed in the river, and he and his mother discussed how Judah learned of Abraham's demise. Ruth was diligent and kept Abraham's most cherished things. Judah valued the pipe the old man smoked the most. Even without tobacco, the smell of the bowl brought back memories of his father.

Judah took just a few coins to cross the ferry and said he would not need more. Ruth gave him what food she could spare, then went to the neighbors to borrow more. To avoid his public appearances, Ruth shuttled between shops, errands and traders to get Judah what he needed for his return trip.

"Let me go with you, Judah. I won't be a burden. I can help row. I want to see Kateri, my grandson, and Four Fingers. Please! I beg you, don't leave me alone!"

"You know I cannot," Judah replied. "It's simply too dangerous. I barely made it here myself. A white woman doesn't have a chance in the wilderness. Warriors will descend on us if they see us in a canoe. They will kill us and scalp me and take you hostage. They'll do it for sport. Go back to Holland, re-marry, and get on with the rest of your life."

Judah worried about his mother and the predicament that she was in. Life was very hard for her where she was, in a rented room working hard for a pittance, living without a husband. He would ask Dirk to check with the trading network, to see if there was anything that could be done for people like Ruth who were widowed and penniless.

It was time for Judah to go and return to his life as Blue Eagle, and Ruth knew the truth. She knew he was right; there was danger in and out of New Netherland. She looked up at Judah one last time. They embraced and separated. Judah began to walk west into the setting sun. Ruth looked at the bracelet on Judah's wrist and asked where he got such a beautiful thing.

"Kateri made this from shells found near the river, Mama. Here—I give it to you to keep as a memory of my beautiful wife." He took the bracelet off and gave it to Ruth.

"I will treasure it forever," Ruth said, sobbing uncontrollably as she took it from Judah's hands.

He kissed his mother one last time on the forehead, as Judah departed for the last time.

Blue Eagle took a more direct path to the ferry on the opposite side of the cultivated field. A few people noticed him in the field, including a few men and women, but they merely looked up from their toil, glanced at him, and went about their work in the fields. He crossed at the ferry point with no problem and asked where he might find the closest trader. Getting home would be easier if he could find a trader willing to share the trip, at least partially.

It was time to camp. He would try again at first light. Judah packed only essentials, but his roll was now heavy with a blanket. The night was moonlit with no rain, but sleep did not come. When it did, the talking rock spoke to him again. It spoke to him of the danger and betrayal of fighting and wars. The rock even spoke of fire and death. He awoke in total darkness to the familiar animal sounds at night.

He slept until there was an unfamiliar nudge on his shoulder. He grabbed the handle of his hatchet under his bedroll and sprang to his paces, the blade inches away from whoever disturbed his rest.

"Whoa there, chief," a voice said in English. "No need to use that here and now, I am meaning no harm."

Judah focused on the threat in front of him. He was an obvious trapper, dressed in skins with belts for pelts. His hands were in front of him, palms facing him, showing no weapons. He did not appear threatening. Judah's tense body began to relax.

"You woke me," Judah said in broken English.

"Just a friendly shake, my friend. You're quick with that hatchet, though. I can't blame you. Would you like some coffee? My name is Blaine, Jim Blaine."

"Okay," Judah replied.

They re-lit the fire. They talked. Each had their own story to tell. Judah disclosed that he intended to walk west to the village to recover his canoe and then paddle home. Blaine said that he was not sure if he could help, but he could accompany him to a small trading post nearby.

While Blaine drew a makeshift map, Judah asked him if there was anything the English could do to help a stranded widowed woman in New Netherland get back to Amsterdam. Baine said that he did not know, but if he could find out he would pass it along on the traders' network. Blue Eagle told him that if he did find out, to tell Dirk Dietrick about it. Blaine said that he knew where the village was that Judah talked about and showed it to him on the map.

Blaine told Judah that he had an old canoe he would like to get fixed and asked if he knew of a way to fix it. Judah told him that he did. Together they used mud sticks and dried leaves to make a mixture when stirred that resembled cement. While not totally waterproof, when layered and dried over a hole it was useful for keeping out most of the water. Blaine was grateful for the advice and asked if Judah could use anything in return. Judah replied that he could use some thin snare wire for snagging small animals. Blaine said that it was one of his regular items and gave some to Judah in return.

Judah then departed west with the map. His journey now as Blue Eagle was west on foot, uneventful but tiring. He used the snare wire that he traded for, more useful than sinew for capturing small animal and birds. A small Lenape village was reached in three days even with occasional rain. At the village he linked back up with is canoe and gave his blanket to a family that had none as a show of his appreciation.

Blue Eagle was on the way home now and headed downriver. He knew that a five-to-six-day journey alone lay ahead if there were no interruptions by unfriendly hunters out for sport or for blood revenge. He would rest and camp at islands in mid-stream when possible. At the fork in the river, he camped at one such island.

Blue Eagle's shoulders ached from the exertions, and he rested even through the midday, rubbing his joints with medicinal leaves. As he slept, he dreamt of his mother toiling in the fields of New Netherland. The rock spoke to him again; this time it said that his mother was not alone and that she would not die in New Netherland. When Judah awoke from that dream, the sky was ablaze with a circle of starlight in many shapes blinking through the trees. His eyes bounced from one group to the next until they made him drowsy with sleep.

Except for two canoes that followed him for about an hour, Blue Eagle had no incidents when going downstream to Bear Village. Nothing mattered except home and family. He put his mother and the rock dream aside to focus his thoughts on what mattered most in his life—family and his people.

CHAPTER 15

Muskets and the Hunt

Blue Eagle would always be his mother's son, but he would never go back to New Netherland again. That was a past life that held nothing there for him now. His future was here at Bear Village now with his family and his people. His goal was to make life better for all of them.

Rich and powerful forces, specifically the English and the French, were doing their best to take from the inhabitants of the New World by almost any means at their disposal. In particular that meant land. Blue Eagle knew about the value of land and homes because he was white. He knew this because his parents talked about how the Jewish people lost theirs to others because of their religion and beliefs.

The Susquehannocks did not know of these things and did not yield any of their lands in Pennsylvania, but Judah knew that. He did not trust the motives of the colonists and was suspicious of their goals when they plied his people with gifts. Trust and friendship were more highly prized than cannons and muskets.

Summer was fading into fall and that meant preparation time

for the hunting season. This was also the time that representatives of the English Calvert government in Baltimore visited at Bear Village. The flotilla of six canoes carrying Captain Nick Marcus came up the Susquehanna River as if they owed the waterway. Blue Eagle was summoned to meet them and spoke to their Algonquin interpreter in a mixture of broken English and Algonquin with hand gestures. Blue Eagle did not trust these English, but he could not know the true motivation of Marcus' visit. He would try to find out.

After pleasantries and small talk, Blue Eagle got down to business. "Please tell me, Captain, why did you come all the way up here to Bear Village?" asked Blue Eagle through an interpreter. "I know that it was not to see our beautiful maidens."

"You are correct, Blue Eagle. Although your maidens are indeed quite attractive, that is not why I came. It is in Lord Calvert's interests to maintain peace throughout this entire region even extending this far north. As you know, the Iroquois and their Confederacy of nations have recently attempted to extend their influence far and wide, not only west but north into this area as well. Lord Calvert believes, as do I, that if left unchecked that influence could undermine the fragile peace that we worked so hard to achieve." The captain said this with a tone of smugness in his half-smile.

"What have you brought with you as a gesture of Lord Calvert's benevolence?" asked Blue Eagle.

Captain Marcus responded without hesitation, "We have a gift of eight muskets and one rifle, with stores of ammunition for your use. The rifle is for you, chief. Am I correct in saying that you are, indeed, the chief?"

"Yes," said Blue Eagle, "I have been chosen as the chief sachem of this encampment."

Marcus then gestured to one of his lieutenants who was waiting outside the longhouse. He brought in one musket and the one rifle. Captain Marcus continued, "My men and I are prepared to stay with the men that you select to show them the proper use of the muskets and the rifle in your defense. Further, if you accept this offer, we will return on another visit with three cannons with ammunition that can be used to deter enemy forces. All of these weapons will be for your village at no cost to you."

After a pause to collect his thoughts, Blue Eagle said, "We are grateful for the generosity of Lord Calvert and his interest in maintaining peace in our area. But muskets and cannon are of no use to us in hunting game. They can be used for defensive positions with proper training. We will need you to train our warriors on the proper use of these weapons. We will provide the food and lodging over the next few weeks for that purpose."

What Judah could not know, and Captain Marcus did not tell him, was that the Susquehannock chiefs near Maryland over nine years before ceded land near Baltimore. This gave the English land to build their forts and settle disputes they had over hunting grounds. The English saw the Susquehannock nation as a blocking force to Iroquois and Confederacy (Seneca) expansion. The weapons were a trifle, since the Iroquois already had them.

Since preparations for hunting season had already begun, Blue Eagle was faced with two immediate problems. He asked the Duck clan sachem, Running Bear, to pick Eagle Claw as the warrior to lead a group of men fit to learn the use of muskets. Blue Eagle explained that these men must be good with their hands, quick on their feet and undeterred by smoke and noise in battle. They would be known as Arrowheads and have tattoos inscribed onto their right shoulders.

Eagle Claw took a full week to weed out the most likely young warriors for the Arrowhead group of sixteen. Eight men would be firers, and eight men would be back-up and loaders, but all sixteen would learn the process. The curious young men stood around in an arc to watch the captain. He went slowly through the steps. At the loading position, they were to reach into the pouch and pull out a premade wad with the ball and powder.

141

Bite off one end and pour a bit of powder into the pan.
Pour the rest down the muzzle with the ball.
Extract the rod from the barrel underside.
Tamp the ball three times hard down the breech.
Return the rod to the musket.
Move the hammer from cock to the full cock position, and listen for the 'click' sound.
Aim and squeeze the trigger to fire.
Return the musket to loading position.

Marcus said that after practice, the process should take no more than thirty seconds. Judah could see that the critical problem was the supply of premade powder balls. The Susquehannocks did not have access to lead smelters or to gunpowder. They would have to depend on trade or the good graces of the Marylanders.

How did the Iroquois do it? Maybe his spies could tell him. For now, three of his warriors dropped out for replacement. They were too slow and clumsy. He told Eagle Claw to find replacements. Practice targets spaced out in the field, and the shots from the ditch and other positions became as natural as shooting as a bow. Cleaning the muskets was a separate chore. The weapon had to be swabbed with boiling water and oil to remove powder residue. The flints also had to be replaced when worn. The Susquehannocks adopted the new armaments that winter.

The sixteen warriors practiced by swapping places for two weeks, but Eagle Claw was worried about ammunition supplies. Captain Marcus gave Blue Eagle separate instruction on the rifle, which took longer to load but was accurate at a longer distance. Blue Eagle did not like it and gave it to Brave Cloud to use. He wanted to reward Eagle Claw and his sixteen Arrowheads, all of whom had now been tattooed. He asked the council and Four Fingers for a ceremony.

With Captain Marcus present, Blue Eagle presented Eagle Claw and his sixteen Arrowheads with eagle feathers. He told the assembled, "These warriors will be the first to fight for your protection and for the defense of the village. They will be equipped with muskets, bow and arrow, tomahawks, war clubs and knives. The tattoos on their shoulders mark them as ready to go at a moment's notice to defend what is most valuable to them—their loved ones, their honor, and their homes. We are grateful to them and to their ancestors before them. We must now prepare for our fall hunt. AYEEEHA! AYEEEHA!"

The captain and his flotilla left that afternoon for Baltimore.

The Hunt

Leaders in Bear Village knew what to expect in the fall hunt, but this was the first time it was led by Blue Eagle. Even though not everyone was in the hunt, everyone in camp was involved in getting ready—that was the communal way. Sachems rewarded individual achievement.

Community effort played the most significant part. Grinding stones, which were usually busy, were now going around the clock. Canoes were repaired and checked for leaks, while supplies such as blankets, fried fish, and meat were wrapped and loaded. Personal weapons, including extra bows and arrows, were checked and loaded. The Susquehannock arrows were smaller and more deadly than their enemies' and used obsidian or flint stone. This in turn was chipped and barbed to penetrate the flesh of an animal or man but pulling them out was impossible without significant injury to a muscle or an internal organ.

Rituals were an essential part of the preparation. Storyteller, with his bangles and seed pods, started in the council longhouse and went around to the lodges to smoke, chant, and pray to their ancestors for a good hunt and safe return of their warriors. When he arrived at the chief's lodge, he found him in deep meditation and turned away without saying or doing anything.

When he returned, he found Judah shaving his face by the fire. He spoke in the Susquehannock dialect. "I understand they call you Blue Eagle," Storyteller said with a twinge of sarcasm in his voice.

"Yes," Judah said in an even tone.

"Do you pray to your ancestors?"

"I pray for good hunting and safe return of all warriors."

"Why do you not pray to your ancestors?" Storyteller asked.

Judah tried to explain. "My ancestors do not know who I am or why I am here. I do not know them. My blood is my own."

"Do you believe that the Great Father brought forth the heaven and earth, and all living things are related? And that we can talk with our ancestors?"

"I believe that the God who created you and I created the fish in the sea and the stars in the heavens and everything around us is as important as the ground we walk on. We live in this world to be a part of it, as we are a part of every living thing in it." Blue Eagle said the words as he looked at Storyteller without blinking.

Storyteller was taken aback. This man was his chief, a white man who spoke in his native tongue. He was a decorated Susquehannock warrior who he respected in many ways. He was like him, but somehow different. It was almost as if he still had one leg in the white man's world. Storyteller concluded that if actions lived up to his name, he would be good for the tribe. He then went on to another longhouse.

The time for preparation was over, and the early morning saw the launch of the canoes and the hunt. A fog was again on the river, and it crept inland to cover the longhouses, fire rings, and storage mounds. Like a vast shroud, the cloud covered the fields, the trees, and even the sleeping owls in the woods. The wind from the east formed small white caps on the river, but it was still time to move on. Storyteller, like some ancient forecaster, assured those gathered on that day that early morning fog could not last and would blow away soon. The village had collected around the riverbank, and children ran up and down the canoe line like warriors in the making, whooping and hollering in barefoot delight. Still, the fog dampened much of the anticipation. The excitement of the moment strengthened when Blue Eagle raised his feathered spear in the air and shouted in a bellowing voice for all to hear:

"May the forests and trails bring great rewards to our people and return our warriors home safe to their loved ones."

Storyteller blessed each canoe as it left the shore and rattled his seed pod for good luck. There were many waves from the shore, but only the young litter bearers waved back; everyone paddled with the moderate current downstream. A rhythmic chant echoed between the banks as the men's voices were heard a great distance away—"umphpapa, umphpapa."

The chant lingered on in Blue Eagle's brain long after the echo faded. The cadence was automatic. The rhythm seemed to have a life of its own. Blue Eagle was in the lead canoe for the first time. It felt good to be in the lead, and a glance to the rear revealed a string of canoes as far as the eye could see, more than fifty. Two lines rowing in unison chanting the same rhythm, oblivious to their effort in tune with nature and the world around them. This was life as it was meant to be. His trusted friend, Brave Cloud, was heading north with almost as many warriors. Almost every clan sent at least twenty warriors splitting directions for maximum effort using every available canoe.

On the way south, Blue Eagle passed two smaller villages, which were probably Susquehannock but from the banks it was difficult to tell their size and their nation. The river itself seemed to widen the further south they went. The day was long, but the paddling was not hard.

The camp was at a bend in the river with islets in the middle where canoes could park for the night. There were so many canoes that the party took up both islands in the middle and the riverbanks on both sides. The river was still wide enough for passage, but canoes seemed to clog the waterways. Fires appeared almost at once on both banks. The group's chatter, laughter, and talk were heard from everywhere. At their campsite, the warriors talked about past hunts, deer size, and even an occasional bear. When the chatter quieted, Blue Eagle told the gathering about his rock vision and then related the vision to the Iroquois bear hunting legend.

"Six great hunters and their dogs searched for a great bear in the forest," he told the gathered warriors. "They searched for days and nights without success. They even searched at night, but they would not quit. The hunters and dogs finally located the great bear high in the mountains. When they went to kill it, the bear just roared, leaped, and threw a net onto the hunters and the dog. To this day, you can see a bear's tail on a fall night in the northern sky like this one."

Then he pointed to the bear tail, the seven stars of the Big Dipper, a constellation in the northern sky. To those who had not heard the legend before, their mouths were agape as they stared skyward at the easily recognized formation. "The white man refers to the rest of the constellation as the Ursa Major and forms the large bear in the sky, and he points to the shoulders and head of the bear. Those stars at night will tell us where the deer will be in the morning. Deer live and feed near the forest's edge five times a day on the tops of grass and flowers. That is the way to find deer."

Another warrior who wore two campaign feathers, whom others called Wolf Eyes, said that he liked to spread corn near water to attract deer. Judah said this was also effective. His story was to lift spirits and prepare for the hunt. The talk around faded with the glow of the flames, and soon the warriors curled up in the blankets for sleep, except those who had to share watch for the night.

The enthusiasm of the first day afloat gave way to the sheer effort of the second. Blue Eagle noted the gradual widening of the river and how the intermittent streams intersected the river's path. He did not know the names of those creeks, but they looked promising as game-hunting sites. Camp for the second night was made on the east side of the river near a creek called Wisconnosco by one of the warriors who had been hunting in that area before. Word that this would be their last camp before their destination lifted everyone's spirits for the next day's push ahead.

The hunt was on, but the party took care to spread out and move with stealth and quiet in all directions. Blue Eagle went north with Wolf Eyes, Hawk Shadow, and three other warriors. In the afternoon, they shot one turkey, one grouse, and a thrush—an abysmal showing. The following morning before sunrise, Wolf Eyes, who carried some corn with him, scattered it near a tree line before dawn while Hawk Shadow scattered flowers and grass tops on top of the corn. The mix was irresistible to deer.

The warriors waited less than ten paces away. When the sunlight stroked the bottoms of the trees, teenage deer came first out of the woods. Warriors notched their bows and waited in a semicircle. The teenagers were followed first by the one doe, then two, then three. At last, a buck shoved his antlers through the brush into the clearing, followed by another doe. Blue Eagle aimed for the neck of the buck, pulled the tight sinew taut, and released. He then gave a signal with his arm for the others to release their arrows. In less than ten seconds, all the deer lay flat on the ground, dead or dying. Knives were already out to sever the necks to ensure a certain death.

In all, the hunt was successful. Hundreds of game animals were slain including deer, some elk, antelope, and even three bears. Blue Eagle and the sachems followed both the traditional and non-traditional methods of trapping the game. The traditional method included using a "V" formation and walking the herds into a hillside where they could not escape. There was also the non-traditional, where small groups are lured into openings using pinecones, flowers and other types of enticements.

Blue Eagle knew that hunting and killing animals could sometimes wear down a warrior's motivation to hunt. That is why he repeated camp-side stories like this one about the Iroquois legend of why the turtle's shell is flat.

An island floated in the sky. Sky People lived a long time ago quietly and happily, and no one ever died, was born, or experienced unhappiness. One day, the Sky Woman discovered she would give birth to twins. She told her husband, who flew into a rage. A tree in the island's center illuminated the island, since the sun hadn't yet been created. He tore up the tree and made a massive hole in the middle of the island.

Curious, the Sky Woman peered into the hole. Far below, she could see the waters that covered the earth below. Water animals already existed on Earth. Two birds saw Sky Woman fall into the hole. Just before she reached the ground, they caught her on their backs and placed her on the back of a turtle. Trees, mud, and other land soon followed. Soon, the turtle was carrying the weight of the earth on his back. That is why turtles have flat shells.

Blue Eagle knew that such legends would help to bind people to their past and to their ancestors. He knew also that the dark side of hunting is the moving of the slain animal back to the village.

The legs of the fresh kills were bound together and drug to the river where the litter bearers would put the animals in canoes for transport back to the village. There, women and older men would drag the animal near the river in a place for gutting, bagging the insides, and then skinning the animal. Then the pro-cess of drying and hanging meat could begin. The meat itself would be separated from the skin and dried to prevent spoilage. This was a difficult and consuming process involving days of transport and preparation to the home village. The undertaking involved the whole community.

Blue Eagle saw the process of hunting as a community cycle where nobody was more important than anyone else. The river was their lifeline, but their togetherness made their success the envy of others. He appreciated the life of the Susquehannock warrior. If one warrior succeeded, they all succeeded. They lived for each other, and they would die for each other in battle.

CHAPTER 16

Diplomacy and Capture – Again

T he intensity of the fall hunt with its hundreds of animal carcasses that needed to be dressed overwhelmed the resources
of Bear Village. All able hands including Blue Eagle, Kateri,
Orenda, Four Fingers and all the clan sachems were busy carving
and slicing the slain animals. It was a community-wide effort to
smoke the moisture from the hides and dry the meat before it rotted
and became unusable. This activity helped to solidify purpose in
the village, because everyone understood it was for the common
good. Their work now would pay dividends in the winter, which
was just around the corner. The building of the palisades around
the village was an effort that had its detractors. They were vocal
about their dissatisfactions, and they were quick to present them to
Blue Eagle and the council.

At the council meeting, the sachems from the Jackal and
Snake clans objected to the plan of having walls and gates built
to surround the complete village compound, including the

planted fields and riverbanks.

"Your plan was too complicated and difficult," the clan leaders argued. "We are accustomed to free access to the river. This wall, even with a gate, would be an obstacle and slow us down, especially the women and children."

Judah countered by saying that the plan would allow people to walk through two at a time and be barricaded at night from the inside for security. "Each clan would rotate nighttime guard duty and watch the canoes. This would prevent a sneak attack by water, at night, the most likely means of penetration into the village."

He went on to explain his idea for the ditches was to extend them five to seven paces each. They would not be continuous and allow traffic between. Their distance behind the walls would vary. The plan was to space the ditches at critical points behind the gates where invading forces were most likely to hit. In that way, archers and gunmen could fire along the perimeter. Each longhouse would be responsible for a series of wall sections. Once complete, they could practice and drill. Practice by the longhouses was essential. Brave Cloud said that he and his crew would finish the wall completely by the end of summer next year.

Reactions from the sachems were mixed. Most agreed, but there were a still a few who did not. Blocking the river was not necessary, they said. It would be difficult for the Confederacy to mount a sizable force by water, assemble along a narrow riverfront, and attack at night. Judah countered that only some men would have to come by water. Once a surprise came by water, and they were inside, the people inside were trapped. The key to long-term survival was to keep the invaders out, period.

A quiet hush came over the group. They looked at each other without saying anything. Heads began to nod one by one.

At last, Dark Moon, the old-fashioned warrior from the Turkey clan, spoke. "Your plan is wise. Our clan will provide the needed warriors first." After that, the two other clans went along, even the holdouts. Judah asked Four Fingers to call for a council vote to approve his final security plan.

There were two more elements of Blue Eagle's plan that needed discussion. The first was the use of spies in the field. There was little doubt that the Confederacy used whatever means they could to put as many spies in the field as possible. Oftentimes they would appear at camp as strangers, dressed as Blue Eagle had, Susquehannocks on a trading mission or lost. Other times they would simply hang out and watch movement.

The second element were alliances. The Iroquois and their Confederacy were famous for their chain of spies that often stretched over several terrain features. The spy network combined with their strong alliances made them fierce adversaries.

Blue Eagle told the council that he did not want to imitate how the Iroquois operated; he wanted to develop his own reliable spy network, together with one or two allies that they could depend on in case of trouble. They were not easy tasks and needed intense development for success even on a modest level. They could not survive alone; failure was not an option. After two more hours of pipe smoking and back and forth exchanges, the security plan was approved and completed.

Four Rivers and Twin Branch were chosen by Blue Eagle again to form a network of spies for long-range intelligence. This time, however, they were joined by Hawk Shadow from the Snake clan as a trio to give depth to the ring. The three, once in place, could scatter in three different directions and meet back up at a pre-determined place and share what they learned. They each took extra blankets for warmth in the winter but had to rely on self-preservation by hunting and trapping small animals through the harsh weather to survive. Nobody said it was going to be easy.

Although the council left the issue of making alliances up to Blue Eagle, it was a difficult process that had to be concluded to maintain long-term survival. The Lenape in the south would be his first start. He had a plan to approach them: first offer token gifts, then propose a joint hunting trip where they could share in the joint rewards of the hunt. After that, develop a shared alliance where they both agreed that the enemy of one is the enemy of the other and they both came to the aide of the other if they were attacked.

Forming alliances with the Mahican tribes to the north would be more difficult, since they had no previous contact with them. Blue Eagle planned to use gifts and the alliance with the Lenape as a springboard with the Mahicans, and another hunt if necessary to cement the relationship. He could not be certain if this would work, adding that he proposed to go to the Lenape in the south first this winter to cement the deal there. In the spring, he would go to the Mahican.

Kateri and Orenda and four other women worked for three weeks on each wampum for these alliance missions. The shelled and beaded strings had to be collected, tell a story, then carefully woven and sewn by hand. The colorful handiwork was difficult and prized by all that held it. When Moving Moon and Blue Eagle set off on their early-winter journey to the Lenape downstream, ice had formed on the riverbanks, but the river itself was cold and still passable.

Canadian geese had set their course south months beforehand, and bears had long since begun their winter naps, but beaver were still busy as ever in the cross streams and flats, building and damming away with unreal energy. Moving Moon and Blue Eagle made their camp at protective tree coves in midstream where stray hunters were not likely to aim at their canoe. A cozy fire kept them warm at night. The winter wisdom that Blue Eagle passed on included a story from Kateri.

Our ancestors say winter provides a time to preserve food like beans and squash underground, protected by grasses and barks stored in pits and wrapped in sumac leaves. Winter was also a time for easy hunting because leaves and vegetation died back, and animals were easier to find, and their meat was easier to preserve. Winter was also a time to have festivals and socialize, tell stories and lift spirits and make use of the long nights. So winter is not just a time to huddle around a fire and do little. It is also a time to know family to get out and do, play games hunt, fish and enjoy.

As the duo eyed both banks of the Siskuhanne, they paddled downriver looking for suspicious activity that might disrupt their movement. They spied mostly women or men by themselves tending fish traps, washing, or looking for game on or near the riverbanks. Then, some distance into their second day, Blue Eagle spotted a group of young men with weapons and buckskins near the bank staring at their approaching canoe.

Not knowing whether the men were friendly or foes, Moving Moon and Blue Eagle paddled quickly to the opposite bank. They put their bows and quivers close by their side and rapidly picked up the pace of their rowing. The goal was to move out of bow shot range as quickly as possible without looking back. Adrenaline now rushed through their bodies. Their backs bent and their shoulder muscles responded to the demand of the moment. Legs and knees gripped the floor of the canoe as it shot past rocks and trees on the bank.

Moving Moon in the rear turned around and saw that they were not being followed and tapped on Blue Eagle's shoulder, a signal for him to let up. What neither of them could possibly see were a group of four teenagers bent over double in uncontrollable laughter, slapping each other for spooking two feathered warriors in a canoe. The duo meanwhile coasted for the next few minutes, letting their bodies adjust to a normal rhythm of rowing, and continued downriver. Blue Eagle told Moving Moon, "You acted well and quickly to that situation—good instincts." Moving Moon responded, "It's the way a warrior should act."

After another overnight camp, the Blue Eagle and Moving Moon pulled into a village that was clearly not Susquehannock. The markings on the canoes, the dress and hairstyles of the women and children, all pointed to an Algonquin village, possibly Lenape. In his limited Algonquin, Blue Eagle asked to speak with the village lead sachem and village mother.

The warriors were led from one longhouse to another but from the manner of speech and dress of warriors they spoke to, they did not believe that they were speaking to the village chief sachem. It was not until they reached a smaller longhouse with the symbol of a wolf on the side and spoke to an old, multi-feather warrior inside that Blue Eagle was convinced that he had finally reached the chief sachem.

"I am called Twin Peaks," the old man said in Algonquin, "and this is Black Braid, our village mother." She sat on a blanket cross-legged and looked to be very old. "Who are you two and why are you here?"

Blue Eagle answered for himself and Moving Moon in his halting Algonquin. "We come from a large Susquehannock village about two days' travel north. We are friendly neighbors and honor and respect the Lenape people and their nation. We bring a special gift from the Susquehannock people to your people as a show of that esteem." With that, Blue Eagle took the wampum belt from his pack. "As you can see, this belt shows the Sis-kuhanne River joining our two villages in an unbroken chain of friendship between our nations, symbolizing our togetherness." Blue Eagle laid out the wampum belt in front of Twin Peak.

Twin Peak and Black Braid examined and admired the belt in great detail for several minutes. Twin Peak said, "This is an excellent and unexpected gift. Your people must have toiled for many hours to prepare such a thing. We have nothing to give you in exchange."

"Please allow me to tell you the full story and the reason for our trip," said Blue Eagle. "Our people and this region are threatened by a vicious and cruel adversary in form of the Haudenosaunee and the allies of the five nations of the Confed-eracy. Their combined force numbers many times the warriors we possess. They will not stop until we and everyone else in this region are either wiped out or absorbed into their circles. Their atrocities are legendary, and their reputation precedes their assaults. Our own village mother had her little finger cut off by one of their chiefs at age six because she spit in his eye. The reason for our presence is to form an alliance between our nations and our villages."

Twin Peak's face grew somber and serious. The color in his cheeks went from sunburn red to ashen gray, then back to sunburn red. "We have not experienced the wrath of the Confederacy as you have. Why should we incite the Haudenosaunee by agreeing to an alliance?"

"Because what they do to one of us, they can do to any of us," said Blue Eagle. "By ourselves we can fall, but together we can win. It is really as simple as that. The reason the Confederacy has remained strong through these years is because they have agreed to stand with each other and fight. If you and your people agree, we can do the same."

"This is a decision that must go through our sachems and council," said Twin Peak, "and they must all agree. There must be no turning back. You will have our answer before spring comes. In the time before that, enjoy our newfound friendship and understanding."

Blue Eagle and Moving Moon stayed overnight at the Lenape village and rested for the journey back home. Over a private campfire they talked about possible outcomes. Moving Moon said, "There is no reason for the council to approve an alliance. They are not threatened by the Haudenosaunee. They have little to gain and a lot to lose—warriors in battle with the Confederacy."

"That is where we disagree," said Blue Eagle. "If they do not commit to an alliance and we lose to the Confederacy, then the Haudenosaunee will taste victory and move further south to conquer and absorb the Lenape who do not have a history of fighting. They are stronger in an alliance than without one. If they do not join with us, we have no choice but to go north to the Mahicans. There is but one certainty, the Confederacy cannot defeat us in a single battle. We are too strong. It will take many battles to overcome our defenses."

Both warriors stared at the fire in deep reflection and curled in their blankets for warmth before falling into a deep sleep. The talking rock came into Judah's dream of his family once again. This time it told him to be wary of dangerous situations that would drive him into perilous behavior. It was dark and the sky as black as coal when he awoke. Moving Moon was still asleep and Judah, wrapped in his blanket, gathered together more firewood and placed it on the dying embers.

Sleep would not come, and Judah couldn't help but think about the dream's warning. It didn't frighten him, but it did make him feel uncomfortable, like a baby that won't stop crying. Sleep then did come, but it was spotty and rough. At daylight the duo packed up their things, bid goodbye to their hosts, and left for the trip upriver.

After an uneventful night at the same island in the middle of the river, they paddled upriver, fighting the current and a bitter northerly wind and fog that slowed their pace almost by half. The wind cleared the fog off both banks and revealed a hunting party of four warriors on the bank closest to them. They did not appear friendly, and the duo instinctively paddled much harder and faster than before.

They were only about fifty paces away when a bevy of arrows was shot at their canoe from the rear and left side. Three of the arrows found their mark in Moving Moon's shoulder and side. Moving Moon slumped downward in silent pain and bled uncontrollably on the canoe's bottom. Blue Eagle was also hit in the left hip but struggled to keep the canoe going.

Two warriors from the shore braved the icy waters at this point and swam hard toward the canoe. The warriors on shore stopped the barrage of arrows for fear of hitting the swimmers. The canoe drifted while Blue Eagle tried to shoot at the approaching swimmers, but his hip wound prevented accuracy. He then broke the shaft of the arrow in his hip but couldn't remove the barbed arrowhead. One swimmer reached one side of the canoe while the other reached the other side. Blue Eagle resorted to using his paddle to beat the swimmer who was trying to climb into the canoe until the man's head split open and he slid under the water. At the same time, the swimmer on the other side managed to get into the canoe, climb over Moving Moon's body, and then swung the other paddle against the back of Blue Eagle's head and neck until he was unconscious. He then paddled to the shore and joined his victorious hunters who grabbed Blue Eagle's body, dragging him to shore.

All three Seneca warriors marveled at the white Susquehannock warrior with four feathers who was now their captive. The loss of their comrade in the river was balanced by the death of Moving Moon in the canoe. They completely ignored the craft in the chaos of the capture and the canoe drifted toward the middle of the river.

Blue Eagle was unconscious at first, but in time he could feel strong hands lifting him up by his shoulders. His feet were dragging the ground and stumbling over logs, leaves, and dirt as they drug him across the woods and around trees. He was not yet conscious, but he could feel the pain in his left side gnawing him awake like a beaver felling a cedar tree. The longer and further they carried him, the more his senses came alive. He had to think and think quickly.

In the corner of his eye Blue Eagle could see one warrior had hefted the carcass of one doe on his shoulders and he was holding its legs in his hands as he walked. This, he thought, could mean only one thing: they intended to stop for the night, butcher the carcass and use the sinew from the muscles to tie his arms and legs. That meant that they intended to carry him intact to their village in this state, where they could torture and kill him. The question then was how to disarm and surprise these three and escape to Bear Village. The fog in his brain began to lift and he developed a plan.

CHAPTER 17

Escape and Evasion

The first part of Blue Eagle's plan was to feign unconsciousness until well after dark. Of course, that meant giving these men enough time to butcher the doe, use sinew to bind his arms, head and legs to a tree, before the men fell to sleep. One of the warriors would still take turns watching him in case he stirred or awoke during the night. All that activity would take time, even for three veteran warriors.

Even though Blue Eagle was fully conscious, he had a terrible headache. The throbbing in his head and in the back of his neck was like an unending hammer on bone that just would not stop. Despite the flickering firelight, he did not think that the warriors could see his constantly moving hands and fingers. They were the keys to his breakout. The wet sinew was not twisted and dried as it normally is to make tight 'rope like' bonds. Instead, it was slippery and came apart easily with pressure and manipulation.

Anticipation of the night and the dangers ahead was not easy. First, there was the arrow in his hip. Although it did not appear to be deep, it still hurt like hell, but trying to remove it under the best of circumstances would be impossible, not to mention the blood loss. Part two of his plan was to kill at least one of the watching warriors and take his weapons to survive on the long way home. Judah re-tied the knots in his legs, head, and hands so they gave the appearance of being taut but were not.

He was tired now but only wanted to sleep a little, just enough to rest for a long night ahead. His eyelids felt very heavy. Judah dreamt of the talking rock again and he squirmed against the tree.

I told you this would not be easy, maybe now you listen. You must survive this ordeal. You have a destiny to fulfill, obligations to meet, a family that needs you, a village that respects you. Kill if you must, but you must live!

His eyes rolled and his head throbbed even more than before. He resisted using his hands for anything. He must stay disciplined. His eyes darted around and he used his peripheral vision to see to the left and right. Except for night sounds of the forest, it was deadly quiet. The warriors were not sleeping side by side, which made his plan easier. Blue Eagle undid the knots one by one, and they fell to the base of the cedar tree.

He crept upright to one warrior who was snoring, sitting up at the base of a nearby tree. He covered the warrior's mouth with his right hand and snatched his knife with his left hand and slit his throat twice ear-to-ear while placing his knee in his back, forcing him downward. He slit the carotid artery to be sure he would bleed out, holding his hand over the warrior's mouth until death was certain. Now armed with a bow and quiver of arrows, a knife, and a tomahawk, Blue Eagle was ready to chance the woods. The only certainty was that the other two warriors would rise onto their feet, hot on his trail when they discovered that their prized captive had left in the night after leaving behind another dead warrior. Judah held the hope of meeting up with Four Rivers and Twin Branch on their spy mission. But that was just that—a slim hope to get help while trying to evade the other two warriors who were sure to chase him.

Having a head start on your pursuers is a good thing, but if you are wounded and they are not, even a few hours won't help if they can run and you cannot, and they know how to track. Blue Eagle calculated that he would have to head northeast and toward the river and he headed that way. Winter was upon them and Blue Eagle had no blanket, only his buckskins. He stopped to lean next to a tree to rest and searched below his waist for the arrowhead on his left side. He could see and feel the tenderness around the wound and high sensitivity of the immediate area. Keeping this wound from infection would be difficult if not impossible. Judah kept moving even though he suspected that his pursuers were closer than the village.

A plan developed in his mind. "Listen to the rock," he told himself. "Kill if you must but survive." When he found a sheltering grove of trees not far from the river, he felt close to home although he wasn't. In sight of the river, Blue Eagle cleared his tracks all around, climbed to a fork in a tree nearby in the early afternoon, notched his arrow, and waited.

A few hours later, a rustle of leaves and broken limbs told Blue Eagle everything he needed to know. They were here. The pair crouched and looked up and around the clearing. That was the only opening Blue Eagle needed. He let loose one arrow after another, sending his prey to the forest floor. Three to four arrows each, but they weren't dead yet. He leapt from his perch like a man possessed, wounds be damned. He tomahawked the pair in seconds, aiming for the throats and showing no mercy. He scalped the severed heads in a rush of adrenaline and with a mighty war cry, spread-eagled his arms wide. He held up the bloody hair in the air and shouted, "AYEEE! AYEEE!" and collapsed from exhaustion next to his prey.

The pounding in Blue Eagle's head was gone, but the ache from his wound on the left hip remained as he awoke to witness his handiwork in the clearing. A cold wind accompanied by a bone-chilling hail and then snow drifted in from the shore. He stripped the clothes from the corpses and wore them for protection from the cold. He slid the naked bodies to the edge of the trees and tossed the heads far away. "Let the scavengers pick away at the remains," he thought. "I'll keep the scalps and weapons." Blue Eagle made a fire to keep warm some distance away from the carnage.

The fire and extra clothes kept Blue Eagle warm through the night, and he slept until morning without a dream that he could remember. Judah passed a restful night despite having murdered four Seneca warriors in the last three nights. He was convinced that when he returned home that the Seneca and the Confederacy would come after Bear Village with a vengeance and blood in their hearts. First, he must return home and take care of his wound.

After four more bitter cold days and nights of walking, Judah finally reached Bear Village. The weather warmed and the Seneca clothes he wore were burned. Kateri, Four Fingers, and Orenda tended to his wound. Obsidian rocks as sharp as scalpels were used to cut away the flesh, and fine bone was used to pry the barbed arrowhead from his hip. The wound was closed with yarrow leaves and soapwort and Blue Eagle rested to recover. Kateri was happiest to have him alive and well. She nursed him back to health and tended to Sosondowah as well.

Each family was dependent on their clan and each clan was dependent on their village for mutual support and connection. They did more than help each other in daily tasks; they lived for each other in their lives. If one succeeded, they all succeeded. If one failed, they all failed. Women were central to the lives of all village members, even the warriors.

Despite winter, Brave Cloud and his teams were busy stockpiling logs and building log sections for the palisades around the village. Where they could not dig holes because of hard ground, they stacked logs for spring. The river stayed open during winter and trade for shovels and axes continued.

The Lenape council had met and was deeply divided when it came to accepting or denying Blue Eagle's offer of alliance. Late in the winter of 1662, two Lenape warriors trapping for fish along the Siskuhanne River found the canoe with Moving Moon's corpse still inside. This had a huge impact on the Lenape council. Those that had been previously against the decision for an alliance realized that if a Seneca hunting party could kill a Susquehannock warrior that close to a Lenape village, then the whole Lenape nation could easily be at risk of annihilation by the Confederacy. They voted for an alliance and sent a messenger to Bear Village to close the deal.

As promised, Captain Nick Marcus returned to Bear Village with two cannons with ammunition in the spring from Baltimore, a gift from Lord Calvert II. Captain Marcus spent about one month with some chosen warriors on the techniques and uses of the cannon in defense. Blue Eagle was interested in the cannon placement at strategic points, near the ditches facing the main entry points into the village and the planted fields. Even though there were only two cannons, they could easily be turned and aimed at almost any point of entry. Although the village was not yet fully enclosed, Blue Eagle and Brave Cloud felt confident about their security.

The two brothers, Four Rivers and Twin Branch, returned to Bear Village at the end of winter with news that the Seneca tribe was seen in force about four or five days' away from the village. They had sent out hunting parties during the winter that made it as far as the Siskuhanne River. This all tied in with the information that Blue Eagle had passed on to Four Fingers and the council about his capture and the death of four Seneca warriors.

In a dire warning to Four Fingers and the council, Blue Eagle said, "Once the Seneca find the bodies of the warriors I killed, they and the Confederacy will come after me and the people of this village with a reign of terror, the likes of which we have not seen before. I say, bring it on! We are strong, we are powerful. We are not afraid of your thunder, because we have lightning of our own! We will defeat you in battle. We are waiting!"

CHAPTER 18

Revenge of the Confederacy

A ngry Skies called for a council meeting to plan the attack on the Susquehannock village. His collection of roving spies told him about the village walls and where the town was vulnerable: the riverfront and the irrigated fields. Even though the village crews worked hard from both ends to finish, their spies did not think the work would be completed by the end of summer. Angry Skies began pacing like a possessed demon. A delay of weeks could mean disaster for an attack. Outside, the sky darkened, and anvil-like clouds rose high behind the hills in the background reflecting the mood of his name.

The council of Confederate tribes met in Angry Skies' longhouse and heard a report from the Seneca nation. A white warrior Susquehannocks, a tribe they called Minquas, had been held captive and then escaped and killed four warriors in a hunting party only weeks before. It was mid-spring; the news inflamed Angry Skies and the rest of the Confederacy.

"The Minquas have strengthened their village and defeated us once. If we don't act now, penetration will be much more difficult. They wear clothes and hides of the finest leather. They trade hides and food with the white man for iron tools and pots. Even now, many of our people starve for food and need clothing. The Minquas know no hunting season. Their life is easy, and their longhouses are full of corn and meat. Our life is hard. Their defenses get stronger by the day; if we wait, it will be too long and many of our best will die at their hands. The time to act is now. The white warrior must die!" Angry Skies stood and spit as he spoke and raised his tomahawk in defiance.

Broken Bow, the Seneca Chief, spoke first. "We want the white warrior they call Blue Eagle more than anyone here—we want to avenge the loss of our warriors, but we cannot do this alone. I can send one hundred fighters with some teenagers."

The Onondaga's leader Muddy Waters asked Angry Skies how many warriors he would send for the fight.

The blood vessels on Angry Skies' neck bulged with anger as he replied, "We will send all that we can, perhaps as many as seventy."

"Good. We all know that you despise Blue Eagle. Maybe this time you will send the Iroquois ahead of the Confederacy, instead of behind it. We were fewer in number than the rest of the tribes and had fewer to spare, but we still sent about fifty."

The Oneida and Cayuga followed, and each said that could afford only about fifty fighters. Angry Skies tallied a number well over three hundred, including teenagers. The Mohawk were too far away and not a part of this plan. Spies could not say how many defenders were in camp, but it was a huge village with many clans. When they counted the dozens of canoes on the riverfront bank and the string of longhouses, their best guess was that the village had hundreds or maybe thousands of attack warriors.

Angry Skies drew a very large circle in the sand to simulate the attack on the ground. "Tearing down the walls and penetrating the village was key to success. Once inside, they could wreck the workspaces, set fire to the camp, and then leave. Taking prisoners, raping women, scalping the men and losing warriors in battle was not as important as killing Blue Eagle. To him, nothing else mattered." The incredulous looks on the faces of the sachems around the circle of sand bespoke a story not only of revenge but of obsession.

Angry Skies' plan was direct and simple. The lead group of scouts would go ahead with canoes through streams, rivers and portages for about two moons to an assembly area. The rest would follow on foot for about two to three moons. They would penetrate the unprotected weak spots first, followed by an assault on the gates. First by water, then by the irrigated fields, then by the gates. Once inside, all would focus on destruction and fire.

"It's one thing to plan, and it's another to execute," said Broken Bow to Muddy Waters in conversation beyond the hearing of Angry Skies.

"Angry Skies is crazy with anger and fear over one white man—Blue Eagle. We must avenge the murders of your four warriors, Broken Bow, but we cannot put hundreds of good men at risk of death over one white man."

"I agree," said Broken Bow. He swiveled his head to make sure Angry Skies was not close. "We must travel far. It is too risky, and we do not outnumber the Minquas. We would have greater success with much fewer men closer in with hunting parties. We must have double the men we have now to defeat the Minquas. We need all the Mohawks, and all the warriors we can muster— a thousand men or more."

"If we wait for a thousand men, the Minquas will have finished their wall and found allies—then there will be a fight that our grandchildren will talk about," said Muddy Waters, raising his voice almost to a crescendo.

"What are you two talking about?" asked Angry Skies in a curious tone.

"I was just saying that this fight will be one that our grandchildren will talk about," Muddy Waters said with a straight face.

"Oh, that is very good," replied Angry Skies.

"We need to set a meeting place where we can come together

and still be close to the Minquas," said Muddy Waters.

"I know of just the place," said Angry Skies. He drew a circle in the sand showing a fork and large clearing where two tributaries met about three days' walk northwest of Bear Village. Angry Skies took his knife and stabbed it hard into the circle's middle and said, "Except for the canoes, be ready to attack in three moons."

Muddy Waters looked at Broken Bow, their backs erect, and both stared at Angry Skies, who was rigid, intense and determined. In a voice filled with anger he said, "Don't you two have enough to do without staring at me like I'm crazy? Get to work!"

The summer of 1662 brought unpredictable weather to central and northern Pennsylvania with a mixture of storms, rain and warm sunny weather. Streams and tributaries swelled with runoff from the hills and headwaters, and trees blossomed while animals nourished on the lush grasses. The two brothers Four Rivers and Twin Branch moved out from the comforts of Sasquesahanough Village and headed southeast, looking for traces of human life forms headed in their direction. They were seasoned spies now and no longer novices. Their sole purpose in life was not to be seen and report back on what they saw.

The horde that was the Confederacy moved northwest in bits and pieces across the streams, hills, woods, and valleys between their camps toward their staging area. Angry Skies and his cadre looked over their collection of sodden and worn warriors, some of whom were showing signs of weariness. He ordered the camp to rest to ease the journey.

Angry Skies sensed that Muddy Waters and Broken Bow were reluctant to fight and didn't possess the fighting spirit that dwelled in him. Leaving home was bad enough but knowing you may not return alive was worse. He had no family to speak of—his path was the way of the pure warrior, free from the burden of a family. Free to pursue reward for reward's sake, free to gain glory for the sake of glory. Camp was the time for fire, kinship, and rest.

The lead group with canoes left two days before everyone else. The plan was to converge southeastward from six camps with daily stops. They would be like locusts on a grassy plain moving to a destination. The plan was for the tribes to meet up after three days' walk and live off the land beforehand. They would rest, talk, and make final plans at the tributary fork. One by one, the tribes arrived. Their dispersal was no secret.

Four Rivers and Twin Forks gave their report directly to Four Fingers and Blue Eagle well before the Confederacy began arriving at the tributary forks. The news was not unexpected and not welcomed. In fact, the mass of Confederate warriors was spotted by a Lenape hunting party a full moon before the brothers gave their report in Bear Village. The force was simply too big not to draw attention.

The Lenape council decided to form a group of warriors to join the fight and enforce the alliance because "an enemy of my friend, is my enemy." An emergency council meeting was called to get everyone ready for an invasion. Sachems needed to spread the word in their longhouses to make ready. The Arrowheads' warriors were to be alerted. Those in charge of cannons should place them with ammunition at strategic points. Assign warriors and women to defend their longhouses and gather torches for night fighting. Make ditch assignments and alert litter carriers that they will be needed. Finally, check and re-check all weapons.

Most in the village knew where the weak spots were located and where the first probes would take place—at the planted fields and at the riverfront. They simply did not know when— that was what readiness was all about.

Blue Eagle told White Tail and Eagle Claw to get men to pile the logs across the open riverfront to slow warriors from canoes trying to enter the village. They would be met by arrows day or night from behind the logs. As warriors gathered behind the wall of logs and in the ditches, Blue Eagle chose a central place where he could be heard by most and chose his words with care.

"Angry Skies and the Confederacy will try to invade and burn our homes, rape our women, and take our children prisoner. We will not let that happen. We will fight to defend what is ours. On my honor and on my life, as a Susquehannock warrior I promise this to you. We fight! YAAAHHH!"

As the sun set in the west, it started to rain. Slowly at first, then it picked up to a steady downpour, turning the clay-like soil into a hard-baked slippery goo. Torches lit everywhere and soon a central bonfire was lit that gave the whole surrounding area an eerie glow.

Muddy Waters led his Onondaga warriors across the wet, planted fields and found the going very difficult. The uneven rows, rising stalks and twisted branches were hard to navigate. Blue Eagle's men fired from trenches dug in the ground in front of fields and cut down the aggressors as they tried to enter midway into the rows. Thick woods surrounded the fields on both sides which made going around them even harder. The few that managed to make it through the rows were met by tomahawks, war clubs, and knives. The second wave of Broken Bow's warriors was more successful because they were able to climb on top of the bodies of the first wave.

Angry Skies and his seventy Haudenosaunee warriors at the end of the second wave were aiming to do the most damage. If it were not for the cannon, they probably would have. The rain stopped just about the first time the cannon let loose on the fields from a corner of the ditch. The explosion and shrapnel of the ball felled about ten men on the spot. Action kept up despite the smoke and arrows.

The third wave, with the Cayuga and Oneida nations in the fields, overwhelmed the ditch in front, but it was backed up by a second line of ditch and cannon behind. This reinforced ditch kept firing against the Confederacy onslaught, which by now had lost almost half of the men who started the campaign. The cannon on the opposing end of the ditch was just as lethal as the first one, firing volley after volley into the oncoming force.

About an hour into the battle, the Lenape came in behind the wave of Confederacy scouts on canoes and started to make a difference in the battle for the riverfront. They sent about thirty warriors in fifteen canoes which almost evened the forces. The men behind the logs were holding off the scouts when the Lenape warriors cut and slashed them from behind.

In the midst of all this chaos, death and destruction, Angry Skies and Blue Eagle stood at opposing ends of the village. Both leaders were surrounded by a circle of loyal fighters as they fought opponents hand-to-hand using war clubs, tomahawks, and if close, knives.

Blue Skies urged his men to fight as if their survival was on the line. "We can and will defeat Angry Skies and his horde. His men must die, must leave. We must protect what is ours, we will win."

Angry Skies was heard shouting, "Kill the Minquas, let them feel the edges of our hatchets and the strengths of our clubs. Fight on—do not turn and run!" But the tide was turning, and the Confederacy was losing. And losing was not something Angry Skies could take lightly.

A roar of muskets in line decimated a row of tattooed warriors charging the second line of ditches. They felled warriors at twenty-five paces, men who grabbed their chests, arms, and legs as they writhed in pain, or lay dead when the smoke cleared. The Arrowheads re-loaded, and another volley from their pouches felled yet another group that dared to get too close to the ditch. A cannon in the corner fired a volley toward the fields to disable yet another group that had made it across the rows.

Blue Eagle's voice was heard over the din. "Destroy them when they stand. Live to tell your grandchildren. They are the enemy."

Bodies were everywhere, in, over, and around each other. Mud reddened and soddened with blood, bone, and sinew. It was blade to blade, hand to hand, and club to club. Neither side showed mercy and neither side gave quarter.

The melee continued and spilled over to the longhouses, where the Confederate warriors tried to set them ablaze. Standing Bear and older sachems stood in their way. They went from longhouse to longhouse to fend off warriors determined to cause havoc. His efforts succeeded, but he was killed in the process.

Although some warriors had retreated, there were many more that were still fighting. Blue Eagle picked up his tomahawk in his left hand and hit a fallen warrior across the neck and sliced his neck almost in half. With his right hand, he plunged his knife into the warrior's chest. Blood spurted up, soaking into the red clay.

"Quick but deadly!" shouted Angry Skies. He half turned as if to escape the blood on the ground completely, but Blue Eagle would have none of it. He snatched a war club from the ground and whirled it at Angry Skies. The knob of the club caught the left thigh of Angry Skies as he turned away. The sharp pain forced him to turn around and face Blue Eagle's sneering glare.

"I'll see you dead before you can run," Blue Eagle called out. Just then, a searing pain in his upper back knocked him to the ground. The bottom edge of a hatchet lodged in his upper left shoulder and was pulled out almost immediately by one of Blue Eagle's men. He thrust the handle into Blue Eagle's hand who heaved the hatchet from his knees toward the escaping Angry Skies. The blade cleaved the left calf muscle of Angry Skies as he climbed out of the fallen log and into an awaiting canoe.

"Gotcha, you son of a bitch, gotcha!" cried Judah. "Try running with that in your leg."

The sachems took over the fighting. Blue Eagle was wounded. The blade had entered muscle, and the wound needed attention. As much as he wanted to, he was in no condition to fight. Even though battle continued, only a few still resisted. Almost all the Confederate warriors were gone. The sachems rounded up the remaining teenagers and gave them the job of hauling the dead bodies outside of the walls. The teenagers were then prisoners who had to remain in the village and be raised as Susquehannocks. It was the accepted way for victorious nations to replace their losses.

Blue Eagle's men took him back to Kateri, Orenda, and Four Fingers to heal. Guards were posted for safety. Kateri and Four Fingers used lavender, garlic, and ginger to treat his wounds. They brewed the concoction and then used broad leaves from a rubber plant held with ligament to keep the shoulder immobile. They added sulfur and cloth that Storyteller left behind. The smell was awful, but the cure was effective. Judah hoped that Angry Skies' wound festered and hobbled him into insanity.

The village lost about sixty warriors, including Standing Bear. The sachems counted one hundred and ninety Iroquois and Confederate warriors dead. All the dead were scalped.

Aftermath

"We are interested in digging graves and mourning our dead," Muddy Waters said. "The battlefield sowed a heavy price." Bodies that were piled up by outside walls were taken to the camps and eventually back home for burial. It was a long and painful process.

The other tribal chiefs nodded in agreement as they passed around the pipe of peace. After the last disaster, the sachems held no confidence or loyalty to Angry Skies. They wanted a new, strong leader who was not obsessed with the murder of the one man. They wanted to focus on diplomacy, new hunting grounds, more food, and better living conditions and treaties with the white man. The Confederacy was not finished with the Susquehannocks. Overwhelming them could come later when they became stronger. They wanted a leader who would help them achieve these things in the future.

The sachems sent word out by runners to strengthen their forces from the lakes, Michigan and Canada to the north, and from the Ohio valleys to the west. The council looked for treaties with Maryland's Lord Calvert to gain rifles, muskets, and steel goods. In exchange, they promised not to invade English towns or their people. Mostly, they wanted to destroy Susquehannock villages south along the Siskuhanne, which were weak. Their plan was to attack Bear Village during hunting season instead of directly, until the Confederacy was stronger again.

The elder clan mother conferred with several other sachems at the council meeting and came up with the name of Tadodaho as the most capable Haudenosaunee leader. He knew a little English and had some negotiating experience. After extensive travel and waiting time, Tadodaho negotiated an agreement with Lord Calvert which yielded two rifles, and ten muskets with ammunition in exchange for not disturbing Maryland land or villages. In addition, the Confederacy could not occupy Maryland land or use Maryland rivers or tributaries to raid other tribal villages.

Angry Skies was exiled alone after his wound healed. In the spring of 1663, he vowed to return with a war party of his own and reclaim his honor. His promise fell on the sachems like a torrent of rain and lightning from a spring thunderclap.

The council gave ten of the largest clans one teenager each to raise as they saw fit, but it was insufficient to make up the loss of sixty warriors. The loss of village strength through disease, low birth rate and additional conflicts made long-term gain impossible.

Storyteller helped the clan sachems and mothers to keep the ritual burial ceremonies going and traditions alive. Each ceremony had to follow strict rules and rites to ensure the dead could travel to meet their ancestors in a proper symbolic way. People would never

forget their loved ones or stop praying for their sacred souls to return to earth as their favorite animals. Memories of their bravery
live on in the hearts of those who survive and are told and retold.
In time, the routine of daily life overshadowed the horrors of the
invasion.

The fields had been trampled by the invaders. Restoring and
re-planting the hectares of damage in time before the preparation of the fall hunt was an impossibility. The best that could be
accomplished in time before the first frost was to restore and replant a small portion of beans and corn that had been damaged.
A team of women picked out the least damaged rows and went
to work. By working together, men and women side by side in an
all-out effort managed to restore and replant about one-third of
the crop.

An important council meeting was held, and Blue Eagle at-
tended while still recovering. He asked the council to have a
separate ceremony outside "to give each clan sachem a hawk or
eagle feather to each warrior who risked their life in battle and
either lived or died in the struggle." It would take a little time to
gather over three hundred feathers, but they promised to do it.

Blue Eagle then asked the council to award Four Rivers and
Twin Branch feathers for their spy work. He also asked them to
give Standing Bear's family a feather in memory of his bravery,
which they also granted. Lastly, the council awarded Blue Eagle
a fifth feather for his leadership in the invasion, which he accepted with humility.

The next item was the wall. Blue Eagle said, "The enemy
came mostly through the planted fields and the river. Brave
Cloud, who fought bravely in the invasion, said repairs to the
fence were underway. The fence should be complete by the
spring, including the riverfront."

The last item was to give Twin Peak, the Lenape chief, a gift
for enforcing their alliance. What Blue Eagle had in mind was a
winter cloak that the chief could wear. He added that he would
take it to him personally and suggested they have a joint hunt in

the fall to solidify their alliance. With that, Blue Eagle said he was tired and ask to be excused.

The night was fantastic. It was toward the end of summer and there was a chill in the air. Judah pushed back on the flap of the longhouse. He felt warmed by the fire inside, undressed, and curled under the blanket on the bench next to Kateri. It had been weeks since they had quiet time together, weeks since his wound had healed, and weeks since they had made love. He held her in a gentle embrace. He stroked her back and she murmured in a low voice. He whispered "konnoronhkwa" in her ear. She smiled. They made love under the blanket. Afterward, he started to tell her about the council meeting. He could see the interest fade from her eyes. He hooked one arm around her neck. They fell asleep without talking.

CHAPTER 19

The Enemy of My Friend...

Bright sunshine filled the early fall morning of 1663 as Sharp Point and Blue Eagle paddled downriver on the Siskuhanne to meet with Twin Peaks of the Lenape village. The canoe glid swiftly with ease through the current, dodging an occasional limb or rock toward their destination. They carried with them a gift fit for a chief: a handsome lined cape made of deerskin that would keep its wearer warm in almost any kind of winter weather.

That cape was a token gesture, given in exchange for sending the thirty-plus Lenape warriors to the Sasquesahanough Village riverfront on the day of the invasion. Two of the warriors were returned to the Lenape the day after, shrouded and tied in leaves and branches for burial, the price the Lenape paid in blood to uphold the alliance, a full measure of devotion to it.

When at camp that night, Sharp Point asked Blue Eagle about his wound and condition. He replied, "Kateri and Orenda did an excellent job of putting me back together. The traded sewing kit and needle from Dietrick helped to close the wound, but I still

179

ache now and then from the healing. Other than that, I'm fine, and I'll be even better after more rest. Thank you for your concern. How are you doing?"

"I'm fine. My wife is with a child who is expected in the spring. It will be our first."

"Kateri and I have one son, Sosondowah, who turned two this spring. We are very proud of him," said Blue Eagle. "I will be asking Twin Peaks to join us for a hunt in one moon, and I hope that he will. We need to strengthen our alliance."

It was a perfect fall night on the island in the stream of the Siskuhanne River. Blue Eagle wrapped himself in his blanket by the fire and stared at the canopy of blinking stars that had died millions of years before but were just now being seen. He closed his eyes and drifted off into a quiet sleep filled with the sound of the forest at night. Hooting owls, chirping birds, scurrying animals.

And then, a dream of the talking rock. *They'll be back, you know—the Confederacy, Angry Skies, the whole lot of them. This time the horde will return like a thundering herd, not like a creeping stream. They are coming for you and your people. Be ready, because fire is their friend—and destruction is their end.*

When he awoke, clouds covered the darkened sky, and the twinkling canopy was replaced by an inky darkness that filled his world. The disturbing dream kept him awake for a long time and he had to use long, slow breaths to put his mind back into a restful, dreamless sleep.

The gift of the cape was presented to Twin Peaks. With Black Braid nearby, all shared a pipe of peace. Blue Eagle told them the gift was an inadequate expression of the grief that his people felt for the loss of their two warriors at their riverfront. He deeply regretted that loss and appreciated their allegiance to the alliance.

On that note, he mentioned that the Lenape people were invited to participate in a joint hunt with their village in one moon west and south of their village. The plan was to unite their two villages in a large hunt with many canoes and warriors, led by the clans of both nations and lasting for at least one and possibly two moons.

Blue Eagle drew a large circle on the floor and pointed to where two tributaries met the Siskuhanne, branching off the main river about one day's canoe ride south. Each clan sachem would lead a group of warriors. If scouts could find herds of game in the woods ahead, they would alert the sachems, who would gather warriors for a V-shaped hunt. If not, each clan was on its own to find and hunt game.

The meeting points would be camps on islands in the river or along riverbanks. Each clan would bring a flag showing their location to avoid confusion. Twin Peaks pointed to Black Braid and said, "You may not know that Lenape women also go on hunts with their men. They stay at the river to butcher the animals, cook the meals and provide comfort to the returning mates. This is very important for the hunt, because it frees up the teenagers to transport the carcasses in a chain back to the village where the game can be stripped, separated, dried and hung for the winter, a very time-consuming process. The women at the river contribute to this process, making it a complete team effort. It gives the warrior-hunter comfort, instead of anxiety."

Blue Eagle was taken aback by this. He thought about it for a minute and concluded that not only was it a good idea, but that it was an improvement on the way hunts should be conducted. It made practical sense, and the only ones that could possibly object would be the old warriors who had not done anything like this before.

Twin Peaks went on to explain that he would have to ask the sachem council to approve the proposal to be ready in one moon. Blue Eagle and Sharp Point said they would await the council's decision. He also promised that they would exchange runners to communicate information. He thanked his hosts for their hospitality and left.

Since they were already on the water, Blue Eagle explained to

Sharp Point they would be visiting another Susquehannock village, much smaller than their own. Storyteller reported it was not in good shape and was not far away.

The canoes at the landing site were in disarray and tossed in all directions, with some on top of each other. There was no one to greet Blue Eagle or Sharp Point, so they simply walked into the closest longhouse. Not only was its appearance awful, but the smell and atmosphere of the village that Storyteller had reported was even worse than he described. Blue Eagle asked a young boy in ragged clothes where he could find a sachem; and the boy pointed to a longhouse which appeared to be in disuse and dilapidated.

After speaking to the man for a few minutes he learned that the few capable warriors and the chief sachem were away on hunts, and only about one hundred men and women remained in the village. Almost everybody else had died from diseases which had swept through the village months before. Others were in the fields retrieving whatever would grow there, or off hunting in the woods for food. Only a handful of mostly sick and old people and few children remained in the village. There was no security that Blue Eagle or Sharp Point could see.

To the west side of the planted fields, Blue Eagle noticed lines of fresh burial mounds near the rotted rows of corn and squash. He and Sharp Point set out for home with little to say to each other on the way except that it would be a sad, sad report back to the council when they returned.

Three days later they pulled their canoe onto the riverbank of Sasquesahanough Village. It was reassuring to see rows upon rows of neatly laid out canoes laden with provisions for the upcoming hunting trip. What a change from what they had just witnessed.

Brave Cloud's wall and gates were now converging from both sides—north from the planted fields and south from the main wall to form a solid palisade enclosure. Tired and weary from their long trip upstream, the pair was ready for a rest. First stop for Blue Eagle was family and Kateri at the longhouse. He overhead Kateri saying to Orenda that her father had a lot more responsibility now than in the past. Orenda said she would do nothing to dishonor her father. Kateri said that she was proud of the way that she helped her father recover from his wound. She also asked Orenda if she had learned things from White Tail during her time in the woods, and Orenda said that she had.

Blue Eagle told them of his travels, and that it was a Lenape tradition to include women in the hunts at their campsites. Women replaced the jobs of many warriors and litter carriers. Kateri and Orenda thought it was a wonderful idea.

Next, Blue Eagle went to Four Fingers and asked for a council meeting to discuss the upcoming hunt with the Lenape. He would tell them what he witnessed at the forsaken village downstream. When the council of sachems met, he told them of the plan for the hunt and the use of women at the clan campsites. As expected, there was resistance from the older sachems who were not used to having women along on the hunts. Black Elk of the Antelope clan said, "Hunting is the job of the warrior and the teenager who wants to be a warrior. A woman's job is to produce babies for the village and to feed and clothe the warrior. She would need extra protection at the hunt from the Confederacy, who could take advantage of their vulnerability."

Blue Eagle listed all of the advantages of having women close by and how their presence added value to the hunt by making it more efficient. A few warriors could be present for protection, if needed. "Nothing could replace the value of having family close by on the hunt," he said. "It provides comfort and security."

The council considered the opposing view and decided that the Lenape cooperation and alliance was well worth the lives saved when it came to the invasion. The council agreed with Blue Eagle's position on having women at the hunt.

After Sharp Point and Blue Eagle briefed the council on the desperate and poor condition of the downriver village they visited, the conclusion they reached was telling but very difficult. If possible, that village should be abandoned and evacuated to Bear Village before the Confederacy destroyed it completely. It was the only honorable and just thing to do. Without security or protection, the people there had no future or chance for survival. It was agreed that after the hunt, teams with canoes would venture over the winter, if possible, to move the people there and absorb them into the village. This would be a difficult but worthy move, since it would save the village from certain destruction. It would also increase the potential for the village to make up for its losses from the last invasion.

Blue Eagle said that the village must now focus on the joint hunt, which must happen over the new moon and carry the village through the coming fall and the new year. Those warriors left behind would continue to work on the wall and defend the village, watch over the children, and fight in case the Confederacy decided to take advantage of the hunt. Each clan would have to decide how many to leave behind but switching back and forth between the hunt and the village could take place.

After some last-minute preparations, the canoes took off downriver to join their Lenape partners in the first joint hunt in the history of the Susquehannock nation. Not all, but many warriors also took their wives with them, also a new experience. The warriors painted their faces and bodies with red and blue, ocher stripes and animal figures, symbols of strength and courage. Pyres sent flames skyward that delivered smoke to the heavens, and prayers followed for ancestral messages. Laden canoes filled the waters as young boys and girls danced for joy and good hunting.

Kateri and Orenda went with Blue Eagle in the first canoe. It was a joyous event. Clan leaders followed in canoe after canoe to make up the long chain. Storyteller chanted and sang over every canoe as it left the landing, his staff and seed pods and feathers dangling.

The river seemed alive as leaves fell from the trees even before the first canoe touched the water. The warriors chanted the paddle cadence as they stroked the water: umphpapa... umphpapa. The two-headed dragon of canoes seemed alive as it skimmed double-file down the river, as if it had a life of its own. There was magic in their stroke. In the lead, Blue Eagle swiveled his head to look back at this marvel. He hoped this feeling would never end.

Since this was their first joint hunt, Twin Peaks thought it best not to gather with the Susquehannock at the clan campsites when hunting game. Although their Algonquin languages were similar, their customs when it came to hunting might be different. The alliance was all about defense and little else. This meant that the Lenape would stick to hunting game near the farthest tributary downriver while the Susquehannock would hunt around the closer tributary. It seemed best to keep the two nations apart unless a huge herd of deer was spotted. Then both nations could combine forces and share in the result.

Except for grumbling by the some of the old warriors, having the wives along went well. Small animals like squirrels and rabbits were found everywhere. Orenda and Kateri showed many of the other women how to trap, butcher and skin these animals. Spreading this knowledge added to the value of having the women on the hunt.

The hunt for larger game went slowly at first but picked up after a few days. The warriors spread out west in search of beaver, muskrat, porcupine, turkey, deer, and duck. The women and teenagers fished and searched nearby for waterfowl and frogs. Litter carriers followed the teams into the woods, and the chain of dragging the carcasses back to the river for preparation began.

Sharp Point went out with Orenda, Blue Eagle, and other warriors to experience Orenda's first game hunt. They passed up on three very small deer and finally caught up with two does and a buck, one of which may have been pregnant. Orenda waited and shot the one that did not appear pregnant. Sharp Point and Blue Eagle shot the big buck, and Orenda was very excited at her first kill.

"Warriors work in teams," Blue Eagle told Kateri later, "not individually, and hunts must follow established rules. Orenda will team up with experienced hunters who will show her the patience and the finer points of hunting. If she listens and learns discipline, she will trust her skills and the skills of those she is with. She will be fine if you trust her."

"I hope you are right," said Kateri.

Although the hunt had yielded a sizable number of deer and turkey, the big kill had not happened. Just before Blue Eagle was going to call off the hunt, the scouts returned with a report that a herd of well over two hundred deer was spotted further west toward the hills. Runners were sent to the Lenape to gather at a point west for a big hunt.

Two forces of about four hundred armed warriors gathered at the meeting point. The scouts led them in a huge V-shape over a valley, heading toward hills in the west. The formation, with a mass of litter carriers behind, walked at a brisk pace at first. Then, as the herd came into view, they slowed their pace to a steady walk and the formation started to close like a noose. The deer had nowhere to jump or leap since the hills blocked their way from behind and the V prevented escape on the sides. Shouts of "ready" and "aim" were heard as they closed within range of the herd. Then, the order of "fire" rang out and the sky darkened as arrows filled the air and found their marks.

What promised to be a good hunt turned into an extraordinary one that filled the canoes of both nations. It promised enough meat to dry and harvest for many moons. The chain of canoes along the banks of the Siskuhanne were clogged and busy with the butchered carcasses of deer going back to home camps.

In addition to being a conduit for supplies, men, and places, the Siskuhanne was also a river of information for the traders and spies of the Confederacy. When word filtered back to Tadodaho that the Lenape and Susquehannock had trapped a big herd of deer not far from his hunting grounds, he was livid and determined to get even. He developed a strategy to net some of what had been shot for his people. Because the Lenape were closer to the Seneca, he asked Broken Bow to send as many warriors as he could down the Siskuhanne to take as many of their canoes as possible.

Tadodaho knew that the Lenape had an alliance with the Susquehannock and that this action would mean conflict with them, but he did not care. He was mad as hell and was going to risk lives to get back what truly belonged to him.

A full week had passed, and the two nations were still dividing up the deer shot in the hills when the first Seneca canoes were seen headed upriver toward the Lenape camp. The Seneca canoes bore distinct markings on their sides. The warriors' headdresses, bows, and painted faces showed no intention of being friendly.

The first Seneca arrows landed on shore and on the canoes lined up at camp. The surprise attack was met immediately by counterfire by the Lenape. Soon, there were about fifteen Seneca canoes with about thirty-five warriors making a raid on the Lenape. Women fled into the woods. Runners and canoes were sent to the Susquehannock. A fight was on.

Teams of warriors were sent down to help the Lenape, but it would take at least thirty minutes to get there. Meanwhile, the Lenape rushed to the aid of their comrades at the river. Although not raised as warriors like the Susquehannock, they fought like possessed demons, firing at all the targets they could find. Off in the distance, Twin Lakes could see more canoes headed upriver toward them.

The second wave of Seneca warriors arrived at the Lenape waterfront at about the same time as Blue Eagle and his teams arrived with Susquehannock warriors. Twin Peaks said, "I am glad you are here. We are almost out of arrows. They got away with eight or ten canoes of deer, but I think we killed at least ten or twelve of their men and lost a few of our own. We are really tired."

"We'll take it from here. Don't worry about the canoes. We'll make up for your losses, we have plenty. Protect your wives. We will go to work now," Blue Eagle said in an excited mood.

With that, Blue Eagle, Hawk Shadow, Strong Oak and their men started to decimate the remaining Seneca warrior ranks. In less than fifteen minutes, all the remaining Seneca warriors were either dead or had left the scene. It was great victory for the Lenape.

CHAPTER 20

Don't Forget About Me

adodaho told Angry Skies to leave the Haudenosaunee camp. "Pack up your shit and leave now," he shouted. His words were filled with venom and hate, spilling like a springtime flood even though it was winter of 1664.

Angry Skies turned back and snarled at Tadodaho. "I will return, and when I do, I'll come back not with fifty men but with five hundred warriors. All of them will be hungry and ready to rip the heart out Blue Eagle's white body and eat it in front of his Mohawk bride. Then, I'll take my rightful place with one foot on top of your dead body."

With his prophesy spent, Angry Skies trudged off downhill. His limp was noticeable but only at a fast pace. He kept up a steady mumbling to himself, vowing over and over again to make Blue Eagle pay. He had a new mission now on his long and seemingly never-ending quest—to gather followers.

The first days, weeks, and moons almost killed him. He was headed northeast from camp, first with a sled for supplies, and when that gave out, he reverted to a backpack. He also had to use his basic woodsman's skills to trap and kill animals. Working just to stay alive in winter and keep walking with weapons made him lean and strong. After walking with a backpack and a few weapons, he paced himself. Angry Skies was no fool, with minimal food, enough for a few days at most. He knew what lay ahead and without shelter or village, living off the land, and alone with his thoughts he was increasingly desperate. His only comfort in the winter was his blanket, the fire and an occasional friendly village that gave him shelter from the snow. He could do it alone—constantly alone. It was how it would be for a while, but not forever.

He had skills he had learned as a young man in the woods alone at night. He could build a fire and shelter, trap food, and live off the land. He had not done this in a long time but could do it again. Sometimes, the gods sent him messages for a purpose. Angry Skies set his mind to only two things. Head northeast, using the sun and the sky for direction. Next, survive at all costs. Nothing else mattered. He could not change anything else. Not the rain, not the sun, not the heat, not the cold, not the dark, not the howl of the wind or chirp of the birds. Only those two things. If he kept his mind focused, he would overcome the obstacles. Self-doubt kept coming, creeping into his mind like hunger that was gnawing in his gut.

After weeks on the trail, survival became easier. Trapping, killing, eating, and living became habits. The hardest part was being alone—alone with his thoughts. He needed followers, people to talk to, anyone. His lone walk molded him hard and lean. He lived on tree bark, grass, and snakes and slept with a blanket, a fire, and a cover of snow.

Angry Skies came across a ragged village of scattered fires and clay pots. He begged like a dog for food and another blanket. The people were friendly, and he made sign language to show respect and need. They took pity on this bedraggled stranger with multiple, faded feathers and polite ways. He was grateful for his stay and rested for days. He asked for directions to the next village.

In that village, he picked up two young warriors and a canoe. There, they managed to paddle upstream to an even larger, substantial settlement of Mahicans. He learned that he was in New York and closer to other nations, where it was possible to talk to groups of young warriors about their stories and tell them his.

"Why would we want to leave our homes and family?" asked a young, no-feather buck.

"I was expecting that question," Angry Skies said, "and here is my answer. The Haudenosaunee are a whole family of nations we call the Confederacy—the Seneca, Mohawk, Cayuga, Onondaga and Oneida. We are one and defend each other in battle and in peace. We absorb other nations into ours; white men make peace treaties with us to keep the peace. They look to us to protect them against nations they fear like the Susquehannock. If you join us, you'll be a part of a great collection of nations that together no one can touch. You will experience adventure, excitement and meet beautiful maidens of other nations. Bring your friends to join you on this adventure, these are the reasons for leaving your family. Who can blame you? I left the group to recruit young men like you."

The speech left the young men tongue-tied. They could not make a counter-argument because those words reached into their inner fears and desires. At that age, they still had strong family ties, but they also yearned for adventure and excitement. Angry Skies had to convince them that forming a party to join the Confederacy in the west was a worthy and just goal. He told them of his past leadership and his plans. Angry Skies stopped short of making them promises, but he managed to convince a few of them to come with him, which was all he needed.

It wasn't what he said as much as what Angry Skies was himself that formed the attraction. He was a dynamic personality full of a magnetism that set him apart from others. He made young people believe in his ideals of freedom against the odds. They believed in his promises of future glory and how he led five nations of people in the north, absorbing tribe after tribe to achieve Hiawatha's dream of a great united nation. Now, they would be the core to rise of glory again.

His mission was beginning. He picked a few good leaders to help him spread the word and gain followers. Success would only come when he had tens or even hundreds of followers like them. Then and only then would he go south. His goal was clear, and he learned patience in the woods. He would stalk villages like he stalked game. Aim for weaknesses; strike when unexpected; seize without mercy. His forces grew every few months, and he was always on the move. No one could stop him. His message was clear—but he never detailed why he left, or why he was exiled, or exposed his hatred for Blue Eagle.

The groups Angry Skies infiltrated came mostly from villages and nations that had suffered from diseases or costly encounters with the Confederacy like the Wendat or the Munsee, or the nations in the upper northeast like the Wappinger, or the Mohegan or the Pequot. He gained followers wherever he could find them, even if they were strays and came one or two at a time. Small groups were better, since their future usually held less promise for young, ambitious warriors like the Pocumtuk, and the Mahican camps.

All this wandering, organizing and marshaling took time. Their forces were arrayed in valleys west of the Delaware River.

Angry Skies filled them with stories about how the Confederacy absorbed other nations such as the Hurons. In many cases villages were in bad shape with weak leadership and security. Often those villages were on the verge of starvation. He told them stories of how the Hiawatha and the great Peacemaker brought the Iroquois and other nations together to form a strong bond that existed to that day. They followed him because he symbolized success over suffering.

Moon after moon passed into years, but Angry Skies felt he had lots of time. He thought it best to count his followers as best he could. It took over two years of talking and training for Angry Skies to gather his forces into a group of over eighty men. A far cry from the promise of five hundred he boasted about much earlier, but a sizable war party, nonetheless.

Angry Skies led this group on their trek from the flatlands of the northeast across the rolling hills and mountains of the Catskills to the sweeping valleys and rivers of central Pennsylvania. A group of mostly young, eager warriors followed Angry Skies. They were filled to the brim with stories of glory and conquest of the mighty Confederacy, determined to follow their great leader to victory!

It was now the summer of 1666, and after their crossing, Angry Skies parked his war party in a valley outside of Seneca camp. He approached Broken Bow, the same chief with whom Angry Skies had disagreed so violently years before.

"Why should we accept you now, Angry Skies, after you were exiled years before?" Broken Bow said in a mean-spirited tone laced with sarcasm.

"Because I brought you over eighty young warriors eager to conquer the weak Susquehannock to the south," said Angry Skies. He was now excited. "They come from the east, where the white man is taking their tribal lands, and their way of life is gone like the wind. They are ready to fight for new land and hunting grounds. Use these men to build an unstoppable army of new warriors that will lead us to victory."

"It is time that you told these men the truth of why you had to leave," Broken Bow said. "If you do not tell them the truth, they will not be accepted into the Confederacy to fight. Go with your leaders now and tell them that you were exiled because your hatred for one man caused the Confederacy to lose warriors in defeat. Go now and tell them."

"As you wish, I will tell them," said Angry Skies. He gathered the men around him that he spent two years painfully accumulating in the northeast and spoke words of admission. "Warriors of tomorrow, before we join the great Haudenosaunee Confederacy of five nations, I must tell you the whole story of why I left this camp.

"Years ago, I was exiled from here because my heart and my

mind became totally obsessed with the death of one man. A white man who is called Blue Eagle, Susquehannock chief of a large village about four days from here. My attempts to defeat this man cost me the injury that I bear to this day, an injury to my ankle. My obsession was also paid in blood to the Confederacy. That is the truth. If you still want to fight, then stay with me and fight for the Confederacy. If not, turn around and go home to your families."

The assembled warriors stared at one another is stony silence. Then they talked and spoke to each other in quiet tones for a few minutes. After a few minutes, a group of two or three gathered to leave. They were followed by another group, and then another three who left together. In about ten minutes, about thirty young men had decided to go back home. When Angry Skies stopped to ask one group why they decided to leave, one young man said simply that he did not want to stay with a person that did not tell the whole truth from the beginning.

"Yes," Angry Skies agreed. "The truth can be a bitter root to swallow."

Angry Skies told Broken Bow that he felt better that his truth was out for all to see and that he had nothing to hide from his men. He also told Broken Bow to tell the council they could now count on these fifty men for the fight. Broken Bow was still reluctant, but he said he would carry the message to the council and ask them to consider the numbers.

Never daunted or discouraged, Angry Skies pushed on. To a man, these were bachelors or men who were separated or never actually married, like himself. He gave these men hope where they had none. After all, the Confederacy was flush with maidens. In Angry Skies' mind, all he had to do now was to wait for the council's final decision, which he believed would be positive. How else could they decide?

Angry Skies had at first hidden his inner revenge against Blue Eagle from his followers. He ignored the bile in his mouth that cast him off in the first place. The hatred lingered there in the core, like biting into an apple that was hard on the outside but rotted on the inside. Now, he was bringing back a war party of more than fifty warriors eager to destroy and take what they could for him from the Susquehannock. In his eyes, the Susquehannock were rich and had more than they could use. Take from those who had plenty and give to those who had little, that was the essence of his plan.

Angry Skies would have to wait for weeks to decide his fate on the full council decision. Broken Bow finally came back and told him that he could keep his men and lead them in battle, but to prove his sincerity, he would not be allowed to go against Blue Eagle until he had proven his leadership in a different raid on a different Susquehannock village. Until then, he and his men would have to build their own longhouse and subsist on their own. He could live near the watchful eyes of Muddy Waters.

Neither Muddy Waters nor Angry Skies were happy with this outcome, but both agreed it was the best they could have expected. Another group of six young warriors went back home to their families when word went out about this decision.

In a separate conversation with Muddy Waters, Angry Skies said, "My past is over. The journey northeast taught me many things. It taught me to be humble in the face of danger. It taught me there is no glory in revenge, only hatred for myself. It taught me that a warrior's victory is to defeat an enemy in battle no matter the costs. It taught that trust among men is more valuable than the recognition that I have come back in peace and honor. I brought almost fifty loyal men from all over the northeast nations. I do not come empty-handed. These men will do as I say for you and the Confederacy. We wish to be a part of the Confederacy legacy forever." Angry Skies stared directly at Muddy Waters when he said those things.

"Those are mighty words, well spoken. We know your history, Angry Skies, and why the Confederacy banished you. Why should we believe you do not come back with revenge in your heart now for Blue Eagle? Perhaps you are using your men only to cover your past."

The fire crackled in a newly built longhouse and sparks jumped across the rocks. There was a chill in the late summer night, and Angry Skies wrapped himself in a blanket to keep warm while he stared at the fire. He rocked as he thought. "Damn that son of a bitch, just damn that blued-eyed, feathered son of a bitch! Damn him! I'll see him dead yet!" The spittle that lay deep in Angry Skies came to the surface and rushed out to the ground in a massive blob onto the dirt floor. That felt better, a lot better.

Ultimately, the men he brought to fight won the day. He could join the battle provided his men stayed with him, not mixing with the others. They could be used as a flanking or backup force, but not as a leading force, since the leaders did not know their languages and fighting abilities.

A partial victory was better than a full one. That was the outcome that Angry Skies would have settled for when he heard the news. He spun the news in his head, returning to his camp. In a quiet moment around two large fires, he told his men. With his arms outstretched, he stood with his back to the fire and said, "Now is our chance to give value to the Confederacy's plan. We will be a part of their next battle with the Susquehannocks. We will camp away from the main party. We will train and practice as they do. We will not waver or disappoint. We will feed ourselves and gather water for ourselves as we have done in our journey here. The warriors pronounced their chance to prove what they could do. We will follow orders and fight!"

What Angry Skies failed to mention was that he was now a part of the war council. He would have a say about when, where, and how the Confederacy planned to attack. This was a fact not lost on Muddy Waters, Broken Bow or Tadodaho. The first chance of that happened in the early summer of the following year, 1667. The Iroquois duo made plans to raid and destroy two lower Delaware Valley Susquehannock villages in full force. The Twin Fork attack meant that a force of about three hundred warriors would have to travel long distances over land and canoes through hills and rivers to reach their destinations. Because of the distance, their attacks would have to continue upriver to destroy two more villages. At least two villages in four to six months. It was an ambitious plan designed to strike fear everywhere.

The Confederacy fanned out like a locust cloud across the summer plains with a rough pre-planned set of movements. Clans and nations generally stayed together and helped each other across difficult passages. Canoes had to portage where there were no tributaries or streams. Groups of men and some women followed the sun and the stars for the southern route. Using crude maps from traders as guides, camps along the rivers and tributaries took days before everyone was in place. A final war council was held at Twin Forks.

The combined outcome was almost over before it began. With little or no security in place, resistance from the weakened villages was meager and pathetic. Crazed hordes of enraged and tattooed warriors pushed down the haphazard logs that fell into the soft soil. Frenzied warriors held scalps high in triumph for all to see before a knife was plunged into the heart of the former wearer. Whoops, victory cries, and dances filled the blood-soaked mud. Resistance from the brave defenders was brief and futile. The hand-to-hand fighting was short and brutal and woefully one-sided.

Angry Skies and his group were ordered to the left flank of the second village, where resistance was surprisingly strong. Instead of ease of entry, they found warriors armed with muskets and rifles. The volleys of balls ripped stomachs open and tore bodies apart at the thighs. The strong defense was well-placed, and the disciplined and practiced men knew how to use the weapons. The first wave of warriors was set back on their heels, and Angry Skies ordered a retreat.

Muddy Waters, as Onondaga chief, saw men leaving the scene and ordered his side to help. It took an overwhelming number of invaders to subdue the second village. The dreams of Confederate

197

glory were shattered among Angry Skies' men, who were expecting unfettered access. Instead, they received unexpected brutality in the face of a strong defense that shattered their hopes. The invaders had to be reinforced by Muddy Waters' men to overcome the village. Deaths and casualties to Angry Skies' inexperienced recruits were high—as many as thirty-five were dead or wounded.

This unexpected result devasted Angry Skies, who fully expected respect and recognition after the raids on the weaker villages. Instead, he received ignominy and defeat with his band of recruits. Instead of falling into the doldrums, he told Tadodaho that he would take the newly absorbed teenagers, the remainder of his men, and any new teenagers in any nation and mold them into true Confederacy warriors, fighters that any nation would be proud to take into battle. "Just give me one year to do it," he asked. Tadodaho agreed, reluctantly.

Every battle had its price, and this one was no exception. Some prisoners were taken, but few knew how many or where to take them. Eventually about fourteen women, teenagers and children were taken from both villages and strapped at the neck and escorted back to the Seneca camp. The second village was more organized than the first. The Confederacy replenished itself by absorbing prisoners. The teenagers would prove more valuable to the Confederacy, since they were given a choice of join or die right from the start. Warriors could burn both villages, but there was no order in retrieving valuables.

The prisoners either decided to be Confederate members or die as prisoners. It was simple. Over time, their nations continued to produce warriors. Their loyalty could not have been more reliable.

There were survivors, but they fled to the woods at first attack, some with families and some alone. The handful that did not die in the invasion or the fire fled to avoid capture. Like deer avoiding the arrow, the fleeing took the path of least resistance. With children in tow, they crossed creeks and streams, forded rivers, and climbed trees. A lucky few managed to find shelter at nearby villages, but most simply vanished in the wilderness never to be seen or heard from again.

Planning and restoration over the winter was necessary. The Confederacy needed rest and recovery to heal the wounded and prepare for the next confrontation in the coming year. It was the way of expansion. The Confederacy had to follow its cycle of hunting, food preparation and storage, expansion of land and of nations, absorption and restoration.

The Haudenosaunee were also interested in making treaties. Living and giving land and weapons among whites, they prided themselves as being diplomatic. Spreading their influence over the land was what built their legend.

CHAPTER 21

Treaties

The winter of 1667 was milder than in previous years, but that didn't stop the smallpox disease from rushing through Sasquesahanough and Lenape villages with a vengeance. The isolation practices of Bear Village prevented widespread loss of life, but the disease managed to take Four Fingers, the beloved village mother. In total, smallpox forced three children and five elderly into the next world. Since Four Fingers had no living relatives, the council decided that the task of village mother should go to Kateri, her dearest and closest devotee.

A new burial mound had to be built. All the clothing and remains of those who succumbed to the disease were burned and placed in the mound with them, accompanied by their favorite trinkets, toys and everyday amulets.

The Lenape village was less fortunate and lost twenty-two to the disease, including their elderly and children. They too needed new burial mounds and pyres for their ceremonies.

Life went on in Sasquesahanough Village, and Blue Eagle called the sachems for a council meeting to discuss disturbing news from the traders coming up from the Delaware River. Confederate warriors had raided and destroyed two Susquehannock villages along the Delaware River not too distant from Baltimore. They took prisoners, but some villagers managed to escape to the woods.

Dozens were stripped, scalped and left to rot on the ground, dead. The traders who came upon the scene later said that it was a ghastly one, with plenty there for the buzzards. The survivors who straggled northward told stories about men who fought with extraordinary bravery to defend their homeland against impossible odds.

When the council and Kateri asked what could be done, Blue Eagle answered, "Unfortunately, nothing can be done about it. We hope they did not attack Flowing Waters' village. The villages to the south are weak and unprotected, without fortifications. Here, we are too far away and helpless to stop attacks on those villages."

Kateri bent at the knees and pounded both fists to the floor. "It's not right. It's not right!" she shouted. "Those poor babies! Those poor people!" Blue Eagle took her outside and away from the council, because such outbursts appeared unseemly. He tried to comfort her, but she sobbed uncontrollably. While he wrapped his arms around her, the normally stoic Kateri was inconsolable.

She calmed down in a few minutes and apologized. "Oh, please forgive me, I'm so, so sorry."

He wiped her face and held her tightly, saying in a low, steady tone, "The Haudenosaunee probably took most of the women with babies as prisoners. They will be raised by the five nations to increase their ranks. Chances are they are not dead." That bolstered Kateri, and she and Blue Eagle returned to the council meeting.

The depressing news of the villages to the south was met by the council with fierce resistance and resolve. In the end, they agreed on a number of measures that would strengthen their defenses and the wall, which was now finished. They voted to keep a constant vigil and alert outside the walls through a network of spies and to continue to practice marksmanship with the weapons received from the British, while still conserving ammunition. The council agreed to continue planting, as well as drying and storing food supplies, despite the wet weather. There was a continuous need to maintain a sense of normality.

One additional practice that the council wanted to keep in place was to keep trading for necessities but maintain strict isolation with traders. They were convinced the reason for the smallpox outbreak was the joint hunt with the Lenape, who did not have a policy of strict trading isolation. A second policy was to increase full immersion bathing to daily instead of weekly, if possible, to prevent spread of diseases. This they knew was going to be difficult for a body of people as large as their own, but making the attempt would help keep their village free of disease.

Blue Eagle raised another item with the council, but he wanted to involve the sachems in his plan to give urgency to his intent. He wanted to evacuate the useful and fit warriors from the Susquehannock villages that he and Sharp Point had visited earlier. By removing the warriors before they were killed or taken prisoner, the Confederacy would be denied their use. By burning down the village, they could not access the stored food and supplies. He asked Dark Moon and Rain Forest for their help. This assured Blue Eagle of council involvement and support.

About one month later, Blue Eagle's plan paid off when Dark Moon, Sharp Point, and Rain Forest recovered warriors from the dilapidated villages and brought them back to Bear Village. The welcoming celebration boosted the dignity and pride of the council and the village. It also brought renewed faith in Blue Eagle and Kateri's reputations as thoughtful leaders of their people. The sachems had come together as one to solve a problem.

The last task the council gave to Blue Eagle and Kateri was to find a way through diplomacy to extend the time it would take for the Confederacy to invade their village. That meant a peace treaty that offered the village some sort of lasting peace in exchange for a promise from the Confederacy not to invade their village or infringe on their right to hunt. Those were daunting demands, since the Confederacy were known not to keep their word on any treaties that they signed.

There was little joy in the village. The simple tasks of living were overshadowed by the threat of the Confederacy attacks, plus surviving the disease. The winter of 1667 bled into 1668, and while not as cold as the year just passed, it snowed or rained almost daily. The wet weather made vegetable storage difficult, since it was challenging to keep the stalks dry. Life was hard. Survival was hard.

Somehow Blue Eagle and Kateri had to find a diplomatic solution to make village life more tolerable. The plan was simple: they would go to the British in Maryland and ask them to meet with the Confederacy and the remaining Susquehannock leaders. Sky Warrior, a young disciple of Storyteller, volunteered to go with Blue Eagle and Kateri to represent the clan members. All agreed.

With the council's blessing and chants for safe travels, Kateri, Blue Eagle, and Orenda set off for Baltimore to make peace with the British. Orenda, now nineteen and grown into a fine woman, went along to see the world outside the village. Except when he paddled and his back was turned, Sky Warrior could not keep from staring at her. The trip would prove to be the village's last hope at peace.

Blue Eagle's eyes scanned the green around him as they slid down the river. It was spring of 1668. A chill in the air did not seem to bother anyone in the canoes, especially Orenda, who enjoyed every minute of their trip. The trees and woods seemed endless.

Camping sites were easy to find along the Siskuhanne. Blue Eagle's favorite was the island in the middle of the river. There was much less chance of disturbance by unknown forces and a higher degree of privacy than stopping on the shore of either side. Kateri told the story of how Four Fingers got her reputation of being feisty even at a young age. Everyone grew sad with reflection and was saddened by the remembrance of her loss. Spirits brightened as the stories around the campfire became humorous. Tasks such as rowing and gathering wood were shared willingly by the group, easing the monotony of the ten-day trip to Baltimore.

Orenda and Sky Warrior became close friends and talked endlessly with each other. This fact was not lost on Blue Eagle or Kateri, and they spoke privately about how they did not object to that relationship.

The Siskuhanne twists and turns as it gets closer to the Delaware. In one of those bends, the canoes stopped at a trading station that happened to be occupied by Jim Blaine, the same English trader that Blue Eagle had encountered years before. After exchanging greetings, Blaine gave them directions to Baltimore in exchange for deer jerky.

The Delaware River was very different from the Siskuhanne. What looked like a peaceful bay opened to choppy and unpredictable waters that made canoeing rough and rugged. Hugging the shoreline led to hidden shoals and islands. The vegetation and trees were so close to the shore that portage was impossible. It took four days of haphazard travel to navigate up to the Baltimore harbor.

The English did not consider the Confederacy, the Haudenosaunee, or the Susquehannock as equivalent to the English, not even with the white man Blue Eagle as a representative. When the administration learned of their purpose, they greeted the group with cautious but friendly introductions. It showed in the way the treaties that were drafted. For example, the killing of an Englishman by a native was punishable by death and worse on his clan. The killing of a native by an Englishman was an excusable minor offense and often dismissed as an accident. The English usually considered the fight of one native against another as a dispute that was not worthy of their interference. They did not want violence on the doorstep of the British settler. They believed that parties would keep their word in treaties, at least for a period. They refused to meddle unless the French were involved.

Blue Eagle conjured up the little English he knew and then spoke Dutch to an interpreter, which impressed the English administrators. They promised to send an envoy to the Confederacy. The Susquehannock had no choice and waited a full moon before Tadodaho could return to Baltimore with his contingent. Their time was spent meditating and fishing the banks with homemade weirs. Orenda and Sky Warrior had a gay time hunting and going barefoot on the beach, catching blue crabs. The crabs made excellent meals along with stews and vegetables.

Animosity ruled the day when the two factions sat cross-legged across from one another. Neither party wanted to sign or mark any document that would even acknowledge the existence of the other, let alone come to some agreement.

Tadodaho said, "Blue Eagle and his nation have taken the best hunting and fishing land for their use. Other nations have starved and suffered at their expense."

Hatchets danced in Blue Eagle's eyes as he uttered his reply. "The Confederacy and the Haudenosaunee have raided and destroyed village after village without mercy. They have taken prisoners at will and bent them to their nation. They are ruthless."

"Humph!" Tadodaho said. "Fighting words from someone close to losing his freedom."

"Come and take it," Blue Eagle shot back, rising from his chair.

Both men stood toe to toe. Sky Warrior held back Blue Eagle, and Broken Bow did the same to Tadodaho. For brief seconds, all in the room shuddered at the thought that the two might come to blows and settle the matter man-to-man on the dirt floor. The boiling point had been reached and passed. The two men sat down. Each stared down at the other and did not exchange words.

Sky Warrior said, "Let us not forget why we are here. We come in peace to share our hunting grounds on the promise that your nations will not raid Susquehannock villages now or in the future. With these terms, we can live in peace. The English will provide both our nations with more muskets and some rifles after one year if we keep this promise."

The Englishman in the room wrote those words on parchment paper. In exchange for joint use of hunting grounds in Pennsylvania, the Confederacy would not raid or take prisoners of the Susquehannock. The British would provide muskets and rifles to both sides to maintain peace. Most of 1668 was spent in discussions that were heated on both sides, then waiting, a waste of time. Finally, maps were drawn, and a treaty was drafted. It was signed in the spring of 1669.

A long silence shrouded the room like a large blanket. No one said a word until Tadodaho spoke. "We will keep that promise if Blue Eagle honors his."

Blue Eagle rose and said that he would. He signed his name. Then he handed the paper to Tadodaho, who made an 'X' mark and circled it with a feather symbol at the end. Neither of the men shook hands or bowed. The entire ceremony lasted only minutes.

The English and the Susquehannock had struck a deal. Summer had turned to fall, and it was time to head home. When alone with Kateri, Blue Eagle said that he hoped the agreement would last but was not sure for how long.

No one answered and they stood in silence and stared at Blue Eagle. Finally, Kateri said, "I am with you, dearest, and will do whatever is needed to move these people back to Sasquesahanough." Sky Warrior and Orenda joined in with Kateri and echoed her intentions.

"Good," said Blue Eagle, "I will need all of your support. Now let's move on."

The trip home upstream took almost twice as long as the trip downstream. The summer season was almost upon them.

Everyone in the canoes had a real purpose: to get home quickly. Then they paddled on.

They did not want to miss the excitement, helping each other was part of the everyday life they enjoyed. There were no plans for a combined hunt as before. There was no mention of diseases, hunts, or treaties. The only talk was getting the villagers out of their predicament and into their new homes.

It was rainy and wet in late summer of 1669. At about midway toward their destination, they reached the muddied embankment of canoes, one stacked on top of the other. They knew right away, from the canoe markings, that it was a Susquehannock village. From appearance of the canoes, it was a village in deep disarray. The four were tired and hungry but did not complain. As before, no one greeted this party, and they walked in unannounced. When they met some ragged children, Blue Eagle asked to meet with the village mother or a sachem. They were led to a longhouse in need of serious repair.

Blue Eagle led the conversation with a middle-aged warrior with two feathers. "Where are your leaders?"

"I am called Long Knife," the warrior said. "The chief sachem and village mother are in a longhouse down the path there," he said, pointing east. They are both recovering from disease along with a few others from the same house. We burned and buried about ten more in a mound close to the fields. There are about twenty healthy survivors left including myself, the women, and the children. No one has left the village that I know about. There is some food and blankets in the house behind us. That is about all I can tell you."

"You have done all that you can, Long Knife," said Blue Eagle. "We have come to take you to our village upriver, the Sasquesahanough. Your people will be well fed and taken care of. The sick will be restored to health and the children will live as Susquehannocks. Together we will help to transport you there. It will be a six-day journey after we start. Before we rest, we will visit with your chief and village mother. What are they called?"

Long Knife said that the chief sachem was called Black Elk and the village mother Morning Dew. When Kateri and Blue Eagle visited these two they covered their faces for protection while they introduced themselves. Although they resisted the idea of moving to Bear Village at first, the pair convinced them that it was best for everyone left in their village to make the move. After adding in the threat of destruction by the Confederacy, there was no choice except to move.

While returning to their canoes, the foursome became somber and almost wordless. The days of anticipation were replaced with determination and purpose as they made their way upriver. Blue Eagle vowed once again to ask the council for help to evacuate this village as soon as possible, this time with twice the warriors.

They paddled slowly past the burned-out village that had been evacuated by Sharp Point and Rain Forest the year before. They saw the utter destruction of the charred remains and were glad that the warriors and leaders who had survived were now safely at Bear Village.

Finally, when back at Sasquesahanough Blue Eagle and Kateri called a council meeting to ask the sachems to gather the necessary transport and supplies to bring the healthy survivors, chief and village mother, and the children back to Bear Village. Several clans volunteered their help and put together a large party to do the job. In less than two weeks, a flotilla was headed to help the needy. The whole operation was completed in under two months including the transfer and isolation of the sick. Torching the infected longhouses and canoes was easy.

The sachems approved the treaty after a short council meeting, although few believed the Confederacy's word would last long. They were hopeful to see it last for least two years. The weapons to be delivered at the end of the following year would be a bonus for the Susquehannock, but they would be a boost as well for the Confederacy.

A public bonding ceremony between Orenda and Sky

Warrior was followed by prayers, cheers, and dancing. A bonfire was mounted, celebrating the event. It was the best of times into the night.

The fall hunt without the Lenape and Confederacy interference was the most successful in years. The practice of women going on the hunt continued since there was no resistance of the older sachems. Due to the huge influx of deer, elk and turkey, two new longhouses had to be erected to dry and store the meat. Leftover meat was taken by boat downriver to the Lenape to replenish their supplies.

Storyteller arranged dances and prayers of thanks for the bountiful harvest. The winter was mild but very wet. Snow with large, soft flakes blanketed the ground, turning into a muddy mess almost as fast as it hit the ground.

Skepticism ruled the day when Tadodaho presented the treaty to the Confederacy. The council pressed Tadodaho on why he would enter such a treaty. His answer was not focused on the promised English weapons. He wanted the Confederacy to regroup and absorb the two raided villages, adding that it was time for more nations to come south before they struck the Susquehannock again. The treaty would allow the Confederacy to use the Susquehannock hunting grounds to feed and replenish its agriculture.

The Confederacy could understand this move, since it proved their resiliency and diplomacy and strengthened their foothold in Pennsylvania. The encroachment on the Susquehannock hunting grounds made it a win for Tadodaho.

Treaties are only as good as the honor of the signing parties. The Confederacy received their expected replenishment of warriors from the north in 1669 and 1670. The British, for their part, provided a small number of muskets and a few rifles in 1670 to both sides. The British considered the number they gave as a trifling amount. The peace, such as it was between the signed parties, lasted only a short while. The British stayed out of disputes between indigenous native tribes and their hunting grounds. As long as British settlers were not involved in local squabbles, there was no need to interfere. The Confederacy stayed away from the Susquehannock hunting grounds until they had the forces and weapons they needed, and that took about two years. They needed time to absorb their prisoners, adapt them into their culture, or kill them outright.

CHAPTER 22

Broken Promises

Tadodaho and his war council met in the summer of 1672. The chief sachems were hardened at the forge and furnace of conflict—ready and willing to sacrifice blood and treasure to achieve their goals. He opened the meeting with strong words.

"We have lived with the Baltimore treaty for a long time now, while our forces have built up strength and supplies to get what is rightly ours. Our people have lived for too long in nearly starving and rundown conditions. Meanwhile, the Susquehannock have enjoyed the best hunting grounds and eaten the best game and stored an endless supply of grain and vegetables. They have gotten fat and well off the land while we scrape the ground to live. This has to end now! When the deer, turkey, beaver and bear are at the ready, we will hunt wherever and whenever we want. The treaty be damned! We shall vote on this now!"

To a man, the sachems of the Seneca, Onondaga, Oneida, Cayuga and Haudenosaunee voted yes. These men were frustrated and fully backed Tadodaho's statements.

Ever since the Baltimore treaty, Tadodaho had sent word out through diplomatic runners to Ohio, New York, Michigan, and Canada that all the nations of the Confederacy needed reinforcement to expand in the south. Over time, warriors continued to arrive for that purpose.

Each of the three modest villages along the Siskuhanne prepared for the fall hunt in their usual way and did not suspect that the Confederacy would try to interfere in any way with their hunt. One village, led by the sachem Spotted Owl, sent a hunting party to the twin tributary area that the English called the Shannhkaha of the Siskuhanne River.

At a council meeting before they left, Spotted Owl said, "We will take our canoes as far up the Shannhkaha stream as we can and then fan out as far as possible. We will follow the game trail as far as it will take us. There are over one hundred of us and we must use this time to provide for our families for the entire year. Our supplies are low and the rains this year have damaged our crops of beans and squash. We should also prepare for interference from the Seneca and Confederacy forces. Put out watches throughout the night and stay alert for the enemy."

Time was closing in for Spotted Owl and his scattered hunting party. The hunt was going better than expected during the first four weeks. The deer and turkey were coming in by the dozen and sleds and canoes were shuttling back to camp as fast as they could. As the warrior teams went further and further west, the scouts noticed signs of human camps and alerted their leaders. These signs put Spotted Owl on edge, and the teams were alerted for possible Confederacy interference.

Except for two night guards posted twenty paces apart, everyone was asleep and rolled in their blankets when a flurry of arrows that were not Susquehannock struck trees, blankets, and bodies.

"Ayeee, Ayeee," shouted the guards. "We're under attack." The shouts spread all over camp.

Bodies sprang up and warriors leapt to their feet. Bows and

tomahawks were at the ready as Seneca warriors led by Raging River, one of Broken Bow's leaders, raided the camp. The fight was on and the numbers were about equal. Blades clanged, edges sliced flesh, blows fell against blows and shadows shifted against shadows. When the fighting was hand-to-hand in the dark, every angle and move could mean life or death. The taller and stronger Susquehannocks slowly gained an edge.

Spotted Owl squared off in a knife fight with Raging River. "You cannot defeat us, we are too strong, too fast, and our cause is just. You bastards are just greedy."

"Hah," countered Raging River, "we have three times your number and we'll burn your measly homes to the ground and rape your women. Your children will be our prisoners."

With those words, Raging River leaned back and laughed, which was a mistake. Spotted Owl lunged and knifed him in the chest—killing him instantly. Spotted Owl turned him over, put a knee into his back and with one swift motion scalped him from the front of his forehead to the back of his head while he bled out.

Seneca warrior leaders signaled for retreat and the invaders melted back into the night after seeing Raging River scalped on the forest floor. The interference was over, but it would not be the last they would hear from the Confederacy. At daylight, the casualty count was six dead and eight wounded, with twice that for the enemy. The hunt continued because it had to. This confrontation was just the opening salvo. Strengthening security to protect the village had to be his first job. Spotted Owl knew he would be fighting the Confederacy again. With help, he could do it in time.

Additional hunting ground raids by the Confederacy yielded similar results throughout the fertile Susquehannock hills and valleys of central Pennsylvania. The net result to the Confederacy was a loss for the season of warriors. This setback forced them to hunt in the scarcer plains to the west.

The situation angered Tadodaho and the war council even further. "I am left with no choice," Tadodaho raged. "Our assaults on hunting parties have left us drained of leaders while our people continue on the brink of starvation. What good are our weapons if we cannot produce results against these Minquas? We must re-group and attack."

With a knife raised in the air he yelled, "Attack!" The other sachems at the council stood up with knives or tomahawks raised and yelled in unison, "Attack!"

Like a pitchfork, they would be a three-element force. The Seneca would mix in the lead with the Onondaga. The next time of the fork would be a blend of the Haudenosaunee and Angry Skies, and the last element was the Cayuga and Oneida. The Confederacy used the winter months to re-group and plan for a spring offensive upon what they believed would be four weakened villages in central Pennsylvania. Now, finally, they were ready to pursue their final reward. The plan was to assemble with overwhelming numbers to attack the weakest link in the chain of villages farthest south.

The southernmost village was the weakest and most exposed. The lead Seneca elements slipped in by canoe along the river while other forces surrounded the longhouses in the adjoining forests on the outside. Broken Bow gave the signal to launch, and all hell broke loose. Flaming arrows fired from canoes lit the sky like fireworks, setting longhouses and storage units ablaze. Warriors emptied out of the canoes and from the woods shouting "Ayee, Ayee, Ayee" and raised their tomahawks in marked defiance. Men, woman, and children scattered like crazed ants fleeing the mound. In the dark, they ran everywhere looking for safety and cover—only to run into the painted bodies of tomahawk-wielding warriors hell-bent on death and destruction.

Some brave souls fought back against the tide of razor-sharp blades that slashed bodies and limbs to pieces. A few lucky souls managed to land death-dealing blows to the invading force, but most were cut down like so much chaff to the blade. The brown clay beneath their moccasins turned red with the blood of their bodies. The carnage was over in less than an hour.

Several women, children and a few old men fled to nearby woods seeking shelter anywhere they could find it. A few managed to climb into canoes that were used by the invaders to paddle their way downstream. They were the ones who would manage to escape the mayhem. The others who sought shelter in the woods would either be caught by the invaders or die from exposure in a few days.

With the help of his leaders, Broken Bow managed to organize his force while it was still dark just before the light of day. His bands of men went out into the woods looking for stragglers to use as prisoners. Anyone who resisted was killed. When the stragglers were rounded up, they were strapped together by their necks and taken back to camp. The village was then burned to the ground and the invaders went back to camp to tell their stories.

Spotted Owl did not know where to turn for help and called for a council meeting after the hunt. "It is only a matter of time before the Seneca and the Confederacy's hundreds take revenge on us. It is far too late to build a wall. What are your suggestions for defense?"

"We could fight or flee," said Crooked Spring, an older sachem. "I suggest we fight to the bitter end!"

"What? And sacrifice our young lives and families so our wives can be raped, and our children taken as prisoners?" Red Hair, a younger sachem, said. "I have more, much more to live for."

"I have a better plan," said Black Elk. "We combine forces with our closest village and burn the weakest village. That way, we stand at least a fighting chance. Together we could put up logs and dig holes. If we go down, we will force them to use greater numbers against us. Maybe more would escape. Maybe we could even have an organized escape."

In the end, Black Elk's plan was accepted, but combining forces meant acceptance by their closest village chief, Hawk Nose and the village mother, White Cloud. The merger into the

Porcupine village would be difficult and would last into 1673. Despite being downstream and only a canoeing day apart, it took a major effort and many moons for both villages to make it happen. They had to overcome individual differences, but there was a general understanding that cooperation was needed for both villages to survive the onslaught that was sure to come.

When the transfer was done, the council sachems of both villages stood beside their canoes holding torches on the riverbank. Hawk Nose and White Cloud said a prayer out loud for all to hear. "May the living continue to live," they prayed. "May our people come together as one and live in peace without fear of invasion. And may our children have children that live in peace together."

With those words, the procession set fire to all the longhouses, storage houses, and crops in the field. The flames lit the sky and smoke billowed upward in great gray and black spirals of embers and dust. In less than two hours, what was once home to over a hundred families was smoldering ashes and swirling clouds.

The Porcupine village was bristling with two hundred-plus warriors over the cold and wet spring. Blades were sharpened, faces were painted, bellies were fed, and the whole village prepared for an attack. Warriors blocked the entrance to the river with logs that would act to deter arrows. They dug holes around their longhouse and covered them with branches. Tall cedar trees were burned at their base and drug into place by twenty men to block entrances and to force invaders into paths that were set up as killing fields. Men equipped with British muskets and ammunition chose the best ambush positions and most likely avenues of approach. In short, warriors from both villages prepared as best they could for what they knew was coming, a full-scale invasion.

As a final resort, old men, women and children left Porcupine Village by canoe and paddled north in search of safety at Bear Village. It was a sad, long journey of almost twenty canoes going upriver to an unknown destination. They motley group would be forced to camp several times, but they were a determined bunch, protective and driven. Their leader was White Cloud, who was the mother to them all.

All the elements of the seven hundred men of the Confederacy pitchfork were now on the move. The Haudenosaunee and Angry Skies were the lead elements going into Porcupine Village. They were followed by the Senecas, which were now last into the village after the raid south. The Onondagas, Cayugas and Oneidas split off into the last two villages in middle Pennsylvania. They did not know that they were going after burned-out villages. To say that they would be surprised would be an understatement.

The hordes of Iroquois warriors came across the Siskuhanne ferried by canoe and raft. They came by the hundreds, then Angry Skies and his few men, and then the Seneca. The horde spread out to the fields and to the woods and surrounded Porcupine Village. Tadodaho saw what lay ahead and stopped his attack, sent out scouts to probe the perimeter.

He held a war council with his leaders and said, "They have strengthened their defenses, so we will strike where they are weakest. We will fire flaming arrows by night at their clusters of men and feign an assault with muskets, here over their logs by the river." He drew a circle in the mud. "The main force will come in here through the fields which will be wet and muddy. The Seneca will come in from the woods—here flanking their clusters in the center. We will all close in like a lobster and crush them in at the center. We will fight until they are all dead! Questions?" Of course, there were none.

Campfires glowed in the dim twilight, while over two hundred defenders waited for darkness and over four hundred attackers awaited a signal. On both sides of a quiet battlefield, men hovered in and around the many fires that lit the woods and fields. Their arms, faces, and legs flashed the red, black, and ocher stripes that signaled their pride of battle. When the moon was high in the sky, a single flaming arrow shot across the log barrier into a cluster of men on the other side.

Almost instantly, the sky filled with shooting flames aimed not at longhouses or storage bins but at clusters of men, some with muskets and some in trees. Some of the arrows found a leg or a torso. Others fell harmlessly into the mud. Knowing an assault was imminent, the defenders notched their arrows and waited. The flaming arrows continued for another five minutes or so and then the assault began.

The cries of "hold your ground" and "save your arrows" were heard over the din of feet climbing and stomping across the log barrier. The first warriors reached the top of the logs with raised tomahawks and leaped on the defenders with pent-up rage and slashing blades. They came in waves over the top, first in clusters, then toppling the wall like so many sticks pushing the barrier back against the defenders.

There were so many coming at them that Hawk Nose thought that they were the main body. It was just about then that tens, no hundreds of men emerged from the darkened fields like mud-soaked, tomahawk-wielding apparitions of the night. Hawk Nose realized that he had been outnumbered and surrounded. Now it was only a matter of time before he and his brave men would be annihilated.

He gathered a few of his men together and told them to look for leaders. "Look for feathers, pick out the leaders if you can and kill them first. Others may follow and give up hope. Shoot them if you can. Followers need direction—kill the feathered ones first."

Hawk Nose pivoted only to turn into a war club that crushed his head like an acorn, and he died in an instant. The bearer of the war club was a Seneca warrior who was covered in mud from head to toe. The fight went on for well over two more hours. Only a few teenage defenders managed to escape to the woods. A part of Seneca warriors who saw them leave chased them down and took them as prisoners. A few of the younger defenders who were not seriously wounded gave themselves up as prisoners.

Dozens more warriors, some wounded, escaped the Confederacy's grasp. They could not kill everyone, but the remaining defenders were battle casualties. Some of those that escaped to the woods were pursued, captured and killed, but many others managed to live on and found sanctuary with the Lenape or the Munee nations.

Tadodaho and the Confederacy satisfied their lust and burned the village but paid a heavy price with over one hundred of their own dead and many more wounded. Although victorious against the Susquehannocks, the Confederacy and the Haudenosaunee would now have to re-group and re-organize.

When the flotilla of canoes from Porcupine Village arrived at Sasquesahanough Village, Blue Eagle and Kateri welcome them with open arms and hearts. The flotilla's expedition north proved to be a weary and tiresome journey filled with pitfalls and close calls. They narrowly missed the incoming Cayuga, Onondaga, and Oneida nations by hiding canoes in a nearby tributary. One of the old men died along the way and a baby was born to one of the women while enroute. It took two moons and a lot of encouragement from White Cloud to finish the journey.

"Our journey has been treacherous," White Cloud said to Kateri and Blue Eagle. "We were nearly discovered and murdered, but somehow with Sky Mother's help we survived. Our husbands and providers are gone. We hope we can pay you back for your kindness, but right now we need food and rest."

Kateri replied, "We have made temporary arrangements for all of you to stay among our clans. Orenda, my daughter, will show you to your new homes. We hope you will be comfortable with your new clan mothers and sachems. We are sorry for your losses and look forward to meeting with each of you personally. We are planning a grieving ceremony to remember the loss of your loved ones."

The village hailed with pride the heroism of those who came through. Although their numbers were few, they showed great courage and tenacity. They proved that the will to live is stronger than the evil to destroy. The whole village lauded them through prayer, thanks to the gods, and joyful dance. But the need for revenge raged like a current under the celebration.

Blue Eagle and Kateri called for a council meeting to discuss possible moves and to celebrate the arrival of the women and children from Porcupine Village.

The matter of the grieving ceremony came first. Storyteller led the discussion. "We should have a bonfire to symbolize the loss of brave warriors in battle, followed by ritual dancing and symbolic burial of one grave in the field."

Everyone agreed. Then Blue Eagle, Kateri and the sachems talked about different ways to inflict reprisals on the Confederacy.

Three Hawks suggested, "Twin Peaks has proven to be able to help us in the past. We need his men now as never before."

"The British have weapons we can use. Maybe they will help us now," Rain Forest said.

Sharp Point added, "Spies with hit-and-run nighttime raids would inflict heavy damage on clusters of warriors."

There were one or two on the council who wanted to capitulate to the Confederacy and be absorbed, to avoid bloodshed and save their families even if it meant certain death to some of their warriors. They reasoned that at least their women and children would be saved.

"Don't you realize what will happen to your women and children?" Blue Eagle bellowed. "Your women will be raped and become slaves. Your children will be raised as Seneca, Oneida, Onondaga, Cayuga and Haudenosaunee and Mohawk warriors. We will cease to be a nation of Susquehannock people forever. You are giving up without a fight, and you will have accomplished nothing in your life. You will die as cowards. Is that how you want to be remembered?"

Blue Eagle suspected, but could not prove, that the source of Tadodaho's spy network came from one or two of these cowardly sachems who wanted to be absorbed into the Confederacy. The only way to prove this would be to plant a false rumor, such as a secret weapon or capability. But that might be tricky, and he decided to let it go.

After a lot of inconclusive discussion, Blue Eagle set out a plan. "Given the huge number of warriors that the Confederacy can launch against us at will, our only chance for survival is to team up with Twin Peaks. Although they were not bred as warriors, their numbers, with our defenses, might be able to stem the tide of a determined enemy."

When news reached Tadodaho of the burned-out villages that escaped his wrath, he became so enraged he wanted to take his horde to Sasquesahanough and take on Blue Eagle right there. Angry Skies and other leaders talked him out of that plan and developed another scheme in its place. That scheme involved luring Blue Eagle into a deal.

The tree-lined woods of central Pennsylvania typically block windstorms in winter coming from the north. In February 1674, the dry winds blew dust so hard that snow seemed to cover all of the earth. Tadodaho wrapped himself in an extra blanket to protect himself against the fierce winds. He and Angry Skies were growing impatient at being unable to conquer the last Susquehannock holdout to the northeast. In keeping with his scheme, Tadodaho said, "When this shitty weather breaks, send a word with a white flag signal to Blue Eagle that we will talk with three of his men about peace." He laughed, almost under his breath.

"Do you mean it?" Angry Skies asked.

"No, especially about the word peace." Tadodaho spit on the ground. "But let's see who he sends," he muttered.

Later, under a white flag of truce three weeks later, Blue Eagle received the messenger. "I smell a trap," he said to Kateri. "But who should I send?"

"Don't force anyone, if you think they won't come back."

"You are right. I will ask for volunteers."

After some discussion, Wolf Eyes and two teenagers volunteered to go. They gathered food and gear to see Tadodaho under a flag of truce. They never got as far as Tadodaho. In front of Angry Skies, the three ambassadors were murdered on the spot. The headband of Wolf Eyes and the belts of the teenagers were thrown over the front gate of the village as proof of their death.

Alone on the bench in the longhouse, Blue Eagle told Kateri, "We are next. It is only a matter of time. There is no talking now." To him, it was simply the end of the line. There was no backing down from the fight. It was kill or be killed. "There is only blood—their blood and our blood. They spoke when they killed our emissaries. We must be prepared."

Kateri did not want harm to come to Orenda or Sosondowah, young people who would be quickly killed or captured in an attack. Both Kateri and Blue Eagle wanted to see their family survive and the story of the proud Susquehannock told for generations. Blue Eagle urged Kateri to take Sosondowah, Orenda, and Sky Warrior to a safe place, but she would not go. She wanted to be by his side but now was not a time to argue. He told Sky Warrior to take Kateri, Orenda and Sosondowah to the Lenape with clothing and gifts as a token of their appreciation.

The goodbye was hurried and heartfelt. Kateri looked into Blue Eagle's eyes and saw herself in his pupils. She simply said, "I will be with you always, and never forget you!"

He hugged Sosondowah, who was now twelve and straight as an arrow. The boy looked at his mother and father and said, "We will always remember you, Father." Blue Eagle then embraced Orenda and told her to take care of her mother, and she said that she would. With their goodbyes said, the foursome went down the Siskuhanne in two canoes to Twin Peaks' village. Always strong and confident, Blue Eagle reassured them that he would see them all soon and told them not to be concerned about him. He looked at his family and told Sosondowah and Orenda to take good care of Kateri and watch over her like an eagle watches over its young.

Blue Eagle's job now was to make final preparations for an attack. A call went out for a volunteer spy mission to get details on the pending attack. High on the list was digging holes outside the fortifications. About one hundred warriors with traded adzes and shovels dug random holes and covered them with brush around the village. The idea was to slow the enemy's advance and cause him to avoid and then have to mark the holes. Spacing them apart every few paces meant that even if marked, enemy warriors could not bunch together without foot injury.

Next was to improve the trench inside by lengthening and widening the fighting positions. They knew it would be impossible to keep out large numbers of crazed warriors. However, once inside, they could concentrate their fire with cannons, muskets, and rifles in critical spots to draw fire. Their goal was to reduce their numbers. The British stopped sending ammunition after the Confederacy broke the treaty.

The village was busy. The barriers would force the invaders to separate and distance themselves from the logs and possibly force them into the holes. Filling in the holes would take time. The strategy was to give the defenders time to go outside the walls and shoot at the invaders. Disruption, delay, and confusion were part of the defense strategy.

The other part of the strategy was cleaning, lengthening, and fortifying the trenches. Once that was complete, the warriors would occupy their time with the dry practice of loading and reloading muskets, rifles, and cannons. The village had accumulated a store of ammunition from the British. The thirty warriors known as Arrowheads were given special recognition for handling muskets and rifles. The Confederacy had at least that many warriors and probably more. They were essential in the fight and could move wherever needed.

Blue Eagle knew that their weak points, if surrounded, were still the vegetable fields and the river. The fence and logs would hold in the fields, but he didn't know for how long. A concentrated force there could topple the walls at any given time. The fields gave him the most concern. The river was a natural barrier to a large invasion. Bowmen could pound incoming canoes outside the fence and ward off attackers coming through the woods. Canoes could be drawn inside and act as a defensive barrier.

The wet spring gave way to a hot and dry summer. As holes were finished outside, men turned to trenches inside. The only thing left to do was to practice and drill. Boredom was never a part of village life, and it would not start now.

Red Tail and Strong Wind became the spy volunteers. They had some experience in the area and spying on the Haudenosaunee. With backpacks of supplies, they set off west and northwest to determine how many and when the five nations might make their move. They knew what the risks were and that their lives were on the line. Torture and an excruciating death awaited them if they were caught. Poor weather, however, turned them around, and they had to inch their way back to camp.

The lush landscape of central Pennsylvania trees, valleys, and rivers turned to freezing rain, snowy plains, icy tributaries, and dangerous rivers in 1674. It was a wet, howling, slick, and snowy winter. Almost nothing moved except hungry squirrels. March was better, but only marginally so. Poor weather slowed but did not stop preparations.

Red Tail and Strong Wind finally moved out of their warm longhouses and started westward when the weather broke in early spring. They did not carry a canoe because it was too heavy over long distances. The fact that they got along and could talk to each other meant a lot. Their previous outings gave them an invaluable bond of trust. They each knew if discovered, the other would not waver, no matter the situation.

Red Tail felt at ease and spoke freely. "Do you think we will survive this?"

"I didn't volunteer for a suicide mission," Strong Wind said.

"Neither did I," Red Tail said, laughing sarcastically. "What will you do if you're caught?"

Strong Wind laughed. "I'll spit in their eye and jump in the fire!"

"Brave talk, brave talk."

Neither warrior had married, which made them ideal choices as spies. It also led to predictable conversations about the differences between Susquehannock women and women from other tribes. Neither had any experience outside their village, but they spoke as if they did.

"So, Red Tail, tell me about the Seneca woman who came to you when you were tied up and captured." He knew no such woman had come to him.

"Well, she was excited. You know I was helpless, bound by hand and foot. Even my mouth was gagged. She sneaked in under the flap when no one was watching. She undid her top and exposed herself. I became immediately excited. I will not tell you more because you think I am merely making this up out of thin air. Then she slipped away." Red Tail's voice faded as he spoke.

Strong Wind knew an exaggerated tale, but he laughed just the same when he heard it. "I suppose you will tell me that every word of that story is accurate."

"Absolutely," Red Tail said without smiling. After a moment, they both grinned ear to ear.

They moved on over the wet ground, camping and pushing further into the forest. Future conversations were about the Confederacy, the direction of and identity of warriors, or whether they would come home alive.

The nations of the Confederacy converged from all points of the compass to rally at the Haudenosaunee camp in northwestern Pennsylvania. It took the entire spring to gather nearly seven hundred warriors and their families. Campfires and temporary shelters covered the plains as far as the eye could see.

After climbing to a hilltop overlooking a valley, the jaws of Red Tail and Strong Wind went agape at the immense circle of humanity and campfires that lit the grasses below. They scanned the horizon and tried to count, but soon lost track of the number. There were simply too many. They looked at each other in disbelief.

"What do you think we should do?" asked Strong Wind.

"I think we should wait a few days and see what direction they take."

"Fine, but we shouldn't wait too long," Strong Wind said.

Broken Bow spoke first. "We need months to prepare. We lost at least eighty strong warriors. We know what is ahead. Blue Eagle is strong, and the fight will be long and hard. They will not give in without a hard fight. We must build an unbeatable force. We need a plan to defeat their walls and then defeat their men inside."

"The nations now combine to about seven hundred with teenagers and prisoners," said Tadodaho. "We have enough to encircle and defeat Blue Eagle. The British will not interfere." The other leaders pounded their bows on the ground in approval.

Angry Skies, who had been quiet to this point, finally rose and gave a short speech. "Most of the men I came with from the East are gone now. I still carry with me their deep hunger for revenge. I burn for the flesh of Blue Eagle. I will not stop until he is dead, or I am dead." Muddy Waters and the other leaders all rose in unison and shouted their approval at this. The enthusiasm for blood in the smoke-filled longhouse was palpable. Tadodaho said that they would meet one more time.

The Mohawk nation was not present at this time, nor were they in past councils, but that did not lessen the strength of the Confederacy. The Senecas outnumbered them all. With well over three hundred warriors plus their families, their zeal for warfare and seizing territory knew no bounds. To them, the Haudenosaunee were tame diplomats more interested in negotiation than battle. The other nations, Onondagas, Oneidas, and Cayugas, simply followed behind the Seneca's lead. Although the Senecas were strong, the Haudenosaunee still took the lead at the council.

Red Tail and Strong Wind could not see the council longhouse, but they saw movement on the ground. Darkness began to descend on the valley. They knew that it was time for Red Tail to return to the village—at least a three-week walk, maybe longer. Their goal was to get there alive before the horde.

Tadodaho spoke to the war council for the last time to give the final strategy. "Our spies tell us they have dug holes around the village to slow us down. First, probe the walls for weak spots. Put teams to work to mark and fill in these holes. Set primary fires at the wall and gate base. The Cayuga will penetrate the approach from both sides of the riverbanks with about one hundred men. The Onondaga and Oneida will attack from the south probe and set many fires to the walls. The weakest part of the village is the northern vegetable fields. The Haudenosaunee and Seneca will probe, fire, and penetrate these walls with over three hundred warriors."

He added that the fight would begin once they were inside. "They will fight you on the ground and from trenches. They have muskets, rifles, and some cannon. You must fight hard and without mercy. Only take prisoners when all warriors are dead or have fled. Their stores, hides, and hunting grounds are valuable. We must have them to survive. Do not burn the village. The signal will be burning arrows."

CHAPTER 23

No Surrender

B lue Eagle called for a council meeting when frustration and a feeling of helplessness was running high. Blue Eagle spoke since Kateri was with the Lenape. They had a strong community bond, where they stood for each other in need. The will to fight was the most important advantage of all.

"Our defenses are strong," Blue Eagle said, "and we can hold out against superior numbers—and we will never surrender or give up the fight."

He listed their advantages, beyond the Susquehannock warrior spirit to defend and keep their families and homes. Blue Eagle became emotional and a little glassy-eyed.

The well-trained warrior corps were ready to fight and ready to defend their homes with muskets, rifles, and cannons knowing that their families were safe with the Lenape. The Lenape had proven themselves a willing and capable ally in the past. They kept that hope alive for this battle. They were surrounded by a fortified village with walls and reinforced defenses not easily penetrated even by a determined enemy.

"We have enough timber for our walls, fireplaces and to replenish our longhouses. We have enough water to supply our need and to put out the fires set by the Confederacy."

They had food and better supplies: longhouses filled with corn, vegetables, squash and beans, potatoes, beets enough to last, dried if needed, for years.

Hides, for clothing and protection.

Meat, to maintain their people for over one year or more.

Trade goods that could last well into the future, including iron pots and pans.

A plentiful supply of dried fish.

Strong outer log defenses against attack.

Finally, a family spirit to hold the village together.

"I could go on," he said, "but the important advantage is the first one. Our ability to stand up to the evil that confronts us. This makes us who we are. This is what separates us from them. Yes, their numbers are great, but we cannot let that overwhelm us. Our ability to fight for our homes and families is greater. With the advantages I have spelled out, we can hold out for as long as it takes to win. They are takers. We want peace—look at what they did to Wolf Eyes and the two teenagers."

The sachems sat cross-legged in stony silence after Blue Eagle's speech. A few even lowered their heads in shame for having even thought about losing to the Confederacy. Others looked about in stony silence, speechless.

Brave Cloud rose and spoke first to second the speech of Blue Eagle. "No one here should doubt Blue Eagle's loyalty or his drive to fight back. No one here should doubt his willingness to make the village as prepared as possible against overwhelming numbers. No one here should doubt his bravery in battle against our sworn enemies. I say to this moment, it is time to stand up and join forces against the evil that would seek to destroy us and our families. Let us join Blue Eagle and put to rest any doubt that we might possess about this. We must raise our arms in defiance!"

All stood and raised their bows as a spirit of unity. The room was electric. No one quiet after those words. The sachems went to each other, grabbed one another by the shoulders, hugged and with tear-filled eyes told Blue Eagle exactly what they would do for him.

Sharp Point said, "My men will guard the vegetable fields and defend against any intrusion into the rows."

Three Hawks said, "I will stand guard with my men at the river. We will make sure we do not falter when the Confederacy tries to invade from there."

Rain Forest stepped in and told Blue Eagle that he and his men would stand guard at the west fence and defend it to the last man.

All the sachems present made similar pledges until the entire village was covered with commitments. It made Blue Eagle very proud. He spread out his arms in a gesture of gratitude and appreciation and said, "Each of you have come forward to express exactly how your men will be used to defend our village. Together we need everyone to do their part. Our plan will use the Arrowheads and cannoneers to position themselves, as we have practiced, and to fire upon the enemy when they break through the walls. Rest easy now. The time of need is near, so spend the time that remains with your family and loved ones. The time for fighting is near."

Red Tail and Strong Wind returned from their spy trek to tell Blue Eagle that the Confederacy horde was on the move. It was hard to tell when the scouts and advance parties would arrive, but their best guess was six or seven days, with the main party a few days behind that. They said the main body was the largest they had ever seen, and certainly enough to envelope the village. Blue Eagle offered them a few days of rest and asked them to go out again and get a closer look then.

The Confederacy would rest only when the Susquehannock ceased to exist. They would not let the last village—no matter how large or how well defended—stand in their way of total domination and final victory over the Susquehannock. Tadodaho knew he would be paying a heavy price for such a victory. But he commanded nearly seven hundred pent-up and half-crazed warriors and he was not worried.

Warriors of both sides tattooed their bodies from head to foot with spotted and striped symbols of masculine dominance. Their regalia included beaded foot bangles, pierced noses and ears, and darkened eye shading designed to ward off evil spirits from entering the body. Their appearance was designed to frighten children and opponents alike. Like apparitions from the other life, they wanted to appear warlike and undefeatable.

Death to the true warrior was a steppingstone to the afterlife. Possessions of this world meant little. The true reward came when he managed to meet his ancestors in the next world or returned to the forest as his favorite animal. He would, of course, miss the previous world and his family, but there was perpetual reward in the next life if he were brave and true in this one.

Confederacy forces were getting closer to Bear Village. Their spies set out in groups of three with scouts and reported on whatever activity they found. The advance parties portaged and paddled about forty canoes upriver, a tedious and time-consuming job. Red Tail and Strong Wind spotted what they were doing but stayed out of sight and circled back to the Bear Village in time to warn Blue Eagle.

Everybody knew they were coming; it was just a matter of time, so no one was surprised. The fact the spies made it back alive was a great reward. The duo did not need a ceremony or feathers as gratitude for a job done well. A good rest meant that they would be in the thick of it. While in the fight with their comrades when the horde came shouting and screaming, they would be ready.

Warriors stood at sharpening stones and the wheels were constantly spinning, grinding away. The men were very close to their weapons and, at first, their nerves were on edge. But they sharpened the same edge twice, three, or four times or until they were completely satisfied, and this calmed their nerves. Those who must wait their turn found something else to do. Their turn at the wheel would be coming soon and then they would take their time. This routine went on into the night.

The defender had the disadvantage of knowing the place but not the exact time of defense, but Blue Eagle had the advantage of patience—the patience of a hunter waiting for his prey. Time was both an enemy and a friend. Time was an enemy because waiting filled the mind with thoughts that the defenders might have missed something in preparation. Time could be a friend because it provided the opportunity to fix what they might have missed.

Blue Eagle sat cross-legged in his longhouse and put his mind in Tadodaho's place and tried to anticipate what he would do if he were attacking this village. Tadodaho's biggest plus was overwhelming numbers; his biggest negative was the village fortifications. If he were attacking, he would wear his opponent down, first by defeating his outside defenses—the holes in the ground, then probe for weaknesses in the walls, then burn down the walls and the trees surrounding the walls, then taunt the defenders. If he were attacking there would be more than one assault. The air would be filled with frightening nighttime charges with flaming arrows and raids that pushed at weak spots. Once those spots were found, he would assault them and exploit with overwhelming and unstoppable force to destroy the trapped inhabitants inside. This would succeed, if, and only if, Tadodaho's leaders and warriors had the patience and time to make this happen.

Blue Eagle could not be certain what Tadodaho would do under any condition. It was time to leave the quiet comfort of his longhouse and inspect his defenses one last time—again and make the rounds on foot before the sunset.

A four-hour walk took Blue Eagle and Brave Cloud all around the walled village. They did not go inside the quiet longhouses. The men needed their rest. They inspected the gates, the trenches, the walls, the ladders, the cannons and the stores of ammunition. The duo talked with the on-duty guards, walked past the rows and fields of planted vegetables. Finally they returned to the riverfront and the stacks of canoes that stood like sentries behind the logs of the walled riverfront.

Twilight faded into darkness as Blue Eagle and Brave Cloud listened and watched for unusual movement and sound. Three stars appeared in one constellation as the full moon arose over the eastern shore. Without any pre-arranged signal, fully clothed, equipped, and painted warriors started to appear near the village center, the walls and trenches. Sachems, feathered warriors, women, and children started to gather near Blue Eagle and Brave Cloud. They knew this thing was going to happen—somehow, they knew.

A teenager climbed a nearby tree and bent a branch to lean over then yelled, "I hear them...they are coming."

The faint sound of paddles touching water could be heard in the distance. Blue Eagle and Brave Cloud started to bark orders. "Women and children inside...stay close to your buckets. Warriors, to your fighting positions. Stay calm, we know what to do and what is coming. Do not panic, stay calm." Everyone scattered like ants, hearing the canoes come closer.

Darkness cloaked the night, and hundreds of attacking men walked in ragged lines while their shadows crept ahead and alongside the figures. They were too far away for bowshots, but were getting closer to the holes in the ground that they could not see.

The forty or more canoes of the advance party fired arrows over the wall at the defenders from twenty paces on the river.

"We're getting arrows from the river," Moving Moon yelled to Lone Peak.

"As soon as you can see their figures fire back and don't stop," Lone Peak shouted back.

Sharp Point, in a moment of unspeakable courage, opened the riverfront gate and led a group of warriors closer to the incoming canoes. He led them around in a semicircle, and with an arm signal, directed them to open fire on the canoes trying to land on the shoreline.

"Spare no one," said Sharp Point. "Let them feel the fury of the Susquehannock warrior!"

A flurry of arrows covered the moonglow in the night sky. More than twenty canoes and their warriors were covered like porcupines, with many figures flailing and falling in the black waters. Sharp Point then led his men back behind the protection of the walls and the logs.

When the other canoes saw the disaster at the riverfront, they signaled down the line to retreat to safer landing ground downriver. There was no place for them to land and most were forced to retreat to the nearby woods to join the other invaders.

Outside the walls, screams of pain and curses filled the night air when warriors stepped and could not avoid the holes. Feet fell and ankles twisted as the fear of moving and injury overcame caution. The smart ones did not advance at all. They were easy targets for warriors who had climbed to the tops of the walls on ladders. The holes had done their work for the night. The Susquehannock warriors who climbed could also see dozens of campfires spread outside the walls like a ring of fire encircling the village. A report on the scene was made back to Blue Eagle who acknowledged it with a head nod.

Susquehannock bowmen crept outside the back gates and took shots at shadows fifty paces away. Even though they had been hobbled by the holes, the Confederacy were not helpless. With the full moon's glow of June 7, they could shoot back and kneel. The bowmen had to shoot and scoot back behind the wall for protection and could not advance for fear of falling in the holes themselves. The long night quieted after the Confederacy crawled and limped back to their leaders. Blue Eagle was restless despite his minor victory, because he knew now what lay ahead.

Tadodaho didn't wait for the morning or for a complete encirclement before sending a messenger with a white flag to the main gate. Speaking through the logs of the gate, the messenger said that Blue Eagle and his village would be annihilated in hours if he did not surrender. Blue Eagle drew his knife, opened the gate and killed the messenger. "That is for Wolf Eyes," he said. He unsheathed a wrapped arrow, dipped it into a nearby fire, and fired the messenger's headband high into the air in a defiant symbol. After that exchange, there was no turning back.

The first light saw a beehive of activity. The invaders knew about the holes but did not bring enough shovels or adzes and used tomahawks instead. They marked the holes with branches, a tedious job. Meanwhile, bowmen shot from the ladders at anything that moved outside the logs. The sight of sticks marking holes that encircled the village infuriated Tadodaho. His answer was to overwhelm the shooters with an impossible number of attackers. The shooters were forced to withdraw to safety of the fortifications or be slain.

Blue Eagle felt trapped inside the palisaded walls of the village. He knew the numbers were against him, possibly as much as three to one. How long were the walls going to last? Two days? Three? The food and water would last a lot longer than the fight, he was sure of that. Blue Eagle was sure his warriors would never give up and he would never let them down. Without hesitating, he ran to tell all his sachems to increase the guards on the walls, especially the gates. The village would be lost if the Confederacy vaulted over the walls and opened the gates.

The three hundred-plus men of Tadodaho and Angry Skies began probing the walls and the two gates of the fields for weak spots. They pushed using their hands, arms, and legs. They then used muskets and rifles to fire where the gates joined the wall. The walls were tall, solid, and reinforced with cross members and would not give in easily. Even though the walls were at the height of two men, it occurred to Angry Skies to vault the gates first and open them up from the inside.

Angry Skies told Broken Bow, "Make human ladders of your men with one warrior standing atop the shoulders of another. With arrows blazing, their support can rush and climb over. The loss of men with the gates open would be the only price to pay."

"That's suicide," Broken Bow said, his face as red as a beet. "My men will be cut down as soon as they reach the top."

"Find a way, you must get over," Angry Skies shot back. "We'll back you up with firepower."

Two warriors proceeded, with one standing atop the shoulders of the other, using cupped hands while a third warrior climbed on both like a human ladder before reaching the top. "This will work if the warrior is brave enough to jump on the enemy below with his body," Angry Skies said. "Or use multiple hatchets to lower themselves down. We must open the gates from the inside."

"You've gone mad," screamed Broken Bow. "This is nothing more than a death wish."

"If you don't want to do it, I'll find warriors myself who will gladly volunteer for it," Angry Skies yelled back. He did try this vaulting maneuver with five or six warriors who were at once backed by bowmen. They were killed immediately by the gate guards, who just waited until they reached the top of the gate and shot them down. Brave Cloud and the sachems immediately increased the gate guards to prevent a possible breach.

Angry Skies tried next to attack with over fifty warriors along the vegetable fields and nearby gates. Some men did manage to vault inside, but the concentration of defenders with arrowheads in the trenches killed them all before a breach was possible.

Instead of wasting warriors on trying to vault over the daytime wall, Angry Skies and Tadodaho decided on an alternate strategy after the first assault failed. The next attempt would be to burn down the walls and push down the logs and gates. They would start at dark that night.

Men were busy all afternoon, gathering firewood and assembling the twisted arrows as torches. It became apparent what the Confederacy would try to do—send flaming arrows into the longhouses while setting fire to the walls.

Women went to the river with all the buckets at hand and filled them with water. Blue Eagle and Brave Cloud passed word that a chain of people between the river and the longhouses had to be formed to counter the mass of fire arrows aimed at the longhouses. Even then, the number of buckets might not be enough to stop the fires.

The flaming arrows lit the sky like fireworks in the night light. Storyteller pranced around the longhouses pulling out arrows while chanting for rain in the darkened night, but rain did not come. Many arrows missed their mark, while others found theirs atop the peaks of the houses. After a steady barrage of arrows, some longhouses were lost to fire, but the storehouses remained intact, thanks to the quick action of the village women and children. The quenched and spent arrows were collected by the villagers and set aside to be used by the defenders against the attackers, yet there were no real targets on the other side of the wall to send the arrows back.

The wall burning went on through the night. Smoke from the logs choked the air all around the village and sent a new threat to both defenders and attackers. The riverbank and canoes seemed to be covered in a layer of smoke that hid their presence. Blue Eagle brought a few sachems together to discuss an idea he knew would be resisted by many but had to be done. He spoke in careful tones.

"To avoid capture and possible rape or death, now is the time for the wives, women, teenagers, children, and old men to leave the village for the safety of the Lenape village. We know that many would not want to leave their loved ones. The old men will have to be protectors for a two-day canoe ride downriver. Leave now and take just a few things with you in the darkness and under the cover of smoke."

Heads lowered, a few villagers muttered words of protest, but they knew what he said was true. They formed a circle. Arms overlapped shoulders in prayer. Blue Eagle raised his head and finished by praying for their safety.

"May the river spirit guide our loved ones to a safe destiny. The hours have come to test our strength and will to survive. We pray that you guide our hands and our hearts in battle. We pray to join our loved ones again in their warm bosom."

Darkness fell on the second night of the siege. The smoke of dozens of fires around the village shrouded the veil of a waxing moon. One canoe after another slipped from the riverbank downriver for the trek to the Lenape village. They traveled in groups of three or four canoes. Each group had old men and teenagers equipped with bows, arrows, and tomahawks for security, plus a minimum of food and supplies. The Confederacy had not used the river since they had not taken canoes with them. It took hours to clear the families from the village.

Wall probing started at first light with the gates, which leaned but did not push over. Dozens of men heaved on the joints. Cracks appeared at first but needed to be wider for a man to slip through. Charred at their bases from the fires, the large cedar logs on both ends were weakening, but not enough for toppling. Men climbed on the shoulders of men below and pushed. The upper part of the door opened farther than the bottom, but more than one person could not exploit the gap at a time. Tomahawks and axes flailed at the bases, but smoke from the continuing fires hindered visibility.

Pushing together, the wall started to lean forward. The field side remained the weakest, due to the softer underlying soil. A wall section next to one of the field gates gave way first. When ten men felt the section give in one of their probes, they called for more men. Twenty, then thirty, then forty men joined them. When they pushed together on the wall, it started to lean forward. They pushed together twice, then a third time, cracking and splitting it even more. It gave way completely, and the section collapsed to the ground.

Alerted by the breakthrough, men from all sides rushed to the opening. Waiting for them on the other side was an avalanche of arrows, both flaming and not, just waiting for their targets. Behind them were rifle musket balls aimed at opening up gaping holes in the painted torsos and arms of warriors. This onslaught of firepower into the bunched-up invaders caused the Seneca and Iroquois leaders to call for a retreat. Over-eager warriors left their many dead and wounded beside the fallen walls of the village.

The Seneca and the Iroquois learned a short and valuable lesson: invading one wall section at a time would lead to disaster. Doing so was sure suicide, because their numbers were too small. Their leaders opted instead for many sections to fall and amass their warriors for maximum effect. In the meantime, they settled for a show of bravado at the wall, raising their arms in mock triumph and stepping over the dead bodies of their own fallen invaders as if human life meant little.

The village's wall sections were getting weaker as the day wore on. It was only a matter of time. Smoke continued rising as the fires licked higher up the logs and expanded into the trees. Blue Eagle could only go around boosting morale through encouragement. One small encounter was fought and won, but there was only one. The worst would come soon enough. He knew Kateri and Sosondowah were safe with the Lenape, but where was Lone Peak and his men? He was expecting their help. He needed it now.

Blue Eagle called for a quick meeting of the sachems to make sure everyone knew what to expect. "By now, your women and children will be with the Lenape, safe from harm. We have an agreement with the Lenape to help against the Confederacy. We must fight regardless. In a matter of hours, the Confederacy will break through. They have already shown they can do that in the fields. We will meet them with flaming arrows, bullets, muskets, balls, arrows, clubs, knives, and steel blades, striking wherever possible. Kill the leaders and the weakest ones. Show no mercy. They will have no mercy on us. Fight in circles to protect those around you. Spare no one. Do not surrender, for only torture awaits you. Show them that you are a proud Susquehannock. We have not given away our land or our right to hunt and fish. We only wanted peace. Brave Cloud is next in line, if I should die in battle. Make your family, your village, and your nation proud."

Everyone stood in a circle and raised their bows in unison. The Storyteller led them in a short prayer. They knew what was ahead and what to expect. They left the circle and went to their men and their positions.

Word came from the canoe landing as battle-ready Lenape warriors started to land, ready to fight. "They're here! They're here!" Brave Cloud said. He caught up to Blue Eagle. "Many, many warriors are now landing with Twin Peaks, perhaps over one hundred. They are ready to rescue us with their fighting."

"I must meet with Twin Peaks," Blue Eagle said, "and tell him where we need him now." Blue Eagle told Twin Peaks to have his men shift to the vegetable rows, because that was where the Confederacy was going to come in first, the weakest spot. "Thank you for keeping our families safe from harm," he told Twin Peaks. "That alone gives our warriors extra reason to fight to the end to protect and keep fighting to the end. We know our loved ones are out of harm's way."

Lone Peak stood proud and defiant as he watched the walls begin to sway and bend. He could sense the end was coming and coming fast. He positioned his Lenape men side by side with Susquehannock warriors in the trench lines facing the fields and told them about the spirit they would use to fight.

"It is your sacred and honorable duty to fight alongside your Susquehannock brothers," he said. "They gave to us in our time of need and now it is our time to give back to them. They have entrusted us to keep their families safe with us. We shall honor that trust with our blood and with the edges of our tomahawks and clubs. We will not be done until the Confederacy is done. They will not be sustained by a victory here. They come after us if we don't stop them here. Kill all who oppose our freedom!"

Smoke from the smoldering timbers of the walls blocked the bright sunshine of the nearly cloudless sky above. The walls swayed in the wind like ocean waves on the shore, but time was almost gone. The sound of cracking and splintering echoed all around. Warriors on the outside shouted their pleasure at the sound. They chanted in unison, "You will die soon! We are coming! You will die! We are coming!"

Inside the walls, men braced in their positions and readied for an onslaught. The cannons pointed toward the cracking sounds of the walls. The staunch defenders stood straight and proud, blades and bows ready. Finally, a loud crack echoed the breaking sound of a falling tree, signaling a final push. The rear gate fell crooked to the ground with a mighty crash. Smoke billowed up from the ground.

Almost in succession, wall section after wall section gave way in the softer dirt. Other sections around the compound held firm. A horde of black and red-painted faces rushed the sections. The pent-up, painted mob met with a hail of bullets, cannonballs, and arrows, all which felled row after row of crazed warriors. The group kept leaping over arms, legs, and torsos to reach the blades that awaited them.

The fury from within and behind the trenches did not hesitate or lessen. It was the third assault and by far the most highly concentrated mass of warriors to date. Orders were to cut them down before they reached the trench. A cannon from the corner fired grapeshot at the mass of Seneca and Confederate warriors pouring over and through the fallen walls of the fields that faced the trenches.

Blue Eagle and Brave Cloud stood atop the trench, looking for Angry Skies and Tadodaho as the hordes moved closer to the trench in a frontal assault. The backup line of Susquehannock and Lenape warriors moved forward past the trench line as the opposing forces came within tomahawk and war club range. Warriors climbed out of the trenches to engage the horde in head-on, hand-to-hand and edge-to-edge combat.

Brave Cloud pointed to the main gate and walls which were cracking and swaying under pressure from outside and yelled at Blue Eagle. "We're holding our own here, the main gate and walls are falling fast, let's go there!"

The pair sprinted to the other side of the village, picking up rows of Susquehannock warriors along the way. The double gate cracked open as they came closer, and more Confederacy warriors started pouring in through the openings. Pairs of invaders managed to penetrate the walls and then opened the gates from inside.

The stream of warriors turned into a flood of half-crazed and starved assailants hell-bent on destruction. Blue Eagle spotted Tadodaho and Angry Skies' warriors at mid-pack pointing to the trenches and longhouses.

The trenches and rows of warriors opened fire as soon as the walls cracked and crumbled. From all around the village center came the cry, "Fire and don't stop! Let them feel your fury!"

The sunlit day turned dark and cloudy, and the sky blackened with clouds. A steady downpour of summer rain followed a stinging hail that turned the dry and cracked ground into a muddy nightmare.

A cannon to one side kept up a volley of grapeshot aimed at the distant walls where men kept pouring in. Men lost their footing in blood-soaked mud beneath their feet. A tomahawk's edge cleaved into flesh and bone like a butcher's knife. Limbs and bodies were splayed open in a horrible display of anger, frustration, and revenge.

Blue Eagle looked up and thought he saw Angry Skies moving to his left. He followed him, but a Seneca warrior caught him off guard and landed a glancing blow with his tomahawk on his back. He spun in the direction of the blow and was able to knife the assailant in the ribs. The assailant went down in a lump, and Blue Eagle wasted no effort in stabbing him twice more in the heart, but he lost sight of Angry Skies in the encounter.

Blue Eagle was proud of the fighting spirit of his men. They were holding their own against the initial assault. The Confederacy was inside, but primary leaders were still alive. The enemy was all around. Brave Cloud came to Blue Eagle's side with two of his favorite fighters, Moving Moon and Eagle Claw. The fight was strength on strength. They stood less than one pace apart. If left apart, they were vulnerable. But in a group of four, they were almost unbeatable.

Blue Eagle then spotted Angry Skies surrounded by a similar group of warriors. He maneuvered his men to begin fighting that group. Their cadres fought, leaving the leaders alone. Blue Eagle longed for this—a shot at Angry Skies.

The two locked eyes, and the fight was on. There wasn't time for sizing each other up—the two locked tomahawks in a deadly embrace. Angry Skies wedged his knee in Blue Eagle's torso and flipped him over his head. He turned and lunged, the knife in his right hand, toward Blue Skies' heart. Blue Eagle spun leftward and struck with his tomahawk on Angry Skies' right shoulder, slicing a gouge in his shoulder.

Angry Skies struggled to his feet, glanced at his bleeding shoulder, and grinned at Blue Eagle with a toothy grin. "I'll get you for that," he said, tossing his knife back and forth between hands.

Blue Eagle lunged for the torso but missed. Angry Skies stabbed him in the back and tripped him. Blue Eagle fell forward but turned quickly on his back to see a knife plunging toward his heart. He twisted again and used his knife to plunge it deep and up and into Angry Skies' ribs to the hilt. In a dying gesture, Angry Skies tried to raise his knife to cut an arc across Blue Eagle's torso, but the blade was knocked aside. Blue Eagle made one silent wish for the spirit of Angry Skies to follow him into the deepest part of GaiWiio, hell.

After finishing with their foes, Brave Cloud, Moving Moon and Eagle Claw rushed to help Blue Eagle. They tried to stop his bleeding using pressure and the skins of the fallen. They were only partially successful. Blue Eagle told them to find and kill Tadodaho. They took Blue Eagle to his longhouse. They called another warrior over to keep pressure on the wound while they searched for pine tar to help staunch the bleeding.

Brave Cloud scalped Angry Skies and held his headband high for others to see. The group of four warriors went looking for Tadodaho, and he wasn't hard to find. He was surrounded by Confederate warriors. Instead of taking that group on in a confrontation, Brave Cloud climbed atop one of the hides' stretching frames and threw his tomahawk at Tadodaho's head to split his face in two. When his body dropped to the ground, the day's battle ended. One of Tadodaho's men hoisted his body on his shoulder and began a retreat out to the fields. The body of Angry Skies was also borne away. Fighting slowed, and almost all the Confederacy warriors began a slow, funeral retreat away from the village.

The dead were scalped and drug outside into the fields. The siege, however, was not over.

Outside the village, a quick council meeting of the Confederacy acted on several urgent matters in a short time. They would pick a new leader—Sarangararo, a sachem from the Seneca nation. Next on the agenda was how to bury Tadodaho and Angry Skies. A quick vote ensued, and the decision was to sled the bodies back to main camp after a short ceremony.

There was no time to bury the dead; their numbers were too

great. The council decided to put them into canoes and leave them in the boats tied up until the siege was over. Sarangararo got down to business by ordering a re-grouping for a fourth assault and to continue to burn the walls which were nearly down. A rest was needed for the fight to continue, but Sarangararo was in a hurry, and all of this took time. Time that he did not have— his men were starving.

The council developed a new strategy for the fourth day: finish pushing down the wall and abandon going around to the fields. They would cave in the walls and destroy the remaining forces. They concentrated their manpower to break into the food supplies and take them.

"I am wounded, but I am not dead," Blue Eagle said. "My bleeding has stopped thanks to quick action by Brave Cloud and others. I will fight to the end to save our village. Angry Skies and Tadodaho are dead, but they have a new leader who will not stop until we are gone. We lost many good men over the last three days. We still have about two hundred fighters against twice that number outside these walls. You have been brave, and now we ask that you be daring for one more day. Rest tonight, but tomorrow, we will fight. We will fight them to our last breath and never surrender. We are proud Susquehannocks!"

The defenders slept by their positions. They wrapped themselves in whatever blankets or coverings they could find. Some sharpened their blades, but mostly they slept and waited. A light rain made walking treacherous on the bloody ground, making combat more deadly.

The same chant was heard outside the walls at dawn. "You will soon die! We are coming! You will soon die! We are coming!"

The main walls cracked and waved as men pushed relentlessly at the weak spots. Smoke rose once again all along the wall structure. Some of the posts were bound to fall soon. The Arrowheads in the trenches checked their ammunition. Their supplies were running low. They needed to make every bullet and ball count. You could swing a weapon when ammo ran out.

The noises outside were louder. The crack in the main gate had been plugged, but only with temporary crossbeams. Men on both sides began shouting with thunderous crescendos of noise. Almost at once a thundering, clasping sound, close to thunder, was heard when the posts started to collapse. The rain did not stop.

Everyone braced themselves. First one wall section fell, then another. Some held, but those that collapsed allowed hordes of men to leap and jump. Arrows and bullets rained down on bodies with a never-ending hail, hitting a flood of arms, shoulders, and elbows everywhere all at once. Hundreds of bodies swarmed through the openings—a wave of humanity without discipline or leadership that swept through the village like a horde of insects. The defenders used all their weapons to stem the flow, like trying to stop the flow of a surging river.

Some of the men of the Confederacy were so hungry they searched every longhouse, looking for dried meat and vegetables. They paid the price for hunger by being shot inside while engorging themselves.

The Susquehannocks fought bravely against the odds. Men fired from trenches, only to find themselves helpless when tens of men leaped onto their positions and smothered their weapons. Bodies lay together broken and dead from contact with bullets and arrows.

The Lenape and Susquehannock warriors fought side by side to slow the attackers and gain some control over the raving and raging mob. The taller Susquehannock men gained an edge in hand-to-hand fighting and managed to inflict heavy losses on the undisciplined Confederacy.

The Confederacy leaders realized that their overwhelming numbers would rule the battle and win the day but since they wanted the stores of food, they wanted the Susquehannock and

Lenape to surrender and give up, which they would not do. They would have to settle for killing every man that would fight.

Blue Eagle found Brave Cloud, Moving Moon and Eagle Claw and reformed their solid circle. This time, Twin Peaks found the group and joined them with a few of his trusted warriors.

Blue Eagle's eyes teared up as he shouted to Twin Peaks. "We are forever grateful to you for protecting our families." Twin Peaks shot back and said, "We have unfinished work to do."

The small group turned into battle one last time, but no one came out alive.

Aftermath

Blue Eagle, Moving Moon, Eagle Claw, Brave Eagle, and Twin Peaks were all killed in the fourth assault on Sasquesahanough Village in 1675. Fewer than fifty Susquehannock and Lenape warriors remained out of a force of over five hundred. Many of those suffered wounds and were not in fighting condition. Their only choices were surrender or death. Many chose the latter and paid the ultimate price. They had the choice to join the Confederacy. Absorbing prisoners was the Confederacy's key to long-term survival.

Sarangararo's force of seven hundred men lost about half of its original warriors. Sarangararo was left to ponder what happened to the village's children, women, and old men. Rumors said that they had gone to join the Lenape before the fight began. He vowed to find out. He told his men to take their fill of Susquehannock food and supplies. After that, they would come back for the remainder of the stores and then burn the village to the ground.

Kateri, Orenda, and Sosondowah lived to tell the story of

Blue Eagle's life to their descendants in the Lenape circle of life. Kateri moved up to be a village mother in the Lenape fashion. Orenda married a Lenape warrior and formed her own family. Sosondowah became a prominent Lenape warrior and deer hunter. He moved up to be a sachem and chief of the Lenape village. The tales of all three are still waiting to be told.

Those that remained told stories of Blue Eagle's exploits. After Kateri passed, Orenda kept the tales alive and passed Blue Eagle's achievements down to her children. She talked of her trip south and the formation of the peace treaty. She also told how Blue Eagle inspired pride in the Susquehannock accomplishments, the nation's fight against the Confederacy and against the white man's diseases. Orenda urged her children to repeat Blue Eagle's stories to their children to help keep his spirit alive for generations.

In time and in this way, the tale of The Last Great Susquehannock Chief became a legend.

Epilogue

The story of the Susquehannock nation began as early as 1550, when villages were established along the upper Susquehanna River and the Powhatan Confederacy was formed. The Susquehannock were an Algonquian-speaking tribe that encountered Mohawk and Iroquois nations with similar origins. Hardened by years of conflict, they overwhelmed the Eastern Algonquian tribes along the Chesapeake Bay.

They encountered John Smith of the British Colonies, who was impressed with their size, deep voices, and variety of weapons. Their height must have been exceptional because the Swedes they encountered in the area also commented on it. The numbers were estimated to be around 7,000 in five tribal groups. Their agriculture set them apart from other similar nations in the northeast. They planted, harvested, stored, and dried vegetables of all sorts, in addition to raising beans, corn, and squash. Some historical accounts attribute the daily consumption of these vegetables to these peoples' unusual height (males averaged about 68–70 inches tall). Other political and cultural ways were also different. The Susquehannock's ability to use drying long-houses to store their vegetables and skins year after year was envied by other nations. It was their insurance against brutal winters and famine.

Algonquin traditional folkways were maternal. A village mother sat in on the council and her decisions were vital. She was sought as a wise counselor and a respected elder matron. She often swayed the council toward the selection of a tribal sachem, a chief also called dogma. She usually would pick a married, responsible man who would contribute to the tribe's well-being, broaden the food store, and its growth. She was critical to the village. If she became incapable or too feeble to make decisions, the job passed to her elder sister or daughter. If none existed, it was up to the clan to decide. Agreements, including war, trade, and peace, were not made without her blessing. She was the continuity in the community.

The Susquehannocks were known as exceptional traders. They often sought the technical wares of the white man as desirable. The colonial trader brought forged and manufactured iron products to the hunter-gatherer, such as iron cooking pots, fishing hooks, hatchets, shovels, axes, knives, muskets, rifles, and blankets. In turn, he was provided skins, especially beaver, plus woven goods, food, beads, and specialty clothing. Susquehannocks had the skills to offer the equivalent to the manufactured goods, but they took longer to produce and often did not last as long. The iron cooking pot versus the clay pot is a good example. The musket and the rifle had no substitute but were often less efficient than the deadly bow and arrow in hunting. The firearms were useful in combat at close quarters.

Although they went through many peace treaties, the Susquehannock tribes rarely traded land for peace, as did many other nations. They guarded their traditional hunting grounds with jealous abandon. This was often a cause for fighting, especially since the fall was the best time to find the game for the winter and the rest of the following year.

Even as hunters, they specialized in using small but deadly arrowheads that were exceptionally sharp. Their distinctive style set them apart from the arrowheads of other nations, who often chipped their arrowheads to make them sharp. The Susquehannocks' smaller and deadlier arrowhead netted more deer and game than other tribes. Being shot by these arrows at the hands of the trained marksman meant a surefire wound or death.

Other tribes also admired their craftsmanship skills. The methods used by women to collect and make wampum, beaded clothing, and woven baskets were extraordinary. The women were also skilled in tannery and molded pottery.

The Susquehannocks adopted much of the Iroquois language, customs, and building techniques; they kept an identity separate from that of the Iroquois, which was an English term. The only forge in the whole of Pennsylvania, Maryland, New York and Delaware during that time period was in New Netherland. Their history, legends, and longhouse building came from the traditions of the Haudenosaunee, the original name for Iroquois. At their peak, the Susquehannock tribe was scattered along the Delaware and Susquehanna Rivers in twenty villages with five to seven thousand warriors. The Haudenosaunee referred to the Susquehannock people as Minquas.

The major village in this text, Sasquesahanough (Bear) Village, focuses on northern Pennsylvania and occupies a large area north of the Susquehannock River near New York. At its peak, it contained well over 400 warriors, sixteen clans, 2,000 hectares including irrigated fields, and twenty-one longhouses and over 20,000 people.

One might think that the Susquehannocks had a lot of favorable positives in their culture at a time when European settlers found the New World such a rich source of natural resources.

The histories that I have encountered point to two significant factors in their population decline from the 1650s to 1675, the time frame of this book. The first points to the significant smallpox outbreaks of 1663 and 1667, including measles, diphtheria,

and typhoid, for which the Susquehannocks had no natural defense. Historians estimate their warrior population declined to
just three hundred by 1676. Historians have traced the diseases
to the poor hygiene of the French and English traders and settlers.

The refusal of colonists, including the traders, to fully and
regularly immerse themselves in a bath was a major cause of
the spread of diseases to others. This contagion and its spread
among local indigenous Americans from village to village has
often been cited as a reason for the demise of the nation. Although diseases were prevalent among settlers and colonists, the
native populations had no natural immunities to these viruses
and their contagion among the villages was rampant. The Susquehannock, as with many other native Americans, regularly
practiced complete body immersion in rivers and pools using
natural soapy plants as cleansers. This book's story shows how
Blue Eagle kept the spread of the contagion minimized, using
isolation of the village from traders and from each other. Dental hygiene among traders and settlers was also deplorable. The
Susquehannocks also chewed on twigs to prevent dental decay.

The second reason for the population decline was the near-
constant confrontation with nations of the Haudenosaunee Confederacy and, on occasion, other tribes in the surrounding
northeast area. The text refers to the Iroquois, Seneca, Cayuga,
Onondaga, Oneida, and Mohawk (later Tuscarora) nations. The
legendary Peacemaker and Hiawatha leaders brought together
these populations.

Although there were periods of peace, fighting between
tribes, especially over hunting grounds, was a regular occur-
rence. The Susquehannock's primary means of movement was
by the river and its tributaries.

This author has a lot of respect for the cultural folkways of
the Susquehannock people. Their superior planting and vegetable farming, their storing and drying methods, and planning for
future use made them the envy of other nations. Had it not been

for the spread of colonists' viruses, and the seemingly unquench-able thirst for Confederacy absorption of tribal hunting grounds in the seventeenth century, the Susquehannock people could have lasted much, much longer.

Judah Joseph, known as Blue Eagle in this story, eventually became a sachem and leader of his people in northern Pennsyl-vania's most significant and last known Susquehannock village. The security improvements he pioneered in the town—the pali-saded log fence, isolation of diseases, and restriction of traders to a single longhouse—enabled the village to become a fortress right up to the last battle in the book.

The village's association with the Lenape tribe in the book's last chapters is fictional. The Lenape were the closest major na-tion to the Susquehannock, and their alliance for hunting and mutual protection was based on their physical closeness, rather than on historical records.

The Demise of the Susquehannock Nation

The historical record shows that the Iroquois nation destroyed vil-lages in the north and west and then turned their attention southward to the Susquehannocks. Colonists, especially in Mary-land, had grown fearful of the Iroquois and hoped that an alliance with the Susquehannock would help block the Iroquois advance-ment. In 1663, the Iroquois sent 800 warriors into the Susquehannock territory. The Susquehannocks repulsed them, but the unprovoked attacks prompted the colony of Maryland to de-clare war on the Iroquois.

The Maryland colonists turned the tables on the Iroquois by supplying Susquehannock forts with artillery. The Susquehan-nocks took the upper hand and began to invade Iroquois territory, where they caused significant damage. This warfare continued intermittently for 11 years. In 1674, the Maryland colonists changed their Indian policy, negotiated peace with the Iroquois, and terminated their alliance with the Susquehannocks. In 1675, the militias of Virginia and Maryland captured and executed some of the Susquehannock chiefs, whose growing power they feared. The Iroquois drove the warriors from traditional territory and absorbed the survivors in 1677.

The natural history is an elongated, sad story. While the Confederacy absorbed some prisoners, a large band of remaining Susquehannocks made its way downriver to the upper Potomac at the invitation of the governor of the British Colony of Maryland, Lord Calvert II. A thousand-man army under the command of Colonel John Washington (the great-grandfather of George Washington) besieged them at an old fort on the Potomac River. A short coexistence existed between the English and French after the British took New Netherland in 1676.

Despite assurances that the English and French were peaceful, the Susquehannocks offered up six sachems as hostages. The colonists took the hostages but killed them when they learned of other attacks in the area. The Susquehannocks abandoned the fort, but a series of retaliatory raids by other than Susquehannock tribes fell instead on the Susquehannocks. This pressure forced the remaining Susquehannocks to move yet again.

In 1677, the remaining 200 Susquehannocks moved north and surrendered to the Haudenosaunee. They were absorbed by the Oneida and the Mohawks, becoming members of the Covenant Chain. They rose to leadership as Iroquois war chiefs but never became truly free.

William Penn signed a treaty with the Susquehannocks, only to learn that they needed Iroquois approval first. The Susquehannocks were ignored in future arrangements with the British government and Pennsylvania.

Finally, the Iroquois relented in 1706 and allowed three hundred Susquehannocks to return to northern Pennsylvania, where they became known as the Conestogas. Quaker missionaries arrived and converted many to Christianity. Those not converted returned to the Oneida in New York or moved west to the Mingo and were absorbed there. The converted became Mahican, a sub-Iroquoian tribe, and moved to join other groups in Ohio. European inhabitants named this town Stockbridge on the Housatonic River. There were only twenty identifiable Susquehannock Indians among the Stockbridge inhabitants. They were peaceful and converted Christians.

Atrocities committed by others in 1763 (the Delaware, Mingo, and Shawnee) incited colonial settlers who just wanted to kill Indians, any Indians, in revenge. Fourteen Conestogas were arrested and placed in jail at Lancaster, Pennsylvania, for their protection. A mob known as the Paxton Boys formed, went to the village and killed six Susquehannock Indians who they found there and burned their homes. They headed for the jail, broke in and took the last fourteen, and beat them to death.

Historians do not take seriously any related claims of survival from that tragedy. The Susquehannocks are now officially considered extinct.

The name Susquehanna is given to the oldest river on earth. The 444-mile-long river is up to 252 million years old, older than the Nile, the Ganges, or the Congo rivers. It has a western branch that extends to Pittsburgh. The name also refers to a town in northern Pennsylvania, a high school, a county, a park, a college, and much more. Our people and children should delve deeper into the tribe's history on whose names we put them. They should understand the culture and way of life of these occupants who are no longer around to tell their stories. Today, the river's rolling hills, and winding banks are home to countless fish and wildlife, and millions enjoy its parks and natural beauty.

In my tale, Blue Eagle's wife, daughter, and son live with the Lenape and re-tell his tale to their offspring. Judah Joseph is forty-five at his death. Eventually, the story of his exploits becomes a legend told repeatedly through lore, handed down from one generation into the next.

Acknowledgments

This author sincerely acknowledges the contributions made in languages, cultures, spirit, traditions, and resiliency of indigenous people that inhabited this continent before the arrival of any colonists. We owe a debt to the tribal nations that lived and settled on this land that cannot be repaid. For generations, federal and state policies systematically sought to assimilate and displace native people and eradicate their cultures and to take and settle on their lands. Promises were made and broken. It is a history that meets the true definition of genocide.

We must do more than name our rivers, cities, towns, and landmarks after the indigenous people who came before us many years ago. Today, we can work together to restore dignity and respect to ensure human rights are grounded in sovereignty for all.